Also by
CAROLE BERRY . . .

Death of a Dimpled Darling

''A very droll detective drama . . . a lighthearted romp.''
—*Midwest Book Review*

The Death of a Difficult Woman

''A pristine whodunit.''
—*Kirkus Reviews*

''A winner!''
—*Murder Ink*

The Death of a Dancing Fool

''An exciting final twist . . . a fast-paced read.''
—*Time Out New York*

''The narrative flow and the character presentations are almost flawless. You'll like Bonnie Indermill.''
—*Vero Beach Press Journal* (FL)

''As always, both Bonnie and the story are lively, amusing and very clever, with Carole Berry's usual array of characters that jump off the page and run around the room.''
—*Mystery News*

(continued on next page)

DEATH
OF A
DOWNSIZER

CAROLE BERRY

BERKLEY PRIME CRIME, NEW YORK

DEATH OF A DOWNSIZER

A Berkley Prime Crime Book / published by arrangement with the author

PRINTING HISTORY
Berkley Prime Crime edition / January 1999

The Penguin Putnam Inc. World Wide Web site address is
http://www.penguinputnam.com

ISBN: 0-425-16614-7

Berkley Prime Crime Books are published
by The Berkley Publishing Group,
a member of Penguin Putnam Inc.,
375 Hudson Street, New York, New York 10014.
The name BERKLEY PRIME CRIME and the BERKLEY PRIME CRIME
design are trademarks belonging to Berkley Publishing Corporation.

PRINTED IN THE UNITED STATES OF AMERICA

10 9 8 7 6 5 4 3 2 1

DEATH
OF A
DOWNSIZER

PROLOGUE

IT WAS EARLY IN THE CHRISTMAS SEA-
son when the warrant for my arrest was
issued. Merry Christmas!

At the time, I'd been temping at Richards & Goode Corporation for a couple
weeks. R&G, as the company is called, is
a manufacturer of consumer electronics.
They've been around for a long time.
Years ago, my brother Raymond and I
sprawled on the floor and watched *Howdy
Doody* on a tiny-screen set carrying their
logo. I can't begin to detail all the things
R&G manufactures now, but whenever you watch a video,
nuke a TV dinner, or get beeped, there's a good chance
something bearing the R&G trademark is involved.

When I started the assignment, Adele, my counselor at
the Pro-Team Temps Employment Agency, told me I had
a good chance of remaining there through the New Year if
I *behaved myself*. Those were her exact words. She was
kidding, but needless to say my continued employment at

R&G was contingent not only upon the quality of my work but upon my remaining out of jail. Once the word got out that the police were looking for me, R&G wouldn't have touched me with a stick, assuming I'd been crazy enough to show my face in their offices.

I wasn't that crazy, though by the time this episode in my life was over, I'd done any number of crazy things. In the beginning they were merely slips in judgment. I spent money I didn't have, and I was taken in by appearances. Who, though, hasn't been guilty of both those minor offenses? And I let myself be pushed into swaggering when I should have kept my mouth shut and my hands clasped behind my back. Well, all I can say about my early behavior is, I've never claimed to have the control of a Zen master.

As things progressed, my mistakes amounted to more than lapses in good sense. There were the misdemeanors—trespassing, and even theft, if borrowing a battered old jacket can be called theft—and, okay, there was a . . . felony. There! I've admitted it! I was guilty of evading arrest. But as it has often been said, desperate times call for desperate measures, and I was desperate.

On the subject of my crimes, the one thing I was completely innocent of was the crime of which I was accused, the crime which made me a fugitive from justice—murder.

1

MY NAME IS BONNIE INDERMILL, AND I support myself with temporary office jobs. I've had more first-days-on-the-job than I care to count. Some of them I couldn't count, actually. They've blended into a mishmash of overloaded file cabinets and clanging phones. Others do stand out, though, and my first day at Richards & Goode's corporate headquarters was one of those.

As a receptionist led me down a corridor, I was struck by the old-fashioned elegance of the place. In an office world that more and more is turning toward particleboard, plastic, and pieces of modern art that look as if they were painted by the participants in an aggression-control program, the employees' wood desks, the oil paintings in ornate frames, the fresh flowers everywhere seemed to be throwbacks to a more genteel era.

The second thing about R&G that struck me was the hush. Of course some of what I'd come to consider normal office noise may have been absorbed by the carpeting that cushioned my feet, and the fact that we were thirty-seven floors above Manhattan's streets took care of much outside noise, but the quiet was somehow deeper than I would have expected. The employees we passed conversed softly if they conversed at all, and the ringing phones on their desks sounded as if they'd been muted.

"You'll be in here," the receptionist said. "You share with a benefits assistant."

The room I followed her to would have swallowed up a good bit of my apartment, but the three desks in it made it seem crowded. Only one of those desks was occupied. When we walked through the door the youngish woman sitting behind it, who was talking on the telephone, shifted in her chair so that her back was to us.

I hung my aging gray coat, along with the red-and-gray scarf I'd bought in the hope of perking the coat up a bit, on a hook on the door's back. The receptionist then showed me the desk that would be mine, told me how to answer the three lines on my telephone, and explained that the phone not only had voice mail but that it also had a display which showed the caller's number, and a redial button which repeated the last number dialed.

"That's pretty *cutting edge*," I said.

"It's helpful," she responded. "I'll leave you now, but someone will be along to show you the ropes of the job."

I pretended to be enthusiastic about this prospect, but to be frank I've spent enough time in enough offices to be able to find most job "ropes" all by myself.

As soon as the woman had gone I sank into the comfy chair behind my desk. My grateful back said, "Ahh," and as I looked around me, my grateful psyche said, "I've made it to temp-worker heaven."

On my left, on the other side of the laser printer that appeared to be mine and mine alone, three sparkling-clean windows looked south to the spire of the Empire State Building and beyond. In front of me, three more windows provided a partial view of the Hudson River. These windows were the old-fashioned kind that could be opened. They weren't open, of course, but it was nice to see that in Manhattan there were still office workers who were not hermetically sealed.

My officemate's desk was as far from mine as the space would allow. The phone conversation she was engaged in was one of those huddled-over-the-mouthpiece ones that not even a creature from another planet would suppose had anything to do with business. I couldn't make out anything she was saying, which was clearly the way she wanted things.

That was okay with me. I had my own personal phone business to conduct. Picking up the receiver, I got an outside line and called Adele at Pro-Team Temps.

"Okay, Adele," I said. "There's got to be a downside."

"What? What are you talking about?"

Adele, known among the temp community as the Scarsdale Screamer, is loud at the best of times. When she is calmly riffling through her humongous Rolodex with her two-inch fingernails, which can vary in color from deep purple to luminescent ivory, her adenoidal screech merely causes my teeth to hurt. When she gets excited, I fear for my eardrums. "You said what to him? Don't you understand he's one of my best clients," she once howled when she learned that I'd told one of her clients to keep his hands off my backside. "How could you?" she shrieked when I quit after a day at an insurance company that easily could have rivaled a day on a chain gang.

I held the phone away from my ear. "I'm kidding. I'll stay as long as they'll have me. You should see this place. There can't be a downside."

"Down*side*? That's what you said? No way! There's no downside. It's like I told you, Bonnie, if you work out there, if you behave yourself and they like you, you can probably count on staying through January or maybe even . . ."

For an office temp, life is one audition after another. If R&G liked me, though, I wouldn't have to audition again for five or six weeks, which would get me through what was going to be an unusually expensive December.

The hourly rate was pretty good for a temp job, too, and the corporation offered some of its company benefits to long-term temps. Not the important stuff, of course. There was nothing so practical as health insurance or paid sick days, but I could get a discount at their company store on their products, which as I've said ran the electronics gamut, and also at a nearby health club. The newest and trendiest health club in Manhattan, Adele told me, her voice leaving no room for doubt, and it was mine for a third of what ordinary mortals paid as long as I was working at R&G.

After I'd told Adele—sworn to her—that one way or another I'd make the powers at R&G like me, I quickly cradled the receiver. Another line on my phone had started ringing softly. One short ring, indicating that this was an inside-the-company call.

"Human Resources," I answered. "How may I help—"

Two short rings, indicating a call from the outside, interrupted the spiel the receptionist had instructed me to recite.

"Please hold for a moment," I said to the first caller. "Human—"

Ring.

Suddenly all three of the lines on my phone had come alive. Feeling a little desperate, I glanced at my officemate. She was still on the phone, but had swiveled her chair in my direction. As soon as I looked at her, though, she again turned her back.

No help there.

It seemed to go on forever. I'd no sooner spit out the words "Human Resources" when another line would start up. Most of the calls came from within the company: "Can I carry over vacation days?" "How many sick . . . ?" "Do we still have casual day before holidays?" "Do the free tickets to the Modern Art . . . ?"

The calls from outside, which were less frequent, were mostly from agencies: "Are you hiring receptionists?"

"Secretaries?" "A replacement for the assistant . . . ?" or from other corporations asking about R&G's former employees: "Marissa Piesman has applied for a marketing position here. Can you tell me . . . ?"

This obviously wasn't nuclear physics, but I had no answers and I didn't know where to find them. While I grappled with taking messages, my officemate—the receptionist had mentioned that she was a benefits assistant, but what on earth did she do around here, anyway?—had time to finish her call, and make another equally huddled one. When she'd finished that, she wandered out of the office with her handbag tucked under her arm.

The barrage of calls had started at about 9:45. While it lasted I was aware of activity outside of my office—phones ringing softly, uniformed messengers dropping stacks of envelopes into in-boxes, people in suits hurrying past. It was all quite officelike, and I was too busy to pay much attention to any of it. Still, I do recall that the same thought I'd had earlier again flickered through my head, this time with some embellishment: *Everyone does everything so softly. The quiet is almost . . . unnatural.*

At exactly 10:45 the barrage of phone calls stopped, so abruptly that I wondered, at first, whether the building's phone lines had gone dead. After a moment I let myself take a deep breath, but before I could exhale there was one short ring. Grimacing, I grabbed the receiver, ready for another telephone attack.

"Human Res—"

"Is this *the* Bonnie Indermill?"

The man's voice was pleasant, but not at all familiar to me. This was an inside call, but no one I knew of worked for R&G. I responded cautiously.

"This is *a* Bonnie Indermill. There are probably others."

"About five-four, reddish-blond hair, likes to dance—"

"Who is this?"

"It's your new boss," the man on the other end of the line said. "I'll be around to see you in a while."

He was chuckling when he hung up.

A moment later my officemate returned, a container of coffee in her hand. Since we were both free of the phone for the moment, I took the opportunity to introduce myself. In response, she told me her name was Louise Gruber, informed me that coffee break was from 10:45 to eleven, and further informed me that coffee break was de rigueur.

"You have to take your break, even if you don't want to. It makes the rest of us look bad if you don't. It's one of the few benefits R&G's management hasn't taken away from us."

"I didn't know anything about a break, but the phones were so busy—"

"Don't worry about the phones. We have voice mail," she said bruskly. "I heard a rumor that you're a temp. Is that true?"

"Yes," I said.

I didn't see any reason why that should have made Louise unhappy, but it clearly did. Though the glasses perched on her nose weren't terribly becoming, and though she was a bit thinner than was flattering, Louise's thick brown hair fell in luxurious waves to below her shoulders, and her features were pleasant enough. Once she had confirmed my temp status, however, the horizontal frown lines in her forehead grew so deep they might have been pounded into her flesh by a jackhammer, and her bottom lip drooped sullenly. It was a look I would come to call her *disgruntled* one.

"I suppose that's not your fault," she said finally as she sat down at her desk.

Even supposing my temp status *was* my fault, it was an odd comment.

"Actually, I enjoy the lifestyle."

That wasn't entirely true. Yes, for a number of years I had enjoyed the lifestyle, but I'd reached a point in life where I would have enjoyed it more if it had come with a retirement plan and paid vacation.

Louise picked up her phone again. Before she dialed, though, she shrugged and said, with a studied carelessness,

"Oh, well. The way things are going around here, we may all be 'enjoying the lifestyle' soon."

"It doesn't seem all that bad," I said, taking in the relatively large, light space we shared with a motion of my hand.

"Don't count on us being in this room much longer," she snapped back. "There used to be three full-time employees in here. That's why we had so much space. Now, with only me and a temp, I'm sure there's a management flunky with his eye on it."

It sounded as if she had a particular flunky in mind, but before I had an opportunity to pursue that, Louise had punched four numbers on her telephone, indicating that she was calling someone inside the company. Within a few seconds she was involved in another whispered conversation and had turned her back to me.

Soon enough my own phone started up again, and what with jotting messages, I forgot about Louise. It wasn't until a few minutes later, when the pitch of her voice suddenly rose, that she again drew my attention.

". . . a good idea to look into the insurance plans your husband's new job offers. We have three different HMOs, as well as Blue Cross," she just about bellowed into her phone. "I'll send you information . . ."

In the corridor outside the office the subtle hush had become complete, which had the effect of making Louise's vocalizing seem even louder than it was. Startled by this outburst, I glanced her way.

The frown lines had disappeared from Louise's forehead, and the sullen turn was gone from her mouth. She was the picture of a happy employee, busy at her work. As she spoke she jotted notes on a lined sheet of paper. Her eyes briefly flickered toward the office's door, and I noticed that she gave a nod to someone there before looking back at the tablet.

"Certainly," she said to the person on the other end of the line. "I'll get that information right out to you."

Cradling the phone, Louise jumped from her chair, threw

open a cabinet built into the wall near her desk, and began flipping through cartons of pamphlets.

Curious about what had brought about this show of energy, I glanced toward the door. A man I would have guessed to be in his mid-thirties was there, speaking to someone just out of my sight. After a moment this man—he happened to be a very nice-looking man—took a step forward as if to go on his way. Before he passed out of sight, though, he glanced back into our office. Catching my eye, he smiled.

It was a nice smile, and though I wasn't sure what I'd done to deserve it, I smiled back. The man's smile widened until it seemed as if he was on the verge of laughter. Then, just before he disappeared from my view, he winked at me.

As I've said, he was an attractive man. I didn't wink back, though. Even if I'd been inclined to, this office didn't strike me as the kind of place where a winker would last long.

"Who was that?" I asked Louise, who was still at the cabinet.

She glanced at the door and, after spotting no one there, sank back into her chair.

"The big man."

"How big?"

"Almost as big as they get. Carl Dorfmeyer. He's the chief executive officer. Reports directly to the chairman of the board. It probably doesn't hurt to look busy when he's around," she added, explaining her sudden fit of animation.

To say I was flabbergasted would be an understatement.

"He seems . . . friendly," I said, keeping the information that the Big Kahuna had winked at me to myself.

"Friendly? We can't be talking about the same man. Dorfmeyer would sooner slit your throat than say 'good morning' to you."

And, as things turned out, we *were* talking about different men. A few minutes later, the winker returned to our office. When he walked in I expected Louise, who had been halfheartedly scrolling through the office E-mail on her computer screen, to leap back into action and start slinging papers around. Instead, she gave this man a curt—almost rude—"hi," and then acted as if he wasn't there.

He didn't appear to notice.

"It really is Bonnie Indermill," he said as he approached my desk. "When I saw your résumé in the bunch the agency sent, I could hardly believe it, but here you are."

There must have been some sensible response I could have made to that statement, but all I managed was, "Yes. Here I am. And you're . . . ?"

"You don't remember? How crushing! Here I've been thinking that I was unforgettable."

Crushed he may have been, but his smile again had widened. Was he flirting? Was that smile a little . . . lecherous? Or could it possibly be that this man and I had, at some time in the past that I'd managed to repress . . .

Please understand. In the total scheme of things I do not have an especially sordid past. I have not made a practice of haunting singles' bars, or of getting blind drunk at parties and staggering into the night with strange men. Still, my past is not totally unblemished. I have no intention of going into a full-out confession here, but in my wild youth, which I often find myself hoping isn't completely behind me, there may have been one or two . . . lapses.

I looked hard at this apparently sane man—he had to be sane, didn't he, to be employed by R&G—who apparently knew me. The question on my mind was, how did he know me?

The lines crinkling at the corners of his eyes suggested that he wasn't quite as young as I'd thought when I'd glimpsed him earlier. Late thirties was more like it, which did nothing to calm my growing fear, the reason being that if I had done something I couldn't remember with a man I couldn't remember, I would likely have done it with someone of that age. On the other hand, despite the smile and the wink, he looked a bit straitlaced for me. His hair, which was a nondescript shade somewhere between dirty blond and brown, was cut conservatively, and as for his gray pinstripe suit, white shirt, and wing tips, think "Brookie" and you've got the picture.

"Central New Jersey High School, 1973," he said. "Right? Drama Club, Cheerleader Squad Captain, Future Homemakers . . ."

That last bit tripped him up. This man may have known me, but he sure didn't *know* me.

"Never!" I snapped. "I was *never* a Future Homemaker of America. You were at Central High? Oh my goodness!"

I recognized him at the same time he said, "Tom Hurley. And don't say that you would have known me anywhere."

I couldn't say that right away, but now that the unfamiliar face had a familiar name, the memory was as clear as day.

Tom Hurley. Tom Terrific. The gray-eyed smile was the same engaging one I remembered, and the hint of mischief behind it was all too familiar. I recalled Tom so clearly that it could have been just minutes before when he'd stood, face pressed against the screen door of the house where I grew up. "Raymond around?" he would ask in a quavery adolescent male voice.

He had changed, of course. Who hasn't? In the late sixties and early seventies, the kid two years my junior—Tom had been in my brother Raymond's class—had worn his hair longer, in the style of the times, and his frame had been more gangly, less fleshed out. The changes hadn't been drastic, though. Tom hadn't gained sixty pounds and developed a cascade of chins, and his hairline appeared to be more or less where it had been.

"Wow!" I said. "You're my boss? That's amazing! I remember when you and Raymond used to take my records—"

"Borrow! We borrowed your records."

"Oh, sure, and you left them on a heater duct, so that most of them ended up warped."

The conversation went along like that for a few minutes, but Tom and I really didn't have much to talk about. When I was a high-school senior he'd been a sophomore, and the way I had looked at things back then, it might as well have been twenty years between us, and not two.

Even if we had been contemporaries, I think it would have been hard, now, to fill each other in on the two-plus decades that had passed. After all, what do you say when someone you haven't seen in twenty years says to you, as Tom did to me, "So, what have you been doing with yourself?" Unless you've led a cloistered life, which I have not, there's so much territory to cover that you can hardly say anything at all.

So perhaps it was inevitable that our brief conversation came to center around Raymond, who, in my opinion, leads a life of stupefying ordinariness.

"He married Noreen," I told Tom. "You remember her? They have four kids now."

"Raymond and Noreen married? Unbelievable! I remember the sweat he was in the first time he asked her out. Junior prom. And now they've got four kids! That's something. How about you? Any kids?"

"Well, no," I said, "but I'm a good aunt."

I could have done the good-aunt thing and pulled pictures of the little darlings from my wallet at that point, but I don't carry any. I was about to ask Tom about himself—married? kids?—but he didn't give me a chance.

"What a shock I got when your résumé turned up on my desk," he said. "I always figured you'd be on Broadway, or maybe living in Hollywood . . ."

That almost succeeded in ending what hadn't been much of a chat to begin with. I smiled, shook my head, and said, "No. I'm a temp." What else was I going to do? Go into a long story about how few dancers really make it on Broadway? Maybe recite my credits to prove that I *had* been on Broadway, and mention a role I'd been short-listed for in a long-forgotten movie?

"That's my good luck," Tom responded. "I've got a lot of work for you. You're going to be very important around here. I've only been here about four months," he added, "but it seems like I've got about a year's worth of projects piled up."

The phone was ringing again, but Tom told me to let the calls go to voice mail. For the next quarter hour or so, he explained what my responsibilities at R&G were to be. There was a lot more to the job than the agency had mentioned, but then there usually is.

The phone work, as it turned out, was pretty simple. Sick and vacation days were explained in a manual on a shelf near my desk. As for responses to employment agencies and people calling about jobs, the answer was an unequivocal no.

"There's a hiring freeze here. For the foreseeable future, we're not hiring. Now," Tom added, "if you'll come with me, I'll show you a couple other things."

He first pointed out a small room down the hall from mine, which was used as an emergency sickroom. The room's window had been raised a couple inches, which let in a stream of cool air, but otherwise it looked pretty comfortable. A cot pushed against one wall was covered with a red blanket and had a fluffy pillow at one end. Grinning, I nodded at it.

"Hmm. I tend to run out of steam after lunch. This could be perfect."

"Oh, please," Tom said with a roll of his eyes, "I've got enough of that kind of thing already. You'll hear about it, if you haven't already."

"Hear about what? I haven't heard anything."

"Staff malingering and grumbling. They hate management. And I'm management," he added. "I suspect that half of them wouldn't mind seeing me dead. As for your roommate back there . . ."

Tom shook his head in what was obviously a gesture of disgust. I was curious, naturally, but when he didn't go on, I didn't probe.

I next followed Tom into a big interior room. Along one wall was a copy machine, above which was a wall phone with many extensions, and a yellowing government-issue poster about equal opportunity laws. The remainder of the room was filled with cabinets, which, I learned, contained the personnel files for both present and former administrative employees.

"We document everything," Tom said. "I believe in keeping records, particularly when anything unusual happens."

I didn't mention this to Tom, but while he showed me how the individual files were arranged, I felt a voyeur's thrill. The room was an absolute font of information about people. The vast majority of it was doubtless as prosaic as the vast majority of most people's lives, but some of it was hot stuff. In one thick file which Tom opened at random, an office squabble over a calculator, which began with an exchange of insults and ended with a punch in the nose, was described in a series of memos. In another file I learned the history of some stolen petty cash. Looking at the profusion of cabinets, I wondered what other riches I might find. Illicit affairs, no doubt, with kisses and who-knows-what-else exchanged in stairwells . . .

". . . all highly confidential," Tom was saying. "I can't stress that enough, Bonnie. Anything you learn here must never leave this department. It's all sensitive information. Okay?"

He had tilted his head slightly, and his gray eyes were impressively serious. Seeing no hint of mischief in them, I assured Tom that torture wouldn't pry any of R&G's employees' secrets from my lips.

"This room is locked up every night," he went on. "The regular office key opens it. I'll get you one. If you're the last person to leave the department in the evening, don't go until you're sure this room is locked."

"All right."

As we continued the brief tour, my feelings about Tom were undergoing a subtle but definite change. He was no longer my kid brother's friend, one of the pimply kids responsible for scratching my Rolling Stones' *Sticky Fingers* album so that the needle always stuck just as the band really got going. He was a grown-up human resources executive, who knew all about EEO and OSHA and COBRA. He was a boss.

And he was cute, too.

I forgave him the crack about Broadway and Hollywood. It hadn't even been a crack. It had been chitchat that had wandered into one of my sensitive areas.

"The files for managers and people on higher levels are kept in here."

Tom had opened a locked door almost hidden by cabinets, to reveal a space about the size of a walk-in closet. Like the outer records room, it was lined with cabinets.

"This room has a special lock, and I can't give you a key," he said. "You can borrow my master key when you need access. It's always kept locked."

"Even during the day?"

"Yes. It's not that managers and directors are any more important than anyone else," he added, smiling, "but some of us think we are. You wouldn't believe some of the egos around here. Speaking of which, I'm sure the big man is wondering where I am."

As Tom shut and locked the door to that little room, I glanced at his left hand. No wedding band. Not that that means a thing, but . . .

Funny. Not half an hour before, the notion that I might have slept with this guy and forgotten about it had given me a minor anxiety attack. Now I found myself wondering how I might react if the opportunity to do just that came along.

I spent the rest of the morning and most of the afternoon up to my ears in time cards for permanent part-time employees who, unlike temps, got all the benefits, though prorated, of full-time employees. During the few moments when I wasn't punching figures into a calculator, trying to figure out how much vacation and sick time they had earned, I was ordering flowers for employees in various stages of happiness or misery, and ordering theater tickets for the ''Employee of the Month,'' and getting said employee photographed so that his smiling face would grace the corridor just outside the cafeteria. And, during my so-called afternoon break, which I had decided was an impossibility, I was typing the letters Tom put on my desk.

Though Louise occasionally took a break from her personal calls to do some work, she certainly never came close to working up a sweat. Not long after lunch, I discovered what Tom had been on the verge of saying about her earlier that day. Standing abruptly, she walked to the office door.

''I'm not feeling well. I'm going to lie down for a few minutes.''

She looked fine, but I got up, hurried to her side, and took hold of her arm.

''Let me help you.''

''Oh, no,'' she said carelessly as she brushed my hand away. ''Five or ten minutes and I'll be fine.''

She disappeared down the corridor and into the little sickroom. When the door closed behind her, I heard the click of a lock. I didn't see Louise again for forty-five minutes.

The question of Tom's marital status was answered near the end of the workday. I delivered some of the letters I'd typed to his office several doors away from mine. Finding the room empty, I took a second to look it over.

It wasn't a corner office, and it wasn't as large as mine, but it held only one desk and not three, and was quite spacious. It was neatly kept, with papers carefully arranged on the desktop and manuals and books arranged with equal care on built-in shelves. The office of an organized person. And, judging from the photos on the top shelf, one with a couple kids.

The two children, a boy and a girl, each had their own photos. The boy was nine or ten, and wore a team uniform. The girl, who appeared to be a few years older, was pictured sitting on a lawn wrestling with a basset hound. The girl had her father's wide-set gray eyes, but her auburn hair, which was pulled back in a ponytail, must have come from her mother. What struck me most about the girl, though, was her smile. It was wide, bright, and displayed a mouthful of braces.

I was examining the photo when the phone on Tom's desk rang two times, indicating a call from outside. Tom hadn't said anything about answering his phone, but he hadn't said I shouldn't, either. When I picked up the receiver the number showed on the phone's display, but initially I paid no attention to it.

"Mr. Hurley's office."

There was the briefest pause before a woman asked, "Is Tom there?"

"No," I said. "Can I take a message?"

I looked at the display for the number. The exchange was 718, which told me the call was from one of the New York City boroughs other than Manhattan. What caught my attention, though, was the long string of 8's, and the two 1's, that followed that exchange. I grabbed a pen from the desktop and was getting ready to jot the number down when the woman said, "No thanks. I'll call back."

Tom walked into the office just after I hung up.

"You had a call. The woman said she'd call again."

He shrugged. "Probably an employment agency. Don't bother answering my phone," he added. "That's why we have voice mail."

"Okay." I turned to the photos on the bookcase. "I was admiring your kids."

"That's Erin," Tom replied, straightening the photo of the girl. "And this is our son, Eric. I was lucky to get that shot of Erin. She's usually self-conscious about smiling with her braces."

"She's darling. They both are."

"Yeah. They're great kids. And that"—he nodded at a photo on the shelf below—"is my wife, Elizabeth."

The photo showed a skier schussing down a slope, her face undiscernible in the flurry of snow around her. Two smaller figures, perhaps the two smaller Hurleys, hurtled after her.

"Elizabeth teaches in a high school near our house."

"Where do you live?"

"Chappaqua. It's about forty-five minutes north of Manhattan."

I knew the area by reputation only. It was a pretty, and apparently affluent bedroom community.

"Elizabeth gets to spend more time with the kids than I do. Especially these days," Tom added.

"What do you mean?"

"I've had to work late so often since I started at R&G that I've been spending a couple nights a week here in the city. I'm sure there are guys who would enjoy that, but I'm not one of them."

What a nice guy! A real family man. Even though I'm not much of a family woman, I sympathized. Poor Tom Terrific, torn from the arms of his Little League–playing, puppy-loving, ski-slope-schussing family. The corporate fast track can sure be a heartless place.

That evening, walking down the curved hill toward my apartment, I passed a place where I could have gotten a back rub and a dose of aromatherapy, had I been so inclined.

My neighborhood in upper Manhattan has been undergoing changes. Nothing so drastic as a wave of Gaps and Starbucks, and don't even try to find a restaurant with the word "brunch" on the menu, but here and there small coffeehouses and art galleries have popped up. In the local butcher shop the display case that once offered shoppers chicken gizzards and tripe—yikes!—is now laden with salmon and other wallet-bruising temptations.

These subtle changes haven't yet made much of a dent in the local street life. The teenage boys in baggy pants who gather in front of the pizza parlor still curse and swagger, and the older guys with their bottles of Corona beer partly concealed in paper bags still leer. Gypsy cabs, unlicensed by the taxi commission, still prowl the streets. And the front of my six-story apartment building still boasts the

unreadable glow-in-the-dark silver graffiti that appeared after a hot Saturday night several years ago. If the neighborhood's gentrification continues, perhaps my landlord will
decide to freshen the building up a bit, but I'm not going
to hold my breath.

My one-bedroom apartment is okay, all things considered, all things being the stabilized rent and the river view.
There are places I'd rather live, but at the end of a workday,
when I turn my key in my formidable lock and push open
my door, I do enjoy the feeling of being "home."

When I walked in that evening, Moses, my big gray cat,
greeted me at the door. He has a prodigious appetite and
I've learned that before dealing with anything else, that
appetite must be appeased. I didn't even slip off my coat
until Moses's face had disappeared into his blue bowl. KID
NEY SUPPER FOR KITTIES, his feast that evening was labeled.
Moses probably would have loved the butcher's tripe.

The red light on my telephone answering machine was
blinking. I generally access my calls remotely at least once
when I'm at work, but hadn't found the time that day. After
hanging up my coat, I pushed the replay button.

The first call was from my sister-in-law, Noreen. She and
Raymond were going to be celebrating their fifteenth wedding anniversary with a dinner party at their home. I'd already accepted the invitation, but Noreen didn't trust me.

"Just a reminder," she said. "I'll call you later this week
to discuss things."

The only thing Noreen and I had to discuss was the thing
she referred to as my "dish." To lighten her load, both my
mother and I were contributing to the dinner effort. I'd
managed to steer Noreen away from the notion that I might
"whip up" an elaborate dessert, but the matter still wasn't
settled.

There was one other matter *pending* between me and my
sister-in-law, but it wasn't something we would discuss. It
was something I simply had to do. I had to chip in on the
present my parents were giving Raymond and Noreen. I'd
actually volunteered, thinking that this would make my life

easier. Noreen's kitchen is a morass of blenders and chop-
pers, and I'd expected to end up coughing up twenty dollars
or so for some minor kitchen doodad. You can't imagine
how shocked I was to learn that my brother and sister-in-
law had wheedled the promise of a side-by-side refrigerator
out of my parents!

My mother had already added my name to the card. Being reminded of what this was going to cost me put me
into a funk. I sped through the rest of Noreen's message.
The last words I heard clearly were *"fois gras."*

There was one other message on my machine.

"Hi, Bonnie. This is a voice from the past. Recognize
it?"

Another one? This day was turning out to be a real walk
down memory lane. I turned up the machine's volume.

"Mike. I'm in town for a while. Staying on a friend's
houseboat at the Seventy-ninth Street Boat Basin. I've got
a river view on all sides. Give me a call. My number's
easy: 765-3333."

Mike. He hadn't given his last name but he didn't have
to. I knew the voice, and I knew the man.

Earlier, I mentioned to you that there may have been a
lapse or two on my part, but I say without hesitation that
Mike had not been a *lapse*. We had developed a relationship, of sorts, and I'd genuinely enjoyed his company. In
fact, I'd liked him a lot. However, Mike had been . . .

What's the best way to categorize Mike? He'd been . . .
unconventional? That hardly covers it. A "free spirit"
comes closer, but the reality is, Mike was free only as long
as he remained out of the United States.

There isn't a best way to categorize Mike. He had been
a criminal. Not a violent one, certainly, but an admitted
lawbreaker.

We'd met on one of the Bahamas out-islands, where he
was Captain Mike, charter-boat pilot and fugitive from the
IRS. We'd spent a lot of time together, and some of it had
been very sweet. When the time came for me to leave,
though, I'd done it without regret. I've never had too much

trouble living in sin, at least for the short haul, but living on the run is something else.

Still, when I settled into bed that night, and Moses had snuggled on the pillow next to me, my mind kept wandering back to those silky warm nights in the Bahamas, and the way the water had lapped against the shore outside the little house that Mike rented from one of the locals.

2

HAVING INITIALLY THOUGHT OF THE REC-
ords room as a deep pit of petty gossip,
a place where I might idle away a few
free moments snooping, it was ironic that
I was in that very room when I got my
first hint that the staff problems at R&G
were every bit as bad as Tom had suggested, and that I got it by eavesdropping.

I was actually in the little room-within-
a-room, the inner sanctum where the
higher-level executives' files were kept. It
was early morning, but already I had so
much work that I couldn't waste time digging around in
the hope of finding a juicy bit of gossip. My hand was full
of end-of-the-year salary-review forms to be filed, and once
I got finished with them, there were letters waiting on my
desk to be typed. And there was always the ringing phone.
In any event, my earlier fascination with the personnel files
was fading. How deeply could I care about office uproars
involving people I didn't know? If something blistering hot

happened to fall into my hands, that was one thing, but most of the *sensitive* information in these files was probably a good deal less than scorching.

I tore a fingernail prying loose a tightly packed file, and was in the process of inserting a memo into it when I became aware of footsteps in the larger records room. This wasn't unusual, nor was the fact that it sounded as if more than one person had entered the room. Everyone in the human resources department had access to it.

What was unusual, though, was that instead of hearing a drawer sliding open when the footsteps stopped, I heard Louise say, softly, "I can't stay in here with you very long. If anybody comes in and wonders what we're doing, tell them we're looking for a file for one of your men."

Louise's male companion huffed. "I'll tell them to kiss my royal you-know-what. I'm the security manager. I go where I want to go."

"Just the same, keep your voice down. I wanted to tell you that I was right about her having connections. You should have seen them. Her and Tom Hurley. Good friends from way back. They grew up together, and went to the same high school. It was sickening the way they were fawning all over each other."

Fawning? She had to be talking about me, but I hadn't fawned. I breathed quietly and steadied the file drawer to keep it from sliding.

"It figures," said the man. "You think there's a little 'funny business' going on there?"

"Not the way you mean it, but it's still funny business. I knew there had to be something going on, for this place to promise her a long-term assignment."

"Cheaper than hiring a permanent employee," the man put in.

"Of course, but they have a lot of nerve bringing her in, after the way they screwed Victoria over."

"You're right there. Just wait until Victoria finds out about this temp. She'll want blood for sure."

"And think about all the other employees who might

want the HR spot," Louise said. "The rumor is that a lot of us are going to be downsized. If there's a job available, why not post it? Almost anybody would be better than a temp."

"What's this temp like?" the man asked, making the word "temp" sound pretty nasty.

"She's typical," Louise responded. "You know what I mean?"

Did he? I wondered. What is a typical temp like? Stupid? Lazy? This was depressing. I felt like a scullery maid might feel hearing herself being discussed by the upstairs servants.

"So what do you think's going to happen?" the man asked. "Do you think they're going to make this temp an offer to become permanent? I thought they weren't hiring anyone."

"That's what they say, but what I'm afraid of is that they're going to get rid of people like us, the ones who have been around for a while, and hire people who will work for peanuts. They'll probably replace you and all of your guys with an outside contractor."

"Why? Why do you say that? Have you heard something?" The man's voice had risen sharply.

"No, no," Louise quickly said. "And keep your voice down. I said that because a lot of other companies contract out their security operations."

"Yeah, but—"

"Dorfmeyer's got a well-earned reputation for cutting back employees any way he can," Louise continued. "He's worked for three other companies in the last ten years. All of them have had serious layoffs."

"Hmmph! He better not have plans to get rid of me, what with my mortgage and my kids' school expenses," the man said. "Besides, since they've moved my whole damned department into the basement, they're probably through abusing us for a while. It's isolated, it's ugly, and it's cold as a damned meat locker."

"Management can do anything they want. That's why we've got to get a union in here."

"There's not going to be any union in here," the man countered gruffly.

"There might be if we unite," said Louise, adding, "I'm trying to get a workers' rally going."

The man chuckled. "You can rally all you want, but there ain't going to be a union."

"You'll see. Anyway, I better get back to my desk now. I've got *her* to worry about on top of everything else. Everyone in the building is nervous about her."

"Just what we needed. A low-level management spy. Is she at least pleasant?"

"So far. You can bet I'm being nice to her, too. I'm not crazy, you know. Good jobs in the benefits field aren't so easy to find. I don't want to antagonize her."

For a few seconds everything was quiet. I was beginning to think they'd left when I overheard Louise say, "Should we ask her to go to lunch with us? I mean, it can't hurt to be on her good side."

Though I'd never seen Louise's companion, I imagined him shrugging and frowning to the point that his eyebrows jutted over his eyes. Like a Neanderthal's.

"It's okay with me. I wouldn't mind picking her brain," he added.

At the same time that I said to myself, *In your dreams, you cretin,* he snickered. The idea of picking my loosely packed temp brain must have struck him as amusing.

"Yeah," Louise responded. "Just be careful how you do it, Casey."

"Hey! I'm an ex-cop. Remember?"

The man named Casey's voice was fading from my hearing when he added, "You're the one who better be careful, Louise. Watch your back with her around. She might turn out to be okay, but if she's tight with Dorfmeyer's 'boy,' she could cause trouble."

The notion that I was tight with Tom, to the point that I might cause trouble for R&G's employees, was so ludicrous that I might have laughed if it hadn't also been so unfair. Knowing that I was causing anxiety attacks all over the company, that when I had passed down a corridor heads would bend together to whisper, "Don't trust her. She's tight with Dorfmeyer's boy," gave me an awful feeling.

And how had Tom Terrific managed to get himself branded with that ugly mark, anyway? From the little bit I'd heard moments before, it wasn't difficult to figure out that R&G was in one of those nickel-squeezing, downsizing modes that most companies go through from time to time. There had been layoffs; there was a hiring freeze. Dorfmeyer, as CEO, surely had a lot to do with this, but in the total scheme of things, Tom couldn't be much more than a minor cog in the downsizing wheel. He'd only been at R&G for four months. How many jobs could he have been responsible for slashing?

My sympathies stayed with Tom as I locked the door to the inner room and headed toward my office. Poor Tom. Hated simply for doing his job, for trying to do his best for his Little League, puppy-hugging kids.

Walking down the hall, I made it a point to smile at the secretary who occupied the corner desk near the records room. It wasn't my imagination that she looked away.

Poor Tom? Hell! Poor Bonnie. Tom was a part of whatever was going on here. He was a player, making a nice fat salary and contemplating the possibility of a lucrative future at R&G. I was lower than low on the corporate ladder. A typical temp!

When I had passed the secretary, I heard her lift the receiver of her phone. She was going to dial a coworker, going to say something about me: "That temp tried to get friendly but I ignored her."

Or maybe she wasn't doing that at all. Maybe she was calling the supply department to order paper clips.

Don't get paranoid, I told myself. *You're not here to make friends. You're here to make enough money to get you through the next few weeks.*

• • •

I pushed the bike pedals harder, until sweat began breaking out across my back. The display panel mounted between the handlebars told me that I was going twelve miles an hour at a slight uphill incline. I'd already done fifteen minutes. Fifteen more and I'd shower and head for home.

There were all sorts of contraptions other than the stationary bikes upon which I might have expended some energy, and perhaps some calories, too—from the prosaic rowing machines and treadmills to strange devices that looked as if they might have seen service during the Spanish Inquisition.

The torture wasn't all physical, either. Had I wished, I could have inflicted psychological torture by monitoring my heart rate while I pedaled. Even more alarming than that, the young man who had signed me up for my membership was just dying to get at me with his calipers to test my fat/muscle ratio. Being reasonably certain that the fat would triumph, I'd put him off. After a few sessions on those Inquisition machines, maybe I'd give him his chance.

Please don't suppose that this place was all sweat and muscle. The health club, which was on the top floor of the new and glittery Royale Hotel, was all that Adele had promised. The sauna, with its heady scent of cedar, was so inviting I was afraid that if I went into it I'd never be able to make myself leave. I felt the same way about the steam room, and if everyone I'd seen slipping into the Jacuzzi appeared to have been born at about the time I was learning to drive, so what? Though I may be deluding myself, it's my belief that cellulite, when submerged in water, becomes invisible to the naked eye.

Those amenities, and the huge swimming pool, were included in the eight-week introductory membership I'd signed up for. Thanks to the R&G discount, it was affordable, but just barely. God help me if anything happened to my gig at the company before that membership expired. The membership cost would triple.

As I pedaled, I tried to calculate, mentally, how much I was going to be bringing home every week for the next six weeks minus the club membership, my rent, transportation, one third of a side-by-side refrigerator . . . How depressing. Not the mental exercise itself. I'm actually pretty good at that kind of thing. What was depressing was the figure I ended up with. I'd been a temp for too long. It was time to find something permanent, something with a future and a generous pension plan.

My gloomy line of thought had distracted me from my pedaling. Glancing at the speedometer, I saw that I'd dropped down to a bare crawl. Gritting my teeth, I pushed the pedals harder, until sweat was gathering above my eyebrows. I refused to slow down. Only ten more minutes to go.

On a big-screen television mounted on the wall over one of the rowing machines, MTV ruled. The rock video in progress featured men and women wearing combat gear and gesturing angrily with their fists and feet. They all looked psychotic. Searching for something more cheerful to engage myself with while I pedaled, I focused on the long lanes of the swimming pool, visible through the plate-glass window that separated the pool from the machine room where the bikes were located.

Every lane of the pool was occupied. A few of the swimmers moved roughly, arms and legs lashing, sending dots of water into the air and leaving rough wakes behind them. Others were smoother, and the swimmer in the lane nearest the window, a man, was the smoothest of all. His arms seemed to cut into the water the way a knife cuts through softened butter, and though he moved rapidly, his feet never rose above the surface. He turned his head and breathed easily on every fourth stroke. His eyes were shielded by black-rimmed goggles. Goggles usually don't make much of a fashion statement, but on this man, moving otter-sleek through the water, they added a touch of *otherworld* mystery.

At the far end of the lane the swimmer turned and headed back in my direction. When he reached the end of the pool nearer me, he stopped swimming and hoisted himself partway onto the blue tile ledge. His swim goggles must have bothered him, because he pulled them from his head and tossed them onto the concrete deck. His back was toward me, which gave me a chance to admire his lean but nicely muscled shoulders.

My distance vision isn't great, and I'm afraid that I was staring intensely—okay, so I was squinting, attempting to bring the undeniably pleasant view into clearer focus— when the swimmer turned. He peered through the window separating us. His gaze caught mine.

Tom Hurley! My boss. And he'd caught me ogling him like an awestruck teenager. Embarrassed, I started to look away but caught myself. That would be more embarrassing still. My hand, and Tom's, went into the air at the same time. Our waves corresponded. Then, to my relief, he slid back into the pool.

My cheeks were warm, and when I realized that my pedaling had slowed to the point where the speedometer was registering less than two miles an hour, they began burning as if I was running a high fever. Upping my speed, and determined to finish my workout, I shifted my eyes toward the MTV war games and did my best to keep them there.

For the next seven minutes Tom hung on the edge of my vision. A couple times my eyes were pulled back, unconsciously, to his body skimming through the water. Each time I quickly turned my eyes away, but he remained very much a part of my awareness. I was relieved when the odometer finally hit that magical six-mile mark. I all but ran to the women's dressing room.

As I showered and dressed, I tried to convince myself that Tom couldn't have realized that I'd been feasting on the back of his shoulders with my eyes. My embarrassment was groundless, I told myself. The next time I saw Tom, I'd mention the gym casually. "So you belong to the health club, too," I'd say. Tom would respond "Yes," and maybe we'd talk treadmills or aerobics classes for a few seconds. That would be the end of it.

The opportunity for this casual little chat came along much sooner than I'd expected. When I emerged from the women's dressing room, Tom was standing at the gym's reception desk in his street clothes, a trench coat draped over his arm. He gestured for me to wait until he had signed up for a pool lane the following evening, and then proceeded to steal my line.

"So you belong to the club, too. Have you tried any of the classes?"

I was a little flustered that my script was already in tatters, and responded like an actor paid to spout the corporate line. "No. I just joined. I took advantage of R&G's discount."

"Smart move. For me the club comes with the territory," he said.

Leaving the gym, we crossed the hall and waited together for the elevator.

"You mean that management gets a free membership?"

Tom shook his head, causing a lock of his still-damp hair to fall over his forehead. The impulse to reach up and comb it back with my fingers was a very tiny one, as my impulses go, and was easily resisted. There are things you just don't do.

"No," Tom was saying. "We get almost the same benefits as everyone else. What I meant was, I'm staying here at the Royale; the gym is part of the hotel package."

The elevator arrived and two men hurried off, gym bags in their hands. Tom stepped aside and let me get on first.

"It's quite a hotel," I said, glancing into one of the marbleized mirrors that lined the elevator. "Very glittery."

He grimaced. "That it is. Frankly I could do with a little less glitter"—we were the only passengers at that point, but he leaned closer anyway—"a few less noisy tourists. You don't know what a heart-stopping experience it is to be woken up at three A.M. by a bunch of drunks bellowing outside your door in a language you don't understand. Actually," he added, straightening, "what I really could do with is going home to my own house, but with the project I've got to have on Carl Dorfmeyer's desk tomorrow morning, there's no chance I'll get home tonight."

"You're going back to the office now?"

The elevator had stopped on a lower floor. Tom nodded as a group of hotel guests—loud-talking men with heavy Middle European accents whose coats smelled of cigarette smoke—stepped into the elevator. Tom and I squeezed toward the back of the car. A few floors lower and we stopped once again. This time three middle-aged couples pushed their way in. They spoke German to each other and studied maps diligently, following the lines of Manhattan's streets with their eyes and their fingers. Tourists on the town.

By then Tom and I were at the elevator's back wall, not quite slammed into it, but without much room to maneuver. Tom was in a corner, with me near enough to him that, in spite of the stale cigarette odor wafting through the air, I picked up the scent of the soap from the gym's shower on his skin. Was he picking up the same smell from me?

I found that notion uncomfortably intimate and wondered if I was blushing. The elevator slowed again and stopped. A large man in a heavy tweed coat blocked my view of the front of the car, but I heard the eager female voices.

"Can we make it?"

"The more the merrier," one of the boisterous men responded.

Isn't anyone but me even a little bit claustrophobic?

The large man squeezed into me, the tweed of his coat scraping my cheek. I'd put on my own coat before leaving the women's locker room. I was uncomfortably warm now, and my knees felt wobbly. As I tried to shift myself and move my face away from the itchy fabric, I was forced even nearer to Tom.

He slid an arm free to accommodate my body, and then laid his hand on my shoulder and patted it lightly. Surprised, mortified, but at the same time comforted, I looked at him.

"It's okay," he said. "We're going express now."

The weak feeling in my knees disappeared. Within seconds the elevator's doors opened on the lobby floor. The invisible women and the various tourists and the loud-talking men burst through them and disappeared, unaware that they'd contributed to my near-anxiety attack, and also to the feverish adolescent crush I'd momentarily developed on my boss.

Tom appropriately and properly moved his arm away from me as soon as there was space in the car, and I'm glad to say that my legs held me just fine as I stepped from the elevator onto the gaudy plaid carpeting. The crush, I realized with relief, had been fleeting. I made a mental note: *Just have to steer clear of those close encounters, Bonnie.*

"My wife gets nervous in tight spaces," Tom said conversationally as he slipped on his coat. "I recognize the symptoms."

Isn't it remarkable how we can experience something that sends our emotions rocketing without the object of our inner uproar even noticing.

And thank goodness for that! I can't imagine what a mess my life would be if, every time I said to myself, *He looks awfully good,* the "he" being scrutinized read my mind.

Like the rest of us, Tom was no mind reader, and as we walked through the hotel's lobby, I got the slightest hint that he might not be an angel, either. We passed a dimly lit cocktail lounge where candles glowed on small round tables. I glimpsed couples, their heads bent together, and heard a peal of high-pitched laughter rising above the tinkling of a piano's keys. My imagination often runs amok, but before I'd had a chance to consider what I'd say if Tom asked me to join him for a drink, he surprised me by doing exactly that.

"Are you sure you're okay?" he asked. "If you'd like, we can stop in here for a drink."

We were just outside the entrance. At the nearest table, a fiftyish man in a green plaid jacket guffawed at something said by his companion, a blond woman whose makeup looked as if it could withstand a mortar attack. I saw the man's hand creep up her thigh. My gaze shifted past an anemic-looking Christmas tree to the bar itself, where a young bartender waited, smug condescension stamped on his face, for a middle-aged couple who already seemed woozy to decide whether another Mai Tai was in order.

The place smacked of something that to me was unappealing. Loneliness, perhaps, and lapses that had more to do with alcohol than passion.

Tom's hand pressed softly into my back, and when I glanced up at him, I thought there was something in his face that I hadn't seen there before. It wasn't out-and-out lust by any means. It was simply a touch of . . . abandon, a hint that the words "We might have some fun" could be running through his head.

"Oh, I don't think so," I said. "I have a hungry cat at home."

"I understand perfectly," Tom said, turning away from the bar. "Our basset hound runs our lives."

Tom followed me through the hotel's revolving door. As we left, an airport bus was disgorging its load of tourists. We dodged a mountain of duffel bags to get to the sidewalk. It was almost eight P.M. and most offices were closed, but the midtown sidewalk was still busy. Tom and I were sandwiched into a crowd as we waited for the light on the corner to change.

"Where are you headed?" he asked.

"The subway stop at Columbus Circle."

"I'll walk you there. Work can wait a little longer."

Tom and I walked together under trees strung with twinkling fairy lights and past red-suited Salvation Army volunteers with their clanging bells. We chatted companionably, stopping a couple times to look at newly arranged Christmas displays in shop windows. The cool air refreshed me, clearing my head of any remnants of the thoughts that had swamped it in the elevator. As for Tom, the little scene by the bar might never have happened. By the time we reached the stairs leading down to the subway station, he had described to me the details of a salary survey he wanted me to work on. We were all business once again.

3

AFTER TOM AND I HAD SAID A QUICK good-bye, I trotted down the subway steps. I was already planning what I was going to pick up at the Chinese restaurant near my apartment—the ever-popular broccoli in garlic sauce and, my personal favorite, cold sesame noodles. Pushing through the turnstile and hurrying toward the platform—was that an A Express coming?—I gave a silent thanks that I'd turned down Tom's drink invitation. Imagining myself settling down at one of those little round tables and gazing at Tom's charmingly boyish face through flickering candlelight was just too mortifying to dwell on for very long. Given the right set of signals—and I was almost certain that Tom had been prepared to send those signals—there was a slim chance that I could have made a major whopping fool of myself.

The train that roared into the station wasn't an A Express. It was a local and of no use to me, and so I began walking north on the platform to position myself at the front of the next A train. On my way, I stepped neatly around a beggar who was jittering his way down the platform, rattling coins in a paper cup and repeating the always reassuring mantra, "I don't want to have to hurt nobody."

Most of the commuters boarded the local. When that train had pulled out, and relative quiet was restored to the platform, I heard the begger going into his spiel with special enthusiasm.

"I'm not going to hurt you, lady. Not at all. Just want to ask you if you could spare . . ."

From the sound of his voice he was at least a couple dozen feet behind me, but I quickened my step before looking over my shoulder. The begger's pitch, I immediately saw, was no longer directed at me. The woman he was now confronting was skirting the edge of the platform, keeping as much distance as possible between herself and the beggar.

She didn't strike me as a regular subway rider. She kept watching the man as if expecting him to rush her, not realizing that you never meet their eyes unless you're forced to. Even when she had passed him, and he had moved on to another prospect, she kept glancing back.

From the little I could see of the woman—she wore a puffy blue knit hat pulled over her ears—she was quite attractive in a patrician, strong-featured way, and well pulled together. Her complexion was of the peaches-and-cream variety and her clothes—tweed slacks and mid-heeled loafers peeked from under a flaring brown coat—tastefully conservative. She could have been one of those Upper East Side women who take the subway only under duress. She sort of looked the part, but then occasionally so do I.

The sound of an oncoming train reached the station. Forgetting about the woman, I quickened my steps. It wasn't so late that I was nervous, but when the trains are almost empty I like to ride in the first car. The motormen who ride in those cars may not be prepared to leap into action at the first sign of trouble, but they do have radios.

I was only vaguely aware of the woman keeping pace with me as I stepped nearer the edge of the platform. The train proved to be a D heading for the Bronx and so I stepped back. The woman, who was about fifteen feet away, appeared poised to board the train, but changed her mind and also stepped back.

The D train pulled out, leaving the station almost deserted. At that point I certainly didn't think the woman was following me. She was simply not accustomed to the subways, I thought. When an A train approached a minute later, I glanced toward her. She had been looking at me, or at least in my direction, but she immediately averted her gaze.

The A train squealed to a stop, and as I moved into position near a door, I glanced once again toward the woman. Almost as if waiting for a go-ahead, she watched me step toward an opening door. From the corner of my eye, I saw her do the same.

I got into the car and took a seat, but after the doors had closed and the train had begun to move, curiosity got the best of me. Standing, I glanced through the window separating my car from the one behind it. The woman in the brown coat had boarded the train. She was in the car directly behind mine.

By New York City subway standards the woman's behavior wasn't alarming. It was peculiar, though. She had seemed out of place and nervous on the platform, but had safety been her primary goal, she would have gotten into the car where I was riding. It wasn't full, but there were sufficient passengers to give an aura of safety. The car she was in was almost empty.

The A train travels a long express route from the tip of Manhattan to the far end of Queens. However, my usual route—from my apartment in Washington Heights to Columbus Circle in midtown Manhattan, and back—involves just five stops, the first uptown stop after Columbus Circle being 125th Street in Harlem. On a good run that segment of the trip, which covers almost seventy blocks, takes about ten minutes, and this was a good run. When the train approached the 125th Street station, I once again moved into a spot that allowed me to peek into the next car. The woman in the brown coat didn't strike me as someone who would be comfortable in Harlem after dark, but I've been wrong about people before.

It looked, at first, as if I was going to be wrong again. As the train slowed she moved to the edge of her seat and gripped her handbag securely. The train stopped and the door next to her slid open. She swiveled and rose partway, using the pole by the door to pull herself up, and stared out the door and up the platform, as if considering leaving the train. When the two-bell ring that indicates the doors are about to close sounded, however, she sank back into her seat.

She repeated this same performance at the next Harlem stop on 145th Street. Was she looking for a sign on a platform that would let her know when she'd reached her stop? Was she on her way to Columbia Presbyterian Hospital to visit a patient, or heading for the uptown bus station at 175th Street? No, she wasn't. At both those stops she stood poised, as if about to leave the car, but changed her mind just before the train's doors shut.

When the doors opened at my stop—181st Street—I glanced at the car the woman was in as I stepped onto the platform. She was standing at the door. Was it my imagination, or did she step through the door only when she saw that I'd left the train?

Several dozen passengers had also gotten off the train. I lagged, making certain that I remained at the back of the group leaving the station. There are two routes out of the station at that exit. Both bring you to the same place—the intersection of Fort Washington Avenue and 181st Street—but the most popular one, for obvious reasons, is the escalator. I only take the other route, a long, torturous series of stairs, when the escalator is broken or on those rare occasions when I feel like my cardiovascular system needs a jolt.

I took the stairs that evening, though, as soon as I was certain that the woman in the brown coat was on the escalator to stay. The stairs—there are seven flights of them—are a challenge, but I generally manage them without taking a break. This time, however, I paused at each landing, took a few deep breaths, stretched my hamstrings, anything to take up time.

At the top of the stairs there are exits on both the east and west sides of Fort Washington. I took my usual west exit, which brought me to the street directly outside the Chinese restaurant. Before walking into its steamy interior, I again hesitated, this time to look around. The street was still busy, but some of the shops—the pharmacy, the hardware store—were closed and shuttered for the night. Pedestrians' faces showed under the illuminated streetlights and were caught by headlights from passing vehicles, but the face of the woman in the brown coat and blue hat was not among them.

Inside the restaurant I gave the counterman my order, then slid into one of the incredibly funky chairs that contribute so much to the restaurant's less-than-haute ambience. Age and wear, or an especially enthusiastic diner, had put a jagged gash in the worn orange plastic upholstery. My new wool scarf caught in this gash, and when I pulled it free, a nice-sized strand of the wool remained behind. Great! Once I'd finally settled myself, I used one of the paper napkins on the table to clean a spot in the steamy window beside me.

I recognized the blue hat immediately. The woman was in the diner on the other side of the street, sitting in a window booth reading a newspaper. She held an oversized white mug near her face and, as I watched, shifted slightly and lifted the mug to her mouth. At the same time, she glanced out the window. Was she looking toward me? Without digging my glasses out of my bag, I couldn't tell. And frankly, I was growing tired of this game. For all I

knew I may have been the sole player. The woman might
have been waiting for a friend. Whoever she was, whatever
she was doing in my neighborhood, the woman in the
brown coat was an unlikely mugger. Besides, the counterman had just waved a brown paper bag in my direction,
and by then, with my stomach making serious inquiries
about dinner, what I cared most about was reaching my
apartment with my Chinese carryout intact.

As I walked down the hill toward my building, I asked
myself why I'd become leery of someone so ordinary, and
so obviously harmless. It had to be the conversation I'd
overheard earlier that day, and Louise's words: *Just wait
until Victoria finds out about her. She'll want blood for
sure.*

Victoria. Maybe the woman in the brown coat was the
woman Louise and her friend Casey had been talking about.
If that was the case, though, how would she have recognized me? For that matter, why would she be out for *my*
blood? I hadn't stolen her job. I was a temp!

Almost certain that I'd been overreacting, I still glanced
up the street before stepping into my building's lobby. As
I did, the headlights of a passing car picked up a glint of
burnished brown. Was the woman on the other side of the
street near the shuttered butcher shop watching me from
behind the trunk of a tree? Or was what I'd seen the gleam
of a brown plastic trash bag?

Another car was coming down the hill. I waited until its
lights caught the shuttered shop. There was no sign of the
woman in the brown coat, but there was no sign of a brown
trash bag, either. The woman could easily have concealed
herself behind a car parked at the curb, but it was getting
late and I was getting hungrier by the minute.

I turned my back on the street and whoever might be
lurking there. As I crossed the lobby of my building,
though, I caught myself saying the name under my breath:
"Victoria."

•   •   •

The Codwallader sisters, who live across the hall from me, don't move as easily as they once did. Eunice shuffles, dragging her feet, and Ethel, who has suffered a mild stroke, now uses a cane, so that hearing the pair of them coming down the hall, I'm sometimes reminded of a dance step. *Slide-slide-tap. Slide-slide-tap.*

That evening their steps were even slower than usual, so much slower, in fact, that I turned down the radio in my kitchen to listen. The sisters have always regarded me as, at best, a questionable neighbor. Still, if anything was wrong with either of them, I'm physically the nearest to them, and the one, logically, to be called upon.

When the sisters reached their door, which is almost directly across from mine, I didn't hear the usual fumbling for keys. Wondering if there really was a problem, I walked to my door and listened closely.

Whispers. That's what I heard. The Codwallader sisters were whispering in the hall. Our hallway doors are metal. Sound carries through them.

". . . always told you she was up to no good."

"You didn't have to tell me. I knew from the day she moved in."

It didn't sound as if the sisters were in trouble, but they seemed to think someone else was. Returning to the kitchen, I turned up the radio and then picked up a bag of trash to carry to the trash chute in the building's hallway.

When I swung open my door, the surprise of finding the Codwallader sisters standing directly outside it, even leaning into it, made me gasp. The sisters gasped, too.

Eunice recovered first. "We were just going into our apartment." She quickly gathered up a couple grocery bags that were on the floor while Ethel rummaged in a coat pocket and pulled out a set of house keys.

"Good night," I said, heading toward the trash room.

The only answer I got from the sisters was the slam of their apartment door.

They'd been listening outside my apartment door, which probably meant that I was the one who was "up to no good." What was it this time? I wondered. I hadn't had any sleep-over boyfriends in months, and the last party I'd had had been an afternoon baby shower. Maybe this had something to do with the woman in the brown coat. Might she have accosted the sisters on the street and told them something about me? That seemed unlikely. Anyway, there wasn't anything the woman in the brown coat could have told them unless she used her imagination. She didn't even know me.

I no sooner was in my apartment when my phone rang. Being in a paranoid frame of mind, I let the machine take the call.

"Hey, Bonnie," Mike's now recognizable voice said. "I guess you're still not there. I had time to kill today, so I drove up to your neighborhood. From the way you described it I expected it to be pretty seedy, but the area doesn't seem half-bad. I checked out the names on the buzzers in your building to make sure you still live there. And you do. So call me. Maybe we can relive some of the good times we had together. I hope you thought they were good times," he added. "I did. Or at least some of them were good."

He left his number again before hanging up. After that there was a click, followed by a sound indicating that my recording tape was at its end. After jotting Mike's number in an address book I carry in my tote, I erased all the old messages and started the tape fresh. While I did this, an explanation for the Codwallader sisters' odd behavior unfolded.

They had come across Mike in the building vestibule as he examined the names over the buzzers. What had he been wearing? It was too cold for the outfits I remembered—the baggy shorts, the threadbare sneakers, the T-shirts with the faded logos—but Mike, living on the edge as he did, could have come up with something guaranteed not only to withstand the cold weather but to set the sisters' antennas quivering. He was living on a boat, which led me to imagine dank blue jeans and a rubber mackinaw stained with fish remains. Maybe he'd worn a black watch cap, pulled so low on his forehead that he seemed to peer up from under it.

Mike, greatly misjudging the sisters, assuming they were being helpful rather than suspicious when they fixed him with their bifocaled evil eyes and asked what his business was, would have mentioned my name. He would have told them he was an old friend, and might have hinted, in a spirit of jocularity and trying to weasel his way into the building, that our friendship had surpassed the ordinary definition of that word. He wouldn't have gone so far as to tell the Codwallader sisters that we'd met while he was on the run from the U.S. government—even Mike wasn't that naive—but he might have hinted that he and I had shared a . . . past.

Thinking about that, I might have become annoyed at Mike. I couldn't, though. Mike was too nice a guy. That may seem an odd thing to say about an admitted felon, but it's the truth. He's a great believer in personal worth, in judging people by what's inside them, and not their exterior. He wouldn't think that the Codwallader sisters would judge him by his greasy jacket and pants, and decide he was a suspicious character because his cap almost covered his eyes. And he'd never think that I'd ignore his phone calls, either. Friends don't treat each other that way. Instead of feeling annoyed, I felt guilty.

I didn't ignore my phone the next time it rang. As soon as I heard Sam's voice, I grabbed the receiver.

At that time, Sam and I had been ''dating'' for about three weeks. You could say that our relationship had run in reverse order. First I'd moved into his house, then we'd gotten engaged, and now, with me back in my own apartment, we'd finally regressed to dates. We had one planned for the following night.

"I got tickets to a show tomorrow," he said. "We'll have dinner first. A friend of mine recommended a place in midtown."

A few weeks earlier, I would immediately have supposed

that the show was the boat show or the auto show or something of that type. Now, though, I wasn't too surprised when Sam said that the show was a musical. A rock musical, yet! The man was trying very hard.

Sam had spent twenty-five years of wedded bliss with a woman who, had it not been for anatomical differences, might almost have been his clone. Forget about the fact that he's Jewish and Eileen was an Irish Catholic. They generally liked the same music, the same movies, the same sports, and the same foods prepared the same way, and on the rare occasions when Eileen wanted to do something— see a musical, for example—and Sam didn't, she did it alone or with woman friends.

Sam had wanted—expected!—me to slip into Eileen's place in his life smooth as a foot slipping into a well-worn slipper. And don't misunderstand. It was a good place. I could have cherished much of it. Not all of it, though, which was why I was back in my apartment in Washington Heights.

Trying to explain why Sam's refusal to accommodate some of my interests became such a problem for me, I can get defensive. Several friends have told me how they would have handled the situation. Sam being an attractive man, and these friends being single, you can bet they all claim they would have handled it better than I did. As for my mother, she persisted in lecturing me, until I sometimes felt as if my relationship with Sam could be a chapter in a bestseller titled *Why Good Men Love Unappreciative Women.*

And don't suppose it was only my mom and my friends who had carried on when I'd returned the engagement ring. I'd gone in for some self-flagellation, too, occasionally whipping my heart raw during the first few weeks after I'd moved back to my apartment. Life with Sam hadn't been all bad. In fact, none of it had been Bad with a capital *B,* and a lot of it had been pretty good.

The phone rang, waking me from a deep sleep. After debating for a second, I reached for the receiver. Probably

Mike. I owed him the courtesy of an answer. He had traveled up to my neighborhood to find me.

"Hi," I said sleepily, certain that Mike was at the other end of the line.

After a few seconds of quiet, I gave a more cautious, "Hello?"

Suddenly I was wide awake. Holding the receiver closer to my ear, I listened carefully. There was someone there, holding the phone, listening to me. In the background there was a tinny blur of sound before the line abruptly went dead.

It hadn't been Mike. That wasn't his style. And it certainly wasn't Sam's. How about that woman in the brown coat, though? Victoria. Hardly conscious that I was doing it, I'd attached that name to the woman. Was Victoria inclined to making hang-up phone calls?

Someone certainly was. Before dawn I got two more, one about an hour after the first, and another at 4:30 in the morning. I took the phone off the hook after that, but I never did get back to sleep. I got up at five and drank coffee as day broke on the Palisades across the River.

4

It was early, but Carl Dorfmeyer's secretary had already chewed off most of her lipstick. The bright red remains of the little that was left had crept into the fissures around her lips.

"Mr. Dorfmeyer is on the telephone. You can go in as soon as he hangs up. And don't be nervous. His bark is worse than his bite."

That may have been true, but I noticed that she kept her voice at a near whisper as she spoke, and her eyes darted toward his open office door. Maybe she wasn't nervous, but she was very much on the alert.

"There won't be anything that isn't routine," she added. "He gives me all his confidential work."

She took a swallow of inky-black coffee from a paper cup, swiveled in her chair, focused on her steno pad, and went back to transcribing the document she'd been working on when I'd approached her seconds before. I glanced at the nameplate attached to the front of her desk. Rose Morris. Her fingers were positively flying over her keyboard. Amazing! Rose Morris could type steno notes faster than I type printed copy.

The Big Kahuna's secretary was swamped, and my boss Tom, the traitor, had volunteered me.

"Just this one time, Bonnie," he'd begged. "I know you took steno in high school. I remember that you used to get Raymond to read you—"

"to read me those disgusting speed exercises: 'Dear Mr. Goodbody: In response to your letter of . . .'"

I hate dictation. I say that unequivocally. I hated it on the first day of my junior year in high school when my commercial-arts teacher, the dreaded Mrs. Utterback—referred to behind her back by her students as "Mrs. Upperbutt"—introduced me to the dot that signifies "a" and "ing." I hated it through two years of short forms and speed tests, and I hated it through a variety of temp jobs. Eventually coming to my senses, I removed every hint of my steno skill, such as it was, from my résumé, substituting the foggy but far more agreeable "administrative assistant." For me, "Bring your pad" are the three most dreaded words in the English language.

So it is understandable that I was uncertain whether my steno skills existed at all. Still, though I was in no rush to get into Dorfmeyer's office and put my skills to the test, when it comes to office work I've always been able to muddle through. I figured things would be the same this time.

"Pssst. He's getting off the phone."

I glanced at Rose, who was tucking a strand of her brown hair into place. She nodded to assure me that the big moment was almost there. In seconds I would be taking a seat in Dorfmeyer's office.

The desk nearest Rose's was occupied by an exceptionally pretty young woman with dark, curly hair, who spent her days as a statistical typist. Glancing her way, I caught her pitying look.

"You can go in now," Rose said.

Just to be sure, I tapped briskly on Mr. Dorfmeyer's door frame.

He was reading through a document, but flicked a stony glare at me.

"I'm Bonnie Indermill. I'm here to take some dictation."

"Do you intend to take it from the doorway?"

That was not the kind of question that requires, or would even permit, an answer. Three chairs were lined up, straight as soldiers at attention, before Dorfmeyer's desk. I chose the one nearest the door. I don't think it crossed my mind that I might want to make a quick exit, but that thought may have been dwelling somewhere in my subconscious.

Whatever Dorfmeyer was reading kept his attention for another minute or two, until my own attention started wandering. I knew little about Dorfmeyer other than the fact that some of his staff hated him, and what I could see of his office offered no clues other than the requisite photos— a wife, three kids, a dog. Only the dog, a black monster that looked like something that should be patrolling a prison perimeter—was not involved in whacking at a ball. For the wife and daughter it was tennis, for the two sons, baseball. Another corporate American's family at play. Makes you wonder where all the quiet bookworm kids have gone. They can't be totally extinct. There must be a few around, but I suppose they don't present much of a photo op.

Apart from the photos, everything visible in Dorfmeyer's office—from the cheap pen gripped in his free hand to the day-of-the-week calendar on its plastic stand—appeared to be straight out of the company's supply closet. Dorfmeyer may have been on the highest corporate level, but if what I'd heard Louise say in the records room was correct, he was a rolling stone. He appeared to have gathered none of the corporate moss that more stable executives pile their desks with—the chachkas out of the Tiffany Corporate Gifts catalog, the "Ten Year" pen-and-pencil sets, and the like.

As he flipped a page over and began reading another

document, I studied him through lowered eyes. If mere appearances had been the sole criterion for judging, I might not have been even slightly anxious. Dorfmeyer was big, yes, but far from a hulking presence. In fact, with his thinning, graying hair and bland features, he was so ordinary looking that you could have plopped him down in any office in the city and he wouldn't have attracted much attention. Only his glare was off-putting, and since that was directed at the reading material, I began to relax.

My gaze slid past Dorfmeyer and out his window, to the spire of the Empire State Building. All these years in New York and I'd never been to the top. Maybe now, with Sam on his "see New York" binge . . .

"Are you ready? I'd hate to interrupt your sightseeing."

Dorfmeyer's voice was so sharp that I felt almost as if he'd slapped me to get my attention, but before I could reflect on my bruised feelings, he started.

"Memo to the manager of office services. It has come to my attention that the fresh flowers placed by a florist in our reception areas every Monday morning are costing the company . . ."

Forty-five minutes later I was handed a file containing letters and memos Dorfmeyer was responding to, and dismissed with the command: "I have an appointment at twelve-thirty. Have drafts on my desk before then."

Most of my right hand, my writing hand, ached slightly. My thumb, however, ached considerably, and could have used a brief massage and a few minutes' rest. The rest of me could have used a visit to the ladies' room, followed by one to the snack bar.

There was no time for any of that, however. Though I had almost two hours to type five or six short memos and a couple of even shorter letters, and I type well enough, I can't type what I can't read and I was afraid I couldn't read my steno. It was even worse than I'd remembered. Each glance back that I'd managed while struggling to keep up with Dorfmeyer had increased my growing anxiety, until

I'd given up trying to scan my notes at all for fear of becoming completely paralyzed.

I hurried down the hall and back to my office with my eyes plastered to a meaningless scratch and the incomprehensible curl beside it. What on earth was this line? And that loop? My only chance was to match the scribbles to the documents in the folder.

"Did Dorfmeyer have anything interesting to say?" asked Louise before I'd had a chance to sit down. "Anything about who's getting promoted, or canned? Any big secrets?"

She hadn't even arrived at work when I'd been called into Dorfmeyer's office, but in a place like R&G news travels fast. I dropped the steno pad onto my desk, plopped into my chair, and stared at my notes. My main interest in what Dorfmeyer had said had been getting it down on that pad, but the truth was that he hadn't revealed even a minor company secret to me. All the hot items must have been saved for Rose, that lucky lady.

All I could have offered Louise in the way of gossip was that R&G's reception areas would no longer be brightened by fresh flowers, but while mentioning that might have done something to alleviate Louise's distrust of me, I kept it to myself. The flames of employee unrest at R&G seemed to be doing just fine without my adding fuel to them.

I shrugged. "It was all routine."

"Well, before you start transcribing," Louise said, "you should take a look at this. It will tell you what kind of a man you're killing yourself for."

"I'm not exactly killing . . ."

Louise laid a large manila envelope on my desk, directly on top of the steno pad. I looked at her, wondering what this was all about, but she simply tilted her head and said, "Keep it out of sight. If anybody comes in, put it in your drawer."

Curiosity, as well as the need to prove to Louise that I wasn't *killing* myself, made me open the envelope. Inside were copies of two short newspaper articles. I quickly scanned one from the *Times*. It was dated almost a year earlier. Under a large, unflattering photo of Dorfmeyer was the headline:

CARL DORFMEYER TO ASSUME TOP ADMINISTRATIVE POST AT RICHARDS & GOODE

Richards & Goode, Inc., the electronics giant, has hired Carl Dorfmeyer away from Butler International, where he has been director of operations for two years. Dorfmeyer, who will join R&G after the first of the year as chief executive officer, has earned a reputation as a tough taskmaster. During the last decade he has held high administrative positions at two corporations in addition to Butler, all of which have experienced downsizings during his term of office. ''Don't think of it as downsizing. Think of it as *rightsizing*,'' Dorfmeyer has been quoted as saying.

The article went on a bit longer, discussing R&G's almost half century of profits, and a recent year of losses. It also discussed the ways Dorfmeyer had cut the expenses, and the staffs, of his former employers.

Louise had returned to her desk, but as I took the second article from the envelope, I was acutely aware of her eyes on me.

This second article had been published in one of the New York City tabloids a couple days after the *Times* article appeared. From the first line to the last, it lambasted Dorfmeyer.

DORFMEYER THE DOWNSIZER LANDS TOP SPOT AT RICHARDS & GOODE!

Heads are expected to roll when Carl Dorfmeyer, the new chief executive officer, swings his hatchet at the employees of corporate giant Richards & Goode. Dorfmeyer earned his nickname, Dorfmeyer the Downsizer, over the last ten years, during which time he oversaw the downsizings at a number of corporations. One former Butler International employee, *downsized* after seventeen years of service, described the corporate atmosphere during Dorfmeyer's reign as "alternately depressing and terrifying." Now it's R&G's turn, and its employees, even the most loyal long-term ones, had better get their résumés in order.

According to a reliable source, Dorfmeyer isn't looking for a long-term slot with any of his employers. His stints have been so short that he spends his weeknights in corporate suites while his wife and children remain in their home outside of Chicago. A heavy contributor to conservative political causes, Dorfmeyer, a self-described "God-fearing family man," sees his own family only on weekends. Interesting behavior for a man who has made no secret of his view that anyone who can't manage a wife and children can't manage a business, either.

"So?" Louise asked when I shoved the *Post* article back into the envelope. "Are you still so eager to please?"

"I'm not *eager* to please, but I am eager to get my work done." I held the envelope out to her.

Louise's expression had been anticipatory—eyes wide behind her glasses, eyebrows raised—but it changed abruptly. The creases in her forehead deepened. Her lips drooped. She was once again disgruntled. My response had been all wrong. Oh, I knew very well what she wanted. She wanted me to feel as outraged about the situation at R&G as she was. She wanted an officemate who shared not only her lengthy coffee breaks but her anger. I couldn't, though. It wasn't that I didn't sympathize—almost anybody who works full-time has my sympathy—but I was a temp, and a nicely paid one at that.

"You wouldn't be here at all if this department was staffed the way it used to be," Louise said, refusing to drop the subject. "There were three people in this office a year ago. One of them, our recruiting assistant, resigned in the spring and was never replaced."

"What about the other person?"

"Victoria was forced out," Louise said angrily. "Management put her in a position where she had to resign. She'd been here over ten years. She was a real professional, and always supportive of the women in the company, too. Now there's just you and me, and you're a temp. What do you think about that?"

What I thought about that was that I suspected her good friend Victoria of following me home the previous night and of making harassing phone calls. I couldn't very well say anything, though. I had no proof that the woman in the brown coat was Victoria, and to falsely accuse someone I'd never even met would have done nothing for my already shaky reputation.

Louise continued looking at me, waiting for an answer. I didn't have one for her, but I responded amiably. Like it or not, Louise and I were going to be spending a lot of time together.

"I've got to get this dictation drafted before I go to lunch," I said, picking up my steno pad, "but I would like to hear about the woman who was forced out."

"Then what about having lunch with me and my friend Casey?"

There it was. The friendly gesture. I wasn't under any illusions about it. Louise and her friend Casey wanted to *pick my brain.* Well, I wanted to pick theirs, too.

"Fine. In the cafeteria?"

"No! Let's go somewhere we can talk. Around here, you never know who's going to hear you. I don't trust just anybody," Louise added pointedly. "There are some sneaks around."

And, as far as Louise was concerned, I was one of them.

"Okay," I said. "If you like Thai food, there's a good restaurant—"

Louise interrupted. "Actually, Casey has already picked a place, if that's okay with you. It's a private club he joined.

Casey has kind of a male thing about being in charge,'' she
added.

''Then let's let him. I'm not fussy.''

Not usually, anyway. I stared through the fog, appalled. The
Little Havana Grill, on Seventh Avenue near Forty-eighth
Street, wasn't far from the office, but only a wildly determined R&G sneak would have followed us very far into
the place.

Viewed from half a block away it had looked sort of
men's club. It was heavy on the maroon—the awning, the
mat extending from the dark wood door, the curtains barely
visible through the windows—and not terribly Havana-like,
but what the heck!

''Cuban food?'' I had asked naively.

Casey shook his head. ''Naw. This isn't that kind of
place.''

Then why was it called Little Havana? Nearing the restaurant, I was still able to see only a vague glimmer of light
through its windows. Louise put what I was thinking into
words.

''It looks kind of dark.''

I expect she meant that as an offhand comment, but
Casey, quick to take offense, did just that.

''Give me a break!'' he snapped. ''The place has got
atmosphere. Hey, speaking of dark, how many women does
it take to change a lightbulb?''

We women shook our heads.

''A dozen. One to change it, and eleven to form a support
group.''

Ha-ha-ha. This could be an awfully long lunch.

Casey, clearly pleased with his joke, used his free hand
to open the door. His other hand gripped the uniquely
smelly fat cigar he'd been puffing on since Louise and I
had met him on the sidewalk in front of the office. Since
the no-smoking law went into effect in New York, you see
smokers gathered in front of many Manhattan office build-

ings, all puffing like crazy. Casey had fit in perfectly with the group in front of R&G. That should have given me a clue.

As Casey crushed out his cigar on the sidewalk, Louise walked into the restaurant. I was right behind her and noticed that she flinched. Not a nanosecond later, when what felt like a wall of smoke hit me, I did the same.

Never mind that to get to the little dining area we had to shoulder our way through a thick crowd—mostly male— that had gathered around the bar to drink and smoke their lunch away. Never mind that a replay of a football game that hadn't interested me terribly the first time around blared from the television over the bar, or that the maroon carpeting was long overdue for cleaning. For me those flaws paled to nothing when compared with the air in the Havana Grill. It was killing, and that isn't merely a figure of speech. The cigar and cigarette smoke was so thick that by the time I was five feet into the place my eyes were tearing and I was sure that I'd soon be gasping for air. Even the big holiday wreath over the entrance to the dining area drooped miserably, as if it was about to expire from lack of oxygen.

I'm not a fanatic on the subject of smoking. I don't start waving my hands in front of my face when someone lights up in the same room. Still, I do have my limits. We'd passed a pizza parlor that in my opinion would have been a definite step up from the Little Havana. As the outsider, I wasn't completely comfortable complaining, but I was ready to. Louise beat me to it, but in a manner that was oddly indulgent.

"Now I know why you wanted to come here, Casey," she called over her shoulder as she followed the maître d' to a corner booth. "Our clothes are going to smell just awful."

"Aw, come on, Louise. How many places are there anymore where a man can enjoy a good smoke? If my wife isn't controlling everything I do, the jerks that run this damned state stick their noses in."

"Well, there's a pizza place. . . ." I began, fearing that once I sat down I was doomed to stay.

"Oh, not pizza again," Louise said, and sportingly added, "This is all right with me. We'll just send Casey our cleaning bills." Sliding into the booth, she reached for some menus that were propped against the wall. She'd made up our minds for us.

As I slid into the booth, I wondered if perhaps Louise had a slight crush on Casey. I didn't much care for the little I'd seen of him, but on the other hand one woman's buffoon can be another woman's fantasy come true. Though his waist was kind of thick, I can't deny that Casey generally looked okay. He was sandy-haired, broad-shouldered, and had about the prettiest blue eyes imaginable. He was in his mid-forties, I figured, but holding up well. Quite well indeed, considering the way he smoked and, as I was soon to learn, the way he drank. Sometimes genes are everything.

Using a tiny guillotinelike device, Casey clipped off the end of a fresh cigar, lit it, and took a long hard draw on the smelly thing. The lighted end glowed red-hot, and when he balanced it in an ashtray on the table, smoke curled into the air, adding its own special stench to the smelly haze around us.

"You women! Nothing but complaints. Tell you what: if you're a good girl, I'll show you my new toy. I've got it in my office. It's a beauty. Deal?"

Louise appeared genuinely intrigued. "A new toy? How exciting. What is it?"

"Like I said, you be good and you'll see. Not right after lunch. Too many people around. Come down to the dungeon this afternoon during coffee break. My staff usually disappears. Just give me a call first in case any of them decide to stick around. Okay?"

Louise nodded, and though I couldn't imagine Casey showing me anything I wanted to see, and his good-girl stuff was getting on my nerves, for the sake of our fragile congeniality I agreed to join her.

"Good! Now, who wants a drink from the bar?"

"Scotch and water for me," said Louise.

"Diet soda," I said.

Casey's blue eyes widened. "Diet soda? You're with friends, Bonnie. You can relax."

"Besides," the unusually perky Louise put in, "you finished Dorfmeyer's dictation. Don't you want to celebrate?"

"I only finished a first draft. He's liable to find a dozen mistakes."

Or more. And how, I wondered, was he going to feel about the numerous blank spaces I'd left? Though I was happy to have muddled through, I didn't think my accomplishment called for a celebratory drink.

I shook my head. "I don't like to drink at lunch. It makes me too sleepy to work."

"That's the idea," Casey said, raising his voice to carry over the excited babbling coming from the television. As he pushed back through the crowd toward the bar, Louise giggled as if he'd said something uproarious.

So, engulfed in smoke but tentatively accepted by two of R&G's disgruntled employees, I studied a big plastic menu studded with brownish burns. Almost everything on it screamed *FAT*.

The Little Havana was turning out to be a real triple threat to the body. If lung disease or cirrhosis didn't get me, there went the old arteries. I'd avoided the evils of lunchtime alcohol but caved in on the smoke. Now either I went for a small salad—probably iceburg lettuce and anemic tomatoes—or sent my cholesterol rocketing.

A waitress passed our table, bringing a plate loaded with meat loaf and mashed potatoes enticingly close. It smelled awfully good. Oh well. I'd already given in on the smoke. Might as well make it two evils out of three and go for the meat, too.

". . . so I say to Tom Hurley, that wimp, 'I'm management like you. You're just one step above me. Director, manager. What's the big difference? How come me and my department gotta move to the basement? They're treating me like

I'm a damned mailroom clerk or something.' And you know what Dorfmeyer's boy says back to me? He says, 'It's the luck of the draw.' Now, whaddaya think of that, Bonnie.''

Like Louise, Casey wanted me to be shocked and angry, but I was still unable to work myself into a lather. I responded noncommittally. ''That's too bad.''

Casey slapped the table with the flat of his hand. My empty soda glass jumped, though my plate remained anchored to the table by the hefty remains of the meat loaf. The stuff weighed in like lead fishing-line sinkers.

''Too bad? It stinks. You wanna know why my department got moved? Because I don't suck up to Dorfmeyer. I'm not scared of him. That's why! I'm no wimp, and I better not ever hear anybody call me one!''

After several drinks—he had made at least three trips to the bar—Casey's disposition, which to begin with hadn't been anything to write home about, had deteriorated, and so had his grammar and his judgment. He seemed to have forgotten about picking my brain. If I hadn't he needed a crash course in diplomacy. Only his looks weren't impaired. Amazing. He wasn't even red-faced. Somewhere, in some hidden closet, there had to be a portrait of this man, growing more hideous with every passing day.

Though hardly in Casey's class as a drinker, Louise was no slouch either. Initially I'd wondered if she'd ordered a drink as a we're-in-this-together gesture to Casey, but that didn't appear to be the case. She'd slugged her first drink down easily and was working her way through her second. Unlike Casey, she was quite flushed by now, but at least she hadn't become belligerent. Every time one of Casey's angry diatribes subsided, she tried changing the subject, either to unions—she came from a long line of union activists, I'd learned—or to Tom Hurley, and specifically my relationship with him.

''I'm not sure Tom is scared,'' she said, looking at me, ''but it does seem that he's awfully deferential to Dorfmeyer. You've known Tom for years, Bonnie. What do you think?''

There was that question again. What did I think? Again, I had no answer that would make Louise happy. Shrugging, I told her that even when I had seen Tom almost every day, I hadn't known him very well.

"He was my kid brother's friend."

"But he's your friend, too," Louise said. "One of the girls happened to see you walking together on the street last night."

She managed to keep any hint of contempt out of her voice, but it showed in the way her lips tightened as she stared at me, waiting for my response.

"What? You're hanging out with that ass-kissing . . .''

That was Casey, who had none of Louise's control.

"Last night Tom and I ran into each other leaving the health club. We walked in the same direction for a couple blocks. That's all it amounted to. Who was it that saw us, anyway?''

"Angela from accounts receivable," Louise responded. "She mentioned it to me this morning."

"Ah."

I didn't believe her. There no doubt was an Angela in accounts receivable, and if that Angela hadn't already been coached to say she had seen me with Tom, she would be soon enough. But it wasn't a clerk from accounts receivable who had followed me home. That I was sure of.

The way I figured it, there were two possible scenarios. The more likely one was that Victoria and Louise had been together on Sixth Avenue when they'd spotted us. Louise had identified me to Victoria, who had then followed me home. Why? Who could say? Maybe she wanted to know her enemy better.

In my other scenario, Victoria had been alone, perhaps doing some Christmas shopping, when she'd spotted Tom and me. If she'd seen us leaving the hotel, her curiosity would have been kindled. She knew who he was, but who was I? Mrs. Tom? When Tom and I had separated at the subway stop, she'd realized that was unlikely. She'd decided to find out for certain by following me home.

Both these scenarios led me back to the thought that it had been Victoria, not Mike, who had spooked the Codwallader sisters? Perhaps. *I'm looking for a woman with reddish-blond hair, about forty. I don't know her name, but she . . .*

. . . picked my pocket? Stole my hubcaps? Whatever Victoria might have told the sisters, it had been sufficient to get them spooked, and to get her my name.

If this second scenario was the correct one, Victoria had later telephoned Louise, who had been only too happy to fill her friend in about the new snake in Richard & Goode's once-happy garden. *Tom came out of the hotel with her? Looks like it was all an act, them claiming they hadn't seen each other in years,* Louise might have said. *There's supposed to be a hiring freeze, but I'll bet that before long she's a permanent employee.*

Having refueled Victoria's fire, Louise may have slept soundly. Her friend hadn't, though, and I'd gotten to share much of her sleepless night with her.

All of this was hypothesis, certainly, and I wouldn't have mentioned my thoughts for anything. Still, the overall picture rang true, and if it was true I wanted to know as much about Victoria, a woman *out for blood,* as she knew about me.

"You had started to tell me about the woman who lost her job," I said to Louise. "Victoria? Was that her name?"

"Her name's Victoria Cerutti, and that's not what happened!" Casey blurted. "Nobody's been let go yet. Victoria quit. After over ten years at R&G she only lasted a couple months with Hurley before she gave two weeks' notice and left."

I glanced at Louise, who confirmed Casey's statement with a nod.

"Then what's the problem?" I asked. "This morning you gave me the impression that Victoria had been forced to resign."

Louise's gaze shifted to the cluttered tabletop. "Maybe we should talk about something else."

Casey, who had begun waving his arm trying to catch the waiter's attention, glared at her. "It's no secret. Victoria was forced out by management. That's the problem!"

Louise was shaking her head. "What happened was, when the former human resources director quit, Victoria was made *acting* director. Everyone thought she was going to get the job. After all, she'd been a manager for almost four years. She knew the company."

"Victoria's single," Casey put in. "Lives with her parents out in Queens. Nice gal. Goes to mass every Sunday. A real career gal, too. Gave more time than she should have to her job. The way I see it"—he leaned across the table aggressively—"over the years Victoria learned too much. Management didn't want her to have a more powerful job because she knew where all the dirt was buried."

Warming to the subject, Louise looked at me. "Either that, or she didn't fit their image of what a corporate director looks like."

"What do you mean?" I asked, thinking of the woman in the brown coat and blue hat.

"Oh, you know. Her clothes aren't always businesslike, and her hair . . ."

Running out of things to say, or possibly feeling guilty about the things she was saying, Louise looked at Casey. He, I expect, had never suffered from a loss of words.

"Victoria's a little wide in the caboose, if you know what I mean," Casey said, "and her nose . . ."

Raising a finger, he drew a hump on his own well-shaped nose.

"Victoria's not *that* bad," Louise said. "She just doesn't look corporate."

"I used to tease her about her hair," said Casey. "Half the time it looked like she hadn't combed it all day."

"Anyway," continued Louise. "The director who retired had been making a hundred and twenty thousand, plus a bonus. Victoria would have expected that much. She was already making almost seventy, and getting a nice bonus, too.''

My head was reeling with those numbers when Volcano Casey erupted again.

"So instead of promoting her, Dorfmeyer brings in that ass-kisser, that toady, pays him five thousand more than the last director was making, puts him in a private office after Victoria's been sharing with two other people all those years—''

Louise interrupted. "The company listed the job with an executive recruitment firm, and also advertised it in the *Times*. Tom responded to the *Times* ad."

"So they didn't even have to fork up an agency finder's fee," Casey said. He slugged down the remainder of his drink, and then took yet another of those dreadful cigars from the miniature humidor he carried in his pocket. "They even made Victoria check his references!" he said as he struck a match to the thing. "What a fuckin' insult! You want to try this?''

He held the cigar toward me. I shook my head vehemently.

"I'll try it," said Louise, taking the cigar from Casey's hand.

"Just try a little puff," he warned.

I don't know whether Louise's puff was little or big, but the coughing spell that followed it was massive. It didn't subside until she finished off the remainder of her drink.

"So," said Louise when she'd recovered, "about eight weeks after Tom started, Victoria gave notice."

"Served the bastards right!"

"Where did she go?" I asked.

"Nowhere."

"She left without a job?"

"Yeah! Victoria's no spineless toady. Anybody with any self-respect would have done the same. Don't you agree?''

I couldn't answer that truthfully without seeming like a spineless toady myself. I've never been what Casey would have called a *career gal,* but I like to eat reasonably well and Moses would sooner starve than eat store-brand cat food. For me and mine, a fat steady paycheck would have gone a long way toward soothing a bruised ego.

"In Victoria's position, I probably wouldn't have resigned until I found another job. There are always things like—" I started ticking off on my fingers the many things that would have kept me working for that $70,000—"rent, food, clothes, dentist bills . . ."

Casey flicked his hand. "Victoria's been making decent bucks for a lot of years, and living at home, she's put away a bundle. Besides, if she goes through with her law—"

"Casey!" Louise said sharply.

She was frowning and shaking her head, sending Casey a message that said clearly, if not loudly, *We weren't going to talk about this.*

"What's the matter, Louise? So Victoria's been to see a lawyer. Big deal." Casey stared across the table at me. "Right after Hurley started, she told us she had an appointment with a lawyer. Makes sense to me! A woman gets forced out of a job, so she files a discrimination suit. Age, sex, whatever. I say, Good for her! Let some lawyers put the screws to R&G. The bastards! What do you think?"

These two were continually asking my opinion about things I knew almost nothing about. I shrugged. "That sounds reasonable."

My response must have made Casey happy. Shifting moods abruptly, he flashed me a smile that might have warmed my heart if I'd liked him even a little. After that, he slapped a credit card down on top of the bill. "I'll expense this one. That's a manager's prerogative. Especially a manager who's been moved to the basement. We talked business. Right?"

That was a stretch, but in a way I suppose we had.

Rose Morris looked down at me almost sympathetically. In one hand she held a cup of coffee, and in the other the hateful manila folder of drafts.

"He wants these in final by four. It's too bad you

couldn't do them in final the first time," she added after sipping at the coffee. "It's not terribly difficult once you get your speed up. Certainly not with short documents like these."

Oh, man! How bad was it? The meat loaf already lay heavy in my stomach. The idea of opening that file folder and seeing the result of my bumbling attempt at steno made me feel as if I'd swallowed a brick.

"You know the old saying, 'If you do something right the first time, you won't have . . .'"

Rose seemed to like those old sayings. I blocked out the rest of the stupid damned adage. Placing the manila folder on my desk, I draped my arm casually over it. To open the thing in Rose's presence was to invite humiliation. Finally realizing I wasn't going to do it, she started to turn away. I peeled up an edge of the folder, trying to be gentle with myself.

"There is a number you can call to build your speed," she said unexpectedly. "I've got it on my Rolodex."

I quickly closed the folder. "Pardon me?"

"There are dictation recordings. You choose your speed by pressing a number. That allows you to build speed gradually, instead of trying to jump right in at a hundred and twenty words a minute."

Well, that was something to look forward to. "Thanks so much," I said to her, while saying to myself, *That'll be the day!*

"Just look on my Rolodex if I'm not at my desk. The card's under *D,* for dictation."

My unspoken response was under *F.* Guess what for.

Before leaving our office, Rose stopped at Louise's desk. "What's Victoria Cerutti up to?"

The question seemed to surprise Louise. "Why?"

"She left a phone message for Mr. Dorfmeyer this morning. They've been playing phone tag ever since."

"Maybe she's really going to sue," Louise said.

Rose had walked to the door. "From what I understand,

Victoria doesn't have a case. Even if she did, this is an odd way of going about it.''

"That's up to her.''

Louise's voice had taken on a sour edge, but Rose didn't react. Working for Carl Dorfmeyer, she'd probably grown immune to sour-edged voices.

Once Rose left I steeled myself and opened the folder to the first of the memos. My eyes immediately glommed onto a note written with a black felt-tip pen: "If you don't understand something, ask! If I'm going too fast, say so!" Dorfmeyer had circled one of my blank spaces, and filled in the missing word—it hadn't been *that* easy a word— with that thick black pen.

I flipped through the other drafts in the folder. With every blank I'd left, Dorfmeyer's handwriting became more savage. His blood pressure must have been soaring by the time he got to a letter complaining about his business-class airline dinner. The black pen had almost torn the paper apart.

"Is it that bad?" Louise asked.

In the total scheme of things it wasn't bad at all. This wasn't the Middle Ages. I hadn't left blank spaces in the handwritten Magna Charta. These drafts addressed matters of brain-numbing unimportance, and furthermore they were all saved on my computer hard drive.

"Not really," I said, shrugging. "I got most of it. It won't take me long to put everything in final."

And it didn't. I managed to finish the whole works while Louise was napping off her lunch in the sickroom. In less than an hour I'd put the final documents on Rose's desk. She was in the great man's office at the time, but her Rolodex was in plain sight. I didn't bother looking through the *D* section for that dictation number, though. There was, I reasoned, a bright side to those blanks that had gotten Dorfmeyer so steamed up. He wasn't likely to want to work with me again, was he?

5

THE BUILDING'S LOWER LEVEL WAS reached either by a freight elevator that ran from the top to the bottom of the building, or a small elevator that ran only between the lobby and the basement.

Louise and I took the cavernous freight elevator. When the door opened after a bumpy ride, we stepped into a maze of narrow hallways. Everything, and I mean everything, from the tiles on the floor to the utilitarian wallpaper to the metal desks inside the few open offices we passed, was gray. No posters, much less oil paintings, broke the monotony, and no bouquets brightened the few open areas. I was reminded of a battleship I'd toured when it was docked at the Manhattan piers. All that was missing was the slight rolling motion underfoot and the occasional passing sailor.

I knew that behind the many closed gray doors people were working. There was a big room for old files down here, and a copy center. Louise and I passed no one, though, and heard nothing but the clicking of our heels on the tile floor.

Casey hadn't exaggerated about the temperature. The halls felt as cold as a meat locker. I'd draped my wool scarf around my shoulders, but as we passed through a set of gray doors and a blast of icy air swept over us, I wouldn't have minded having my coat.

"Terrible working atmosphere, isn't it," said Louise as we turned into yet another monochrome hall. "Cold and ugly."

I tightened my scarf around my neck. "And confusing."

"The security department's new space is near the lobby elevator," Louise said. "It's easy to find from there. We'll leave that way."

A couple more stretches of gray, a couple more turns, and ultimately we reached the new security area.

Corporate-office-space rearrangements are nothing new to me. In flush times they're caused by expansion, by the need to fit in more employees. When less flush times come along—and don't they always?—they're caused by contractions as companies give up space. I knew that was the case here, but still, considering what R&G's upstairs offices looked like, the thrown-together quality of security's new home was a surprise. The small room set aside for Casey's staff, visible from the corridor through a plate-glass window, was crammed with mismatched desks and chairs, some lopsided file cabinets, and a few unlit security monitors.

Casey's own office was next to the room with the plate-glass window, just across the hall from the lobby elevator. I knew it was Casey's room before I even glimpsed him through his half-open door. The stench of his uniquely smelly cigars was heavy in the air.

He was on the phone, his head bent over a newspaper. When Louise tapped on the door frame, the newspaper disappeared, at something near the speed of light, over the back of his desk.

Covering the receiver with one hand, he indicated we should come in, mouthing, "Just be a minute."

Swiveling his chair, Casey finished his conversation in monosyllables, and uncharacteristically quietly.

"Yes . . . Fine . . . Eight-thirty A.M.? . . . All right . . . I am, too. Good-bye."

While this was going on, Louise looked around the room, her signature disgruntled expression settling over her face.

"Disgusting," she said. "The way they treat people is criminal. If I were you . . ."

What Louise was seeing was exactly what I was seeing, but we were seeing it from slightly different viewpoints. What Louise saw was an underground sweatshop where Simon Legree bosses housed their slaving workers. To me, however, the room wasn't all *that* disgusting. In square feet Casey's office was manager-sized, and the metal furniture, though hardly elegant, was in good shape and, unlike the rubble in his staff's room, matched.

For a moment I tried to imagine myself with this basement office. Could I live with it? Probably, if I enjoyed my job, and my paycheck was decent enough. Still, there was no way of pretending this was a window office with a view. On the lower level of R&G's corporate headquarters, the great outdoors was only a memory.

". . . call the attorney general's office and report this," Louise was saying. "There must be some law about access to windows or daylight or . . ."

I seriously doubted that there was any such law on the books. Even if there was, what state or city agency was going to rip into R&G, a major big-time taxpayer, because an ex-cop had been moved from a window office to a basement one.

Just as Louise had played her disgruntled role, I played my sympathetic but noncommittal one. "It's not so bad. A coat of fresh paint, a couple posters . . ."

As I stepped farther into the room, my eye was caught by Casey's one bit of . . . decor. On the wall opposite his desk, he had taped a copy of the photo of Carl Dorfmeyer that had appeared in the *Times*. It had been embellished with some not-too-surprising anatomical alterations: horns, crossed eyes, and fangs.

"Guess you're not expecting him to stop by," I said.

"I doubt if Dorfmeyer's ever seen the basement," grumbled Casey.

"I keep telling you, if we can get a union in here . . ." Louise began.

Casey's response to this song Louise had been singing an awful lot was about what I expected. "We'll have a union around here about the same time pigs start flying over Manhattan."

"You just watch!" Louise snapped.

"Yeah, yeah. Now . . . down to business." Casey checked his watch. "One of my staff's going to be back in exactly ten minutes. You secure the premises—"

He was looking at me. I stared back, not understanding.

"Close that door behind you and lock it," he barked. "Then you're in for a special treat."

Considering the source of the promised *treat*, I wasn't exactly tingling with anticipation. Nevertheless, I did as ordered. Once Casey had watched me turn the lock, he slid open one of his desk drawers and took a smallish wood chest from it.

"Now, if either of you women mention this to anyone around here, my ass will be in a sling. Got it?"

"Got it."

The top of the chest was hinged on one side. Casey lifted the lid so that only he could see the contents, and smiled down at his toy the way another man might smile at his newborn in a crib. He looked up at us then, and his smile grew less tender, more teasing. Perhaps he expected to find us panting with excitement. I'm not sure if what he saw on our faces gave him the kick he wanted, but finally he turned the box toward us so that we too could admire his toy.

Louise, completely unprepared, raised her hands in shock and took a couple of healthy steps back. "Oh God! You better not let anybody see that."

My reaction was more restrained. The box's size and Casey's secretive manner had forewarned me. "Um," I said.

"So? Whaddaya think? Isn't she a honey? Have you ever seen lines like these? And just look at this detail work here. You know what this baby goes for retail? If I didn't have a friend in the business I'd never be able to afford a beauty like this. It's an exact replica of the one Buffalo Bill Cody used in the Indian wars."

The three of us stared down at the item nestled in the box's blue velvet lining, Casey all but smacking his lips over his baby-beauty-honey. If he wasn't crazy, he had to be very very stupid.

It wasn't the first revolver I've ever seen, and it wasn't the biggest. I'll actually admit that it may have been the prettiest, if a gun can be described as pretty. The barrel was blue black, the lines sleek, and the butt ivory.

"It's not loaded, I assume."

Casey snapped at me. "Of course not! How big a dimwit do you think I am? I'm an ex-cop. I know you gotta treat sidearms with respect. The bullets are in here."

Reaching into the drawer where the gun had been, he dug out a small cardboard box and showed us the brass bullets packed neatly inside it, side by side. "I'll give you women a lesson in how it's done."

Casey took the revolver from its carton, opened the barrel, and spun it so that air showed through the six cylinders. "You see? Empty. You want to load it, you put one of these babies in the cylinder."

He had taken a bullet from the box, but I shook my head. "That's not a good idea, Casey."

I don't know how far Casey would have gone to demonstrate his unquestionably monumental skill with a gun, but when Louise agreed with me by saying, "She's right, Casey," he returned the bullet to its container.

"Are you allowed to keep that here?"

"Allowed? I've got a license, if that's what you mean. Now, of course"—he flashed a sly grin—"if the big shots upstairs got wind of it, I'd be out on my ass. I'll be bringing it home by the weekend, once all my buddies here have gotten a look at it."

"You better keep your desk locked in the meantime," said Louise.

"Yeah. Sure. My office is locked when I'm not in it, and it takes a master key to open it. But you know what your problem is, Louise? Your problem is, you're uneducated." He looked at me. "You and Bonnie both. You're scared of guns 'cause you've never been taught anything. Typical of most women. I guarantee you that if everybody in America was trained to use a gun and was armed, we wouldn't have any crime at all. Guns don't kill people. People kill people. You two are ignorant . . ."

Casey's blustering was almost more than I could stand, but I didn't want to get into a gun-control argument with him. He wasn't smarter than I was—I was certain of that— but he was a lot louder, and all too often, loud wins. Nevertheless, I would rather have added five pounds to my hips than let this moron call me ignorant or scared. I'd given in on the smoke-filled restaurant, and what had that gotten me but over an hour of his buffoonery and possible lung disease? I'd played the adaptable woman to Casey's macho man enough!

"I'm not scared, Casey," I said, my voice hard. "I know a lot about guns. I've had years of experience with them."

That was by no means an outright lie. Several years earlier a nasty Saturday-night special had been pointed at my head. More to the point, though, my friend Tony LaMarca, an NYPD homicide detective, had once given me a few brief lessons in handling guns.

The idea that a mere female office worker might know about guns must have taken Casey by surprise. Not only that, but on some level, I believe he thought that I was challenging his manhood. He stepped nearer to me, cocked his head to one side, and regarded me through narrowed eyes.

"Sure you have," he said, a mocking bite in his voice.

"Tell you what: you don't trust *me* to handle my own weapon, so why don't you show me and Louise exactly how it should be done. How you'd load it and aim it."

I'm hardly a violent person, especially when the possible object of my violence is bigger than I am, and a coworker to boot. Nevertheless, I can still almost feel the primal urge that vibrated through me. My fist balled, and I remember thinking, *I would like to punch this obnoxious bag of wind* . . .

Casey nodded at the gun. A grin, closer to a sneer than a smile, spread across his face.

It was that sneer that did it, that pushed me over the edge into making a very big mistake. Considering what this incident later generated, it's really too bad that punching was out of the question. In the long run I would have been much better off if I'd just taken a swing at the guy.

I stepped to the far side of Casey's desk and motioned for him to move aside. He chuckled under his breath as he moved.

When I reached to pick up the gun a small voice—a trace of common sense breaking through whatever was going on with my ego—said to me, *You shouldn't do this. You don't have to prove anything to this bozo.* My gaze dropped to the floor. Funny, the irrelevant things that can make an impression. The newspaper that had been on Casey's desk moments earlier was opened to the want ads. One of them was circled. Casey was job hunting. Probably a good idea.

"Well?"

That was Casey, and the taunting edge to that one word eradicated my brief episode of common sense. Looking back up, I drew a deep breath and lifted the gun from its box. Without a moment's fumbling, I was able to release the barrel.

"I won't load it, but if I was going to, I'd take one of these"—I took a bullet from the cardboard box—"and slide it into this chamber"—I demonstrated the empty chamber—"and then . . ." I clicked the cylinder shut.

Then, keeping my hands from shaking by sheer force of

will, I released the gun's safety and assumed the two-handed position familiar to anybody who's ever seen a cop movie. Aiming carefully at the photo of Dorfmeyer, I pulled back the hammer and said, "Bang! Right between the eyes."

Louise, who had been silent through all this ridiculous grandstanding, clapped her hands. "You see, Casey? Bonnie does know what she's doing."

"Looks that way," Casey said, which was as close to surrender as he was likely to get.

After checking the cylinder a final time and giving it a breezy spin that would have done Billy the Kid proud, I reengaged the safety and carefully laid the revolver back in its velvet nest.

Louise and I left Casey's office a minute later. Just before I got on the elevator, I glanced back and saw him returning the wooden box to his desk drawer.

It wasn't until I was back upstairs that I realized that my scarf was no longer draped around my neck. Thinking over the last few minutes, I knew that if it had been on my shoulders when I'd aimed the gun in Casey's office, it would have gotten in the way. Somewhere between that first door after the freight elevator and Casey's office, I'd misplaced it.

I made a mental note to call the security office to see if anyone had turned it in, but late that afternoon things in the office got so hectic that it slipped my mind. In between fielding phone calls and sending great-résumé-but-we're-not-hiring letters, I did manage to tap into my home answering machine. Mike had called again.

I wasn't sure seeing Mike was a good idea, but I didn't want to ignore him, either. I dialed his number and, when he didn't answer, left my office number on his answering machine. At least I'd made the effort.

Even Louise was wildly busy that afternoon. It wasn't clear whether she was busy with R&G's work or her own, but she fluttered and flew from copy machine to fax machine to computer so feverishly it was hard to believe she was the same woman who had spent almost half an hour on the cot in the sickroom recuperating from lunch.

The reason for Louise's frantic activity was revealed to me late in the day.

"Take a look at this," she said, thrusting a sheet of pale green paper at me. "It's next Tuesday at noon."

It was a noontime rally. "WORKERS! UNITE AGAINST RICHARDS & GOODE'S MANAGEMENT," the oversized type shouted. "Come together in front of the building next Tuesday at 12:30. Don't sit on the sidelines and let management take your jobs. Speak up! Make a difference! Organize!"

"Who's going to be there?" I asked.

"Everyone!"

"I mean, is an existing union getting involved?"

Louise responded elusively. "One of them has said they might be interested. I'm hoping a representative will show up."

Hope is such a wonderful thing.

I spent the last half hour of my workday in the records room filing the pink change-of-address forms that had been accumulating on my desk. I was just about finished when it occurred to me that I'd been incredibly *thick* when it came to learning more about Victoria Cerutti. She was right here in these files. Not in the flesh, but years' worth of records can tell you an awful lot about someone.

Victoria's file was right where it should have been, and it was nice and fat. A good solid dozen years' worth. I was about to pull it when the wall phone rang. My line was flashing. Slamming the file drawer shut, I hurried to answer.

"Bonnie Indermill."

"About time I catch up with you," Mike said.

Oh boy. The sound of his voice without an answering machine as a buffer brought back some real pleasant memories. Before we had time to exchange more than a few words, though, Tom walked into the records room.

"Can I call you back?" I asked Mike.

"Sure. Or why don't you just drop by after work?"

"Not tonight, but—"

"Almost any night's good for me. Just call first. Got a pencil? Boat's called the *Little Brown Jug*. Ugliest boat at the Basin. Pier E, Seventy-ninth Street."

A stray pencil lay on the counter beside the copy machine. I grabbed it and, lacking anything else to write on, jotted the boat's name and address on the EEOC poster above the machine. When I'd finished, I promised Mike I'd drop by soon and quickly ended the call.

"Defacing R&G property, I see," Tom said. "That's grounds for dismissal. And for a personal call?"

Thinking he just might be serious, I grew flustered. Tom's features spread into a smile.

"You're blushing. Must be a man. New boyfriend?"

"Mike's an old one, actually, but new in town. He's been out of the country for years."

"Ah. Well, you didn't have to hang up, but since you did, I'll tell you what I need."

Tom elaborated on the salary survey he'd mentioned the day before. He assured me he couldn't have given the job to a typical temp. So maybe I wasn't so typical after all.

It was simple work, more computer input than research, actually, but sounded more interesting than the kind of thing I'd been doing at R&G.

"Are you comfortable with computer spreadsheets? We use QuattroPro."

I nodded. Work in enough offices and you dabble in all the spreadsheets.

"Okay. We'll talk more about it tomorrow."

When Tom had gone I went back to the file drawer and pulled Victoria Cerutti's file. I didn't have time to look at it then, and probably wouldn't have time that evening, either, but you never can tell. I carried the file, its label hidden, to my desk. There was surely some R&G rule about "borrowing" someone's personnel file, but in the spirit of knowing my enemy, I slipped it into my tote when Louise wasn't around.

As I rushed from the building that evening, it occurred to me that it would only take a few minutes to go to the lower level and try to find my missing scarf. My workday had ended later than it should have, though, and Sam was waiting. We had to get finished with dinner and be at the theater by eight, and keeping Sam calm and content in Manhattan was more important than retrieving a scarf that was already unraveling.

The restaurant Sam had chosen was the Little Havana's antithesis in most respects. It was smoke-free, big, quiet, elegant, and expensive. The walls were hung with etchings depicting Old New York. The only thing it had in common with the Havana was big meat.

The maître d' showed me to the table where Sam, and a glass of red wine, were waiting. He stood up and kissed my cheek—Sam, not the maître d'—and pressed me against him.

"It's good to see you," he said. "You look terrific."

"Thanks. It's good to see you, too."

I meant it. I felt comfortable sitting down across from him. There was something almost . . . familial . . . about it.

"I told the waiter we had to be out of here by seven-thirty," he said. "This place is famous for its steaks. But maybe you want to see a menu . . ."

Memories of the meat loaf no longer weighed heavy in my stomach, but I wasn't particularly hungry. Even if I had been, I ordinarily wouldn't have eaten a big beefy dinner after having a big beefy lunch. I'm not certain how much damage one day of overindulgence would do to my cholesterol, but I know my thighs all too well. They're a rapid-response team. One day I overeat; the next day they jiggle.

Nevertheless, though I could have picked my way down the menu and come up with something else—the inevitable chicken breast or sole almondine—I said, "Filet? Terrific."

Why? Because Sam had driven into the city and parked in an outrageously expensive midtown parking lot, two of the things he hates most in the world. Because he was taking me to see a show, a rock musical, that he had told me months earlier wasn't his *thing*. These were not monumental compromises, but they were more than he had usually been willing to do, and if Sam could try to enjoy my things, I could try to enjoy his.

A waiter appeared at Sam's shoulder, pencil poised over his pad.

"We'll both have the filet," Sam said. "Make mine rare." He looked at me. "Medium rare?"

There is no way Sam can forget that I draw the line at blood on my plate. Still, he persists. I try to be understanding. After twenty-five years with Eileen maybe he can't help himself.

"Medium well," I said, but I said it with a smile, and kindly, as if the subject had never before come up between us.

I took a sip of wine and, as the waiter jotted down the rest of our order, glanced around the restaurant. As I told you, it was a big place. There were two good-sized rooms on the main floor and others up a flight of stairs. Sam and I were at a corner table, partly concealed from other diners by a row of leafy philodendrons, and though the lighting at the restaurant's front was bright, our little nook was darker, lit by candles and filled with romantic shadows.

When I put my wineglass back on the table, Sam's hand slid over mine, warming it, warming my blood. The touch of excitement I'd felt a few moments earlier returned, stronger. Candlelight reflected in his brown eyes as they held mine.

Here you go again.

The thought was so clear that for a second it seemed I'd said the words aloud. Sam massaged my knuckle—my ring-finger knuckle, if you must know—with his fingers. Then, without saying anything, he slid his chair around the corner of the small table and moved his place setting, so that we were almost shoulder to shoulder.

"This is how we should have done things in the first place," he said. "Dating, getting comfortable with each other, before . . ."

"Before jumping into bed together?"

He grinned. "I wouldn't go that far. But I'm enjoying these dates. They're . . . special. Don't you think so?"

In answer, I leaned closer and touched his lips with mine. It was the most intimate, seductive gesture I'd made toward Sam since we had begun this *dating game* a month earlier, and frankly, I surprised myself with it. Was it too forward? I sat back in my chair, suddenly and unaccountably bashful, as if I hadn't spent a good bit of the past year in Sam's bed.

If Sam was caught off guard, he recovered quickly. We talked quietly, oblivious to the restaurant's growing bustle.

"You might not be ready to talk about this, but maybe you are," Sam said. "I still have that ring. It's sitting there in that little box in my dresser drawer. I'm not very good at living alone, and—"

The waiter was there with our salads, interrupting Sam, giving me a moment to think. "This is something I'd like to talk about," I said, but added, for my own comfort, "maybe in a few weeks."

"Got you."

Was he hurt? With Sam it was sometimes hard to tell. Our steaks arrived and we ate companionably, as if nothing had passed between us, but all the while I wondered what he was feeling. Sam has great self-control, sometimes to the point of seeming to be without great passion. He had told me, though, that he experienced the same emotional upheavals that I did, but in a quieter way. He didn't drop rivers of tears onto friends' shoulders or subject them to long, weepy phone calls. My way is moist and noisy. Sam's is stoic. I wonder what Eileen's was. He'd never mentioned it. Perhaps, with Eileen, there were no upheavals.

The check for dinner came, as promised, before 7:30. I knew better than to open the maroon leather folder that concealed it. Sam settled that early in our relationship. It had nothing to do with my fragile financial condition. The way of the world—Sam's world—is that the man pays for dinner.

I looked away while Sam figured out the tip, almost as

if what I might see on that slip of paper would bring a blush to my cheeks. Never mind that I have an affinity for math, that he had trusted me with the bookkeeping for the company that he was part owner of, Finkelstein Boys Movers. Never mind that that complex bookkeeping had always given him such an awful headache. When the dinner check arrives, the woman looks the other way.

The restaurant was packed now, dinner hour in full swing. Rather than the theater crowd you get in Manhattan's West Forties, this was a business crowd. At the table nearest ours, three men and two women in suits bent over their almost raw meat, talking up a storm between bites. I picked up snatches of their conversation. It was all mergers, share prices, interest rates. At a farther table, a quartet of middle-aged men, having just ordered their dinner, huddled once again over their drinks, heads close and voices low.

My gaze flickered toward Sam. He was taking his gold card from his wallet. Circumspect, I looked away again, this time toward the restaurant's brightly lit entrance.

What I saw shook me. She was there! Her blue hat was nowhere in sight, but there was the same peachy complexion, the same patrician nose, and the same flared brown coat. Victoria!

If the restaurant hadn't grown noisier, if the waiter hadn't been picking up the maroon leather folder and Sam hadn't been half-turned in his chair, surely they would have noticed the way I abruptly ducked so that the row of plants shielded me.

She had to be insane to have followed me home, to have made hang-up calls, and then to follow me to a restaurant the next night. Could Victoria Cerutti, who had held a responsible position in a major corporation for many years, be that nuts? Possibly. In the course of my vast experience in the working world, I have run into a number of lunatics in high places.

After a moment, when my heart had stopped pounding, I straightened and peeked through the greenery. A short stout woman of about fifty, who was wearing one of those long-haired raccoon coats that short stout women should avoid at all costs, had joined Victoria.

The two women paused near the coat check, but chose to keep their coats with them. They approached the maître d', and just before they reached him, something the older woman said caused Victoria to shake her head vigorously. Her auburn hair, which she'd piled loosely atop her head, broke free from whatever secured it and fell haphazardly down her back. Grabbing the mass of it, she quickly formed a rough bun at the back of her neck, but she still struck me as very Pre-Raphaelite. I couldn't tell whether or not she was chubby with that brown coat flaring around her, but I thought she was stunning. Still, I could see why she might not fit R&G's corporate image.

The maître d' indicated that the two women should follow him. A second later I realized that he was leading them to the room behind the one where Sam and I were seated, which meant that they had to pass our table. I quickly shifted in my chair and pretended to study the etchings on the wall behind me.

My subterfuge probably wasn't necessary. As the two women passed through the door to the back room, I glanced at them from the corner of my eye. Victoria's head was turned away from me as she said something to her companion, who was nodding briskly. Neither woman paid me any attention.

"Good evening, Mrs. Obus. How nice to see you," I heard a waiter say as the women passed from my sight.

Mrs. Obus must have been a regular at the restaurant. What, I wondered, was Mrs. Obus's first name.

A few minutes later I partially solved that small mystery for myself while Sam was doing the manly thing and collecting our coats from the coat check. The reservation desk near the restaurant's door was temporarily deserted. On it was a huge reservation book, unguarded. It was turned toward the back of the desk, and I was at the desk's front, but whoever had written in the reservations had big, clear handwriting. The letter *G* in front of the name Obus was

quite clear. Mrs. G. Obus was either Victoria's friend or
her business acquaintance. She could have been both, of
course, or a relative, for that matter, but considering the
type of restaurant this was, and the grim set of Victoria's
jaw as she'd listened to the other woman, I guessed that
the two had business, rather than friendship, on their minds.
Whatever was on their minds, though, it probably wasn't
me, and it now seemed unlikely that Victoria had followed
me to this restaurant.

I didn't give Victoria, or Mrs. G. Obus, much thought
for a while after that. The musical was everything the reviews had promised, exhilarating, engaging, and wrench-
ing. When it was over and the applause had finally died,
when Sam and I had joined the swell of theater goers surging down Forty-sixth Street, we both felt too emotionally
high to go home. A crowded, boisterous Theater District
bar with a Tex-Mex motif drew us inside, and no sooner
had we pushed our way to the bar than—

"Bonnie Indermill? Is that . . ."

Talk about memory lane! The bartender was an actress
named Dorian whom I'd met years before. We'd worked
together in a Broadway musical that had opened and closed
in not much more than a New York City second. I hadn't
seen Dorian in ages, and we spent an hour, maybe more,
catching up and reminiscing. Oh, that show. The reviews
had been so scathing that at the time I'd wanted to crawl
into my bed and never let my "too-cutesy chipmunk
cheeks" be seen onstage again. Viewed from the perspec-
tive of the Tex-Mex bar, though, and through the rosy glow
of memory, the experience struck us all—me, my old
friend, a number of other people in the bar, and Sam, too—
as howlingly funny. So funny, in fact, that my friend and
I entertained the others by throwing the script's "abomi-
nable dialogue" back and forth to each other, sometimes
laughing so hard that we could barely get the "unbelievably
clanky" words out.

It was a great evening, the kind you want to go on forever. Too bad it was a weeknight. I remember how, when

ordering my second margarita, a tiny voice whispered to me. *You're going to hate yourself in the morning,* it said, but the morning was hours off.

Sam and I walked in to my apartment at about two A.M. The way that things developed after that, I ended up having quite a night.

What developed wasn't what you might be thinking.

"I was serious earlier in the restaurant," Sam said.

His hand still gripped my apartment door, as if he was ready to leave. I first thought—hoped—he was talking about something he'd said in the Tex-Mex place, but looking at him, at the way his face had lengthened, I realized he was talking about our aborted discussion at the steak house.

"This dating, like a couple kids, is ridiculous," he continued.

"You said you were enjoying yourself."

Sam shrugged impatiently. "Maybe I'm a better actor than you were. I want to know when you're coming back."

I stood there quietly with no ready answer.

"That's what I figured," he said. "You can call me if you change your mind."

Sam left, closing the door hard behind him. I was devastated, and too stunned even to cry. As I fed Moses I kept thinking, "Oh no! What have I done?"

Victoria Cerutti's personnel file was in my tote, but she leaped to my mind only once that night, when my phone rang at three A.M. and my caller hung up after hearing my voice.

I woke early the next morning, feeling rotten, and glanced through Victoria's file as I crunched dry toast, the only thing I felt would stay down. The memos in the file were all run-of-the-mill. Victoria had never gone out on disability, had never had a serious dispute with anyone, and had never had disciplinary problems. There was nothing among the later papers about a threatened lawsuit. Looking through Victoria's annual reviews, however, I did discover that she hadn't been quite an A student.

"Victoria's performance has been good this year," a recent reviewer wrote, "but she still has a tendency to become overly emotional." "Shouldn't take personnel matters so personally" an earlier joker had written. In addition to these remarks, an interesting, and probably illegal one, had been made by someone who initially had interviewed Victoria for her position at R&G. "Not an R&G front-office type," this interviewer had said. A nasty comment, and not necessarily accurate, but I suppose that each corporate culture decides what its own front-office types should look like.

Victoria's application form was the first document in the file. After twelve years it was dog-eared, but it was completely legible. She'd lived in Howard Beach, Queens, then, as she did now. There were no questions on the application about height, weight, or date of birth—those have long been illegal—but Victoria had included the date of her high-school graduation. Assuming she'd graduated at about eighteen, she'd be thirty-seven now. That was about right for the russet-haired woman in the brown coat. Turning to the back of the application, I saw that one of Victoria's references had been a parish priest.

I was about to slide the complete stack of papers back into the file when my eye was caught by a pink change-of-address form midway in the file. The address on it, however, remained the same as that on the application. Only Victoria's phone number had changed. I remembered, then, that all the boroughs but Manhattan had changed to the 718 area code a few years earlier. I glanced at the number, and did a doubletake when I saw the long string of *eights*: 718-888-8811.

I'd had a seriously bad night, and perhaps my memory wasn't working as well as usual, but unless I was in even worse shape than I realized, this was the number of the woman who had called Tom Hurley, the woman who had refused to leave a message.

Nothing really odd about that, I reasoned as I showered a few minutes later. There was no reason why a former employee shouldn't be in touch with a new one. In this case, though, the former employee was rumored to have resigned because she resented the new employee. I knew she'd called Carl Dorfmeyer, perhaps with regard to a threatened lawsuit, but why would she be calling Tom? If she needed benefits information or wanted gossip, her buddy Louise would provide both.

According to her reviews, Victoria was a woman whose emotions might run high. Thinking about that, I wondered if perhaps she'd called Tom to threaten him. Not with violence. That didn't seem likely. But there might have been a general "You haven't heard the last of me!" If that was the case, though, why hadn't Tom, who was so hot on record keeping, put it in writing and stuck it in her file?

All very interesting. Before I left the house, keeping my know-your-enemy spirit alive, I jotted Victoria Cerutti's address and phone number in the address book I carry in my tote.

6

"Bring your pad."

I could hardly believe what I heard.
Dorfmeyer said those very words. No
preamble. No "Good morning, Bonnie."
No "Are you busy right now?" Just a
quick appearance in my office door, a
flash of that stony-eyed glare I'd found
off-putting on first sight and now loathed,
and "Bring your pad."

When he was out of sight I grumbled,
loud enough for Louise to overhear, "I'd
like to bring my machine gun."

"Glad to see you're coming around," she said as I
stalked from our office, pad in hand.

Rose wasn't at her desk. Her desk, in fact, had a *locked-up* look to it. No paper coffee container, no open steno pad.
When I saw that the green "on" light on her computer was
dark, my mood, which had been sinking rapidly, plum-
meted. She wasn't in yet, though it was well after nine. Did
that mean she wasn't coming in? Was I *it*?

Standing at Dorfmeyer's office door while he growled into the phone at some other underling, I prayed to the God of secretaries that when this call ended, another would follow, and another, until finally it would be time for me to go home. The way I felt, I would have preferred standing there all day to another session of dictation.

My nerves jangled like the ring of a phone in the middle of the night. My stomach felt queasy, my skin oily, and my hair had reached a new personal low. The little voice that had warned me against that second margarita had been right. It was morning, and I hated myself.

But not as much as I hated Dorfmeyer right then.

"I'm ready!" he barked at me once he'd hung up.

God, would I have loved to have barked back, "I'm not." For a moment I stared back at him, thoughts of sedition clanging in my head. *I should just drop this steno pad on the floor and walk away. Or maybe I'll toss it on his desk and say, cool as an ice cube, "I quit." I would walk out and soak my cares away in the Jacuzzi at my health club.*

Health club. That did it. The thought of the whopping amount of money I'd owe the place if I left R&G got me moving. Walking into Dorfmeyer's office, I once again sank into that chair nearest the door.

"Take a letter to . . ."

It went on and on and on that morning, a stream—no, a surging river—of bureaucratic blather. Letters to accountants, memos to managers, to supervisors. Everything was about money, about spending less of it. No more free coffee and tea for employees, no more baskets of potpourri in the rest rooms. Talk about micromanagement. This nitpicking maniac was going to nickel-and-dime R&G's bottom line back into shape, and decimate employee morale in the process.

How many times did I ask Dorfmeyer to slow down, or to repeat himself? Dozens. His reaction was always the same. He would draw back his head and curl his lip, appalled, as if I'd asked him about his bathroom habits or something. He would then articulate the words I'd missed syllable by syllable, glaring all the while. Sometime in the midst of this torture session my stomach began churning in earnest and my thumb, which had been a minor annoyance the day before, was seriously aching.

It ended as abruptly as it had begun.

"That's it for now."

For now? When I dragged my wilted body out of Dorfmeyer's office and saw that Rose still hadn't arrived for work, his meaning became obvious. I willed myself not to dwell on it. It would have been like dwelling on a bully's threat. Ultimately the apprehension can become as bad as anything the bully might do.

Back in the corridor, the curiously hushed life of R&G's employees went on. Morning break was long over, and except for Rose, everyone was there. The clerk typist with the curly black hair whispered into her phone while a plump woman at the next desk tapped numbers into a calculator. I was beginning to recognize faces. The dour man walking toward me with a stack of computer printouts in his arms was in charge of payroll. Behind him was a younger man who had something to do with the company's computers.

"Bonnie!"

My name is hardly the stuff of marching commands, but the way Dorfmeyer barked it stopped me in my tracks.

I turned. He was at Rose's desk going through papers that had accumulated in his in-box. Flicking me a quick, sour glance, he said, "I've got more important things to do with my time than play fill-in-the-blank with you. Keep that in mind."

The words rolled like peals of thunder across the open area, and even when Dorfmeyer was finished with me and his attention returned to that in-box, they seemed to hang there.

Looking back now, I find myself wondering if Dorfmeyer was trying to be . . . amusing. I'm not suggesting that he *was* amusing. Maybe, though, he thought he was funny.

It stands to reason that his sense of humor would have been warped by all those downsizings he'd orchestrated.

Whatever the case, I was in a very shaky condition, feet still on the ground but head, thumb, and stomach dangling over the edge of a cliff. Dorfmeyer's words pushed me into the abyss. There's no other way I can account for my reaction.

Tears welled in my eyes. I tried to fight them back, but at the same time a burning lump rose in my throat. Several snotty responses ran through my head, but I was afraid that if I opened my mouth I might sob, and right then I would sooner have cut my throat than let this jerk know he'd made me fall apart.

The dour payroll man was staring at me, apparently dumbstruck by what he saw, and the dark-haired young woman had a distressed look on her face. They were both close enough to see my tears. After a second the woman got up and took a step toward me, as if wanting to help. Shaking my head to let her know I was all right, I hurried back to my office.

No sooner had I shut the door behind me than the tears poured. It was a short, but noticeable torrent.

"You poor thing. What did that snake do?" asked Louise.

"He . . . he . . . embarrassed me. In front of everyone out there."

For a few moments I carried on, becoming everything Louise had wanted me to be. Hurt, humiliated, angry. Outraged! I didn't merely think sedition. I talked it, in a hot ranting blast. I was going to take that steno pad and throw it in Dorfmeyer's face. I was going to quit without transcribing even one of his ridiculous memos. Or better yet I'd transcribe one and leave a dozen blank spaces, and before I left I'd tell him exactly what he could do with those blanks.

My outburst didn't last long. I suspect it was the way Louise was acting, as much as anything else, that cooled me down. There was no point in both of us having a tantrum, was there?

"He's disgusting!" she was saying. "Someone should put him in his place. I'd like to see him on the unemployment line. When my father was in the union, if a boss had ever spoken to a worker that way, a union rep would have . . ."

She paced our office, ranting on and on about picket lines and walkouts. My eyes dried. As Louise described a job action someone in her family had begun against some unspeakably vile management action, my gaze flickered to my steno pad. Sensation had returned to my thumb, and my stomach had stopped churning. Maybe letting off steam had helped. If I started transcribing now . . .

". . . and they initiated a slowdown that went on . . ."

All of Louise's carrying-on had something to do with sympathy for me, I suppose, but my personal plight was a very small part of her anger. I was a catalyst. If my problems with Dorfmeyer would have served her greater purpose—an employee walkout or slowdown—she would happily have chained me to that chair in his office without a moment's hesitation.

Only half listening to her diatribe by that time, I nevertheless tried to envision myself as a leader of the union movement that Louise was so certain was about to sweep the corrupt management out of R&G. The picture simply wouldn't come into focus. Sure, I'm capable of getting worked up—outraged!—about a lot of things, and of nurturing that outrage for a good while, but generally not about temp office jobs. Maybe I've just been lucky, but for me, if one doesn't work out, there's always another one waiting. Ditto men with big egos in big offices. Yes, Dorfmeyer was a fungus of a human being, but in the total scheme of my life he didn't amount to anything more than a minor itch. He certainly wasn't worth wasting my long-term outrage on.

In any event, the bottom line was that R&G would have a union when pigs flew over Manhattan, just like Casey had said. I would have bet my rent-stabilized lease on that. And frankly, unless Louise was truly nutty, she must have had some inkling of that.

"Well, I'd better get on with this," I said, interrupting her mid-sentence.

She stopped pacing and frowned at me. "You can't mean it. You're still going to do his work, after the way he treated you like a mangy dog in front of the entire staff?"

"I'm not sure it was really that bad, Louise. The thing is, last night . . ."

I tried to make Louise understand about the night before—about Sam and the margaritas—but she was no more interested in hearing about my rapidly dwindling social life than I was interested in hearing about her relatives on the picket line. Sensing that her anger was about to shift away from Dorfmeyer and onto me, I propped my steno pad against my typing stand.

"If I start transcribing now while my notes are still fresh, I shouldn't have too much trouble."

That undoubtedly knocked the hell out of what, if anything, was left of my *leader of the movement* image. The hope Louise had held out for me, however briefly, had been extinguished. In the workers' revolution at R&G I was persona non grata, one step away from that awful label *scab*.

For the rest of the day, Louise spoke to me only when necessary, and the atmosphere in the office was chilly. Late that afternoon, to escape her silence for a few minutes, I wandered out to the reception area and borrowed a Manhattan phone book from the receptionist. There was no Mrs. G. Obus in the listing of residential numbers, but there was one in the professional listings. Mrs. Gladys Obus, attorney-at-law, had her office on East Forty-seventh Street. I was so certain that she represented plaintiffs in employment discrimination cases that I didn't bother calling to check.

"I'm sorry about this morning, Bonnie," Tom said. "I hear Carl was kind of rough on you. I understand his secretary was at the doctor all morning. Apparently she has a preul-cerous condition.''

That didn't surprise me considering what she did for a living, but by that time I was tired of it all. I had a life, and Dorfmeyer was just a tiny blip in a tiny part of it. "It was as much me as him," I responded carelessly. "I was in a . . . sensitive . . . frame of mind."

"Just the same, if I'd known he was going to need help again, I would have gotten another temp. The agency has a man on call who has won shorthand competitions."

"You're kidding. Is there such a thing?"

Tom grinned. "That's what the agency told me."

Though I will defend temp workers with my dying breath, you find nuts in every field, and this steno champ sounded like one to me. Still, if he could keep Dorfmeyer away from me, more power to him. I'd transcribed that morning's dictation without nearly as much trouble as I'd expected, and the drafts I'd returned to Dorfmeyer had been free of blank spaces this time, but stenography was not a skill I wanted to continue honing.

Tom had discovered me in the big records room, where, after returning Victoria's file to its proper place, I'd spent a good part of the afternoon filing the staff's year-end performance reviews. He picked a few out of the stack and began filing in another drawer. Guilt can be a terrific motivator.

"Did you read any of these?" he asked as we worked.

I said, "Not really," with a shrug, and ignored my own slight twinge of guilt. Curious about Louise's review, I'd pulled it from the stack immediately and ducked my head into a half-empty file drawer to read it unobserved. Tom had written most of the comments about Louise, but several other management types had added remarks. On a scale of one to five, Louise had received a three for work performed and a one for attitude, which rounded out to an abysmal two. After that, in the process of filing her review, I'd thumbed through her file. Louise may have considered herself a fine example of a worker, but it appeared as if the pinnacle of her performance had been the solid three average she'd maintained during her first two years on the job.

"I have the evaluations for managers, too," Tom said as we worked. "I'll give you the master key and you can—"

The ringing of the wall phone interrupted him. There were two rings, indicating the call was from outside the company. I was closer to the phone, so I answered.

"Hello?"

"Who is this? Bonnie?"

It was Dorfmeyer. Was he after me again? My stomach lurched and my mouth suddenly felt parched. Relief came, though, when I glanced at my watch. It was 5:35. Five minutes later than my stated quitting time. In one of those union shops Louise was always harping about, the whistle already would have blown. If I worked in one of those places, I'd probably be in the parking lot by now, climbing into my pickup truck.

"This is Bonnie," I said, belligerence strengthening my voice. *Just let him ask,* I was thinking. Hoping. *I'll tell him I'm out of here. If he doesn't like it, maybe he'd like to deal with a union-organizing drive.*

"This is Carl Dorfmeyer. I must . . ."

Here it came, and I was ready for it. My breaths were quicker. Like one of Louise's Teamster brothers, I was going to take on the slave-driving bosses.

". . . reach Tom Hurley. He's not in his office. Have you seen him? It's very important."

I'll never know for sure whether I was disappointed or relieved. Perhaps a bit of each. I hadn't gotten to make my *outraged worker* speech, but that was probably just as well. Judging from the way my heart was pounding, my speech might have come out as an incomprehensible sputter.

"He's right here. Just a second." I motioned to Tom and mouthed Dorfmeyer's name as I handed him the receiver.

For the next minute or two I pretended to file. My ears were pitched toward that phone, and my eyes kept flickering in that direction. Tom hadn't achieved Louise's phone expertise—he didn't turn his head away, which made it easy for me to see his grimace.

"This is Tom." There was a brief pause. "The list is in my desk." Tom's next pause was much longer, and as he listened to Dorfmeyer, the color drained from his face. "Impossible," he said sharply. "Where did you hear . . ."

What had begun as a minor grimace was now a major one. Whatever Dorfmeyer was saying was making Tom very unhappy. "I do have plans tonight," he finally said after drawing a deep breath. "My train is at six-ten." Pause. "Yes, sir. Your office, tomorrow at nine-thirty A.M. . . . The files? Well, if Rose . . ."

It seemed as if the subject had changed. Tom's white-knuckled grip on the phone loosened.

"Oh, I see," he said. "Yes. She is still here. She might be willing . . ." Another pause. "Yes, I know your suite number. I'll see that you get them all."

Tom was staring straight at me, leaving me no doubt who *she* was. When he had replaced the receiver, he opened his mouth to say something, but then clamped it shut and averted his eyes. To be specific, he looked down at his feet. Fascinating, those shiny brown wing tips.

I broke the silence. "I must be *she*. What is it I might be willing to do?"

"Well . . ."

He didn't look up right away, and when he did he had a hard time meeting my gaze. What I feared was true. Tom Terrific had handed me over to Dorfmeyer, just like he might hand over a piece of office equipment.

"I'm desperate, Bonnie. Tonight's my son's last soccer match of the season. I've got just enough time to finish up here and make my train."

"No way." I waved my watch in front of him. "It's after five-thirty. I don't do steno on my own time."

"Carl doesn't want to dictate to you. He's at his hotel. He just needs—"

By then I was really worked up. "I don't make house calls, either, so don't even think—"

"Bonnie. Please. Carl's secretary is going to his hotel this evening to work. If he wants to dictate, he'll dictate to her. All he wants is to get some personnel files delivered there. He needs to finalize some things."

"Such as?"

"Increases. These people will be getting the minimum. Two percent. Carl's already signed off on their reviews."

I was shaking my head vigorously when Tom added, "There are only fifteen or so files. You'll be paid double your hourly rate for whatever time it takes you to pull them and take them to his hotel. And if you want to finish up your filing first"—he nodded at the stack of evaluations—"that will be double time, too. Carl doesn't need the files immediately."

My brain, apparently acting without consulting my spirit, which moments before had been ready to throw itself into the workers' revolution, digested that information. Pacing myself, I could stretch my time in the records room to an hour and a half, and then walk slowly to Dorfmeyer's hotel. As much as two hours at double time could come of this. It wouldn't amount to the mother lode I needed to get through the holidays, but it would help.

The deal was clinched when Tom added, "And of course, the company will reimburse you for your cab home, even if you decide to go to the gym first."

That cab home finished off what was left of my resolve. Tom went to get the list of files that Dorfmeyer wanted while I went back to filing performance evaluations. As I filed, I planned my upcoming scene with Dorfmeyer. I would knock on his suite door and, when he opened it, say briskly, "You wanted these," and shove the files at him. And if Dorfmeyer asked me to come in, if he so much as stepped back and made an *enter* gesture with his arm, my response would be a firm no.

"This list is for your eyes only," Tom said when he hurried back into the records room minutes later. "No one else around here should see it. It would cause all kinds of trouble."

He had on his overcoat and hat and was ready to run out of the office. I glanced quickly at the list, my principal interest in it being its length. I liked Tom, but when people are desperate to get away from the office, there's no telling what depths they'll sink to. To Tom's credit, the list was no longer than he'd said. Not only that, but it was in alphabetical order, which would make pulling the files easy.

Noticing both Louise's and Casey's name on the list, I again asked Tom why Dorfmeyer wanted the files. Though Dorfmeyer was a nitpicker, I couldn't imagine him figuring percentages when he had an entire accounting department at his disposal.

"It's a formality," Tom said.

"Formality for what? He already signed off on the reviews. Anybody can figure two percent of—"

"Bonnie! Haven't you heard the expression 'ours is not to reason why'?"

" 'Ours is but to do or die'?"

"You've got it. This opens the inner records room," he said, handing me a key. "One of the files is in there. Just put the key in my top drawer before you leave. It's an extra, but I have to keep tabs on it. And remember, no one should see that list or the files."

"Don't worry about anything," I said. "Just make your train."

"Thanks for helping out, Bonnie," Tom said. "If I don't make that soccer match, Elizabeth's going to be so upset that I might have to move into that hotel permanently."

Tom hurried off to catch his train, and I tucked the list and key into my skirt pocket and went back to my filing. About half an hour later I slipped the last evaluation into its file. It was 6:15, and the realization that if I got two hours overtime out of this I'd make a decent starter payment on that side-by-side refrigerator cheered me as much as something of that sort can.

I pulled Tom's list from my pocket and examined it. Casey was the reason I needed the key to the inner room.

I set his name aside in my mind. His file would be the last I'd pull.

Bernice Adams was the first name. I found her file in the first drawer, right where it should have been, and quickly glanced at her performance appraisal. Whatever Bernice did at R&G, her appraisal indicated that she didn't do it very well.

"Minimum raise for you, Bernice," I said, tossing her file onto the copy machine. "Or maybe worse."

Tom's story just hadn't rung true. My guess was these people were being let go, and Dorfmeyer wanted to give their files one last look to be certain there wasn't some cause for a lawsuit buried in one of them.

Pulling the files ordinarily would have taken little time, but I stretched things out by looking over the papers in them. Though departments and lengths of service varied, the employees on this list all had one thing in common: *marginal* performance appraisals for at least the past two years.

I had gotten through almost the entire list when exhaustion began creeping through me. My arms had grown fatigued and my head heavy. My bed beckoned. There'd be no gym for me that night.

I yawned. A splash of water on my face might help, but more than that, I craved a soda. Thirst, no doubt brought on by the abuses I'd inflicted on myself the night before, intensified until it couldn't be ignored. I left the records room, pulling the door shut until it clicked, but not locking it.

The lights in my office were still on, but knowing Louise as I did, she surely had gone. I didn't see anyone else until I got to the other side of the reception area. There I passed the curly-haired statistical typist. She glanced up from her monitor and we exchanged smiles, but she never stopped typing.

A couple minutes later, after finishing up in the ladies' room, I went into the room with the vending machines and dropped some change into the soft-drink dispenser. No

longer able to postpone gratification, I opened the icy can
of soda the second it popped through that rubber flap. I
leaned against the wall and finished the entire drink right
there.

When I returned to the records room, the door was partly
open. I'd closed it behind me. I was sure of that. Pushing
it wide, I called out, "Anybody in here?" No one answered, but I peeked behind the bank of file cabinets anyway.

Satisfied that I was alone, telling myself that maybe I
hadn't shut the door tight, I reached for the list atop the
stack of files on the copy machine.

It was gone! Someone had been in the room and taken
it! I'd not only let eyes other than mine see the top-secret
list of names, but I'd let someone take the damned thing!
And before I'd finished pulling the files. There had been
only three or four files remaining to be pulled, but Casey's
was the only name I recalled.

I was considering my options, none of them appealing
and all of them involving playing dumb, when something
crumbled under one of my feet. I glanced down, and if I'd
been in a spunkier mood, I might have let out with a happy
little yip. The list had fallen to the floor.

It took me another minute or two to dig out the remaining
files. After pulling Casey's, I glanced through the cabinet
for Tom's. It should have been in the same drawer, but I
didn't find it. It had probably been misfiled, but I wasn't
curious enough to bother searching very hard.

After locking the inner room, I tested the door to make
sure it held tight. Then, out in the corridor, I double-
checked the main records-room lock. Though the soda had
done some good toward waking me up, I no longer trusted
myself.

My own office was now dark. Twenty minutes before
the lights had been on. That first struck me as ominous.
Perhaps Louise *had* been there earlier. If she'd heard me
talking to Tom, she would have been curious. More than
curious. For a chance to get a peek at the list, she might

have been willing to do what, according to her performance appraisal, she hadn't done all year: hang around R&G after quitting time.

I loaded some of the files into my tote and secured the remaining ones with big rubber bands. As I prepared to leave, I wondered how Louise would react to seeing her name on the list. She'd probably think exactly what I'd been thinking—that the people on this list might be let go—and she'd definitely think that I was a turncoat. A scab. How nice.

On the way out I stopped in Tom's office and put the master key in his drawer. On top of his desk, in plain view, was a folder marked PRO-TEAM TEMPS. Opening it, I found a bill for my services, as well as an evaluation form from Adele. Tom had already completed it.

"Bonnie's the greatest, Adele. A fabulous employee. I wish we could clone her."

He'd probably left it there on purpose for me to see, but that was okay. I left the building smiling.

Carl Dorfmeyer's hotel was nothing like the glittery one that housed the health club, and Tom Hurley. Its face did not shout "welcome," at least not to the likes of me. No budget-minded tourists would ever pile out of airport buses and drag their matching his-and-her duffel bags into the shelter of the royal-blue awning with the discreet gold lettering—THE IVY LEAGUE CLUB—and up to the wooden door, much less past the elderly but formidable doorman standing at attention just inside it. No salesmen in plaid jackets would have had the nerve, or the desire, to yuck it up on the sagging sofas in the lobby. As for illicit lovers, none of them would want to cross the mouse-colored carpeting and break the quiet by asking the ancient, forbidding desk clerk about available rooms.

It was a fluke that I was able to enter the way I did—unnoticed. All of the doorman's attention was commanded, at the moment I walked under that awning, by two elderly women who had just gotten out of a black car. A very light snow had begun falling, and the two women waited under the awning's shelter as the doorman began lifting out pieces of hard-sided luggage from the car's trunk.

I crossed the Ivy League's lobby and stood at the marble-topped check-in desk for several seconds, waiting for the desk clerk to look up. This clerk was clearly a man who did only one thing at a time, and at this time he had turned his back on the lobby and was reading through a hand-written list. Reservations, perhaps. This place didn't look as if it had been touched by the information age.

"Excuse me—" I began.

"Just a moment," he said crisply. Picking up a pencil, he began checking off items on the list. I stood there for another few seconds while that pencil moved with what I found agonizing slowness.

My tote was growing heavier on my shoulder, and the files cradled under my arm no longer felt so manageable. After staring at the back of the clerk's head for another few seconds, I gave up. Carl Dorfmeyer was in room 503. Where else would that be but the fifth floor? And if I got there unannounced, big deal.

As I waited for the elevator, a sixtyish couple walked past the growing stack of luggage by the door and through the lobby. Her autumn-haze mink coat must have been going in and out of fashion for decades. These days it was out, pinched at the waist, flaring at the hips, and ending just below her knees. The man with her was a study in tweed. Merely looking at him made me itch.

The couple didn't glance my way.

On the far side of the lobby, past the elevator and a door that may have led to a stairwell, was a restaurant. Like everything else in the Ivy League Club, it did not team with action. Its double doors stood open, allowing the very quiet hum of voices to filter into the lobby.

"Mr. and Mrs. . . . ."

The man who met the couple at the restaurant's entrance must have been eighty. He stood aside as the couple passed him, and then followed behind them. He didn't appear to notice me.

The lobby was still again, until a few seconds later when the elevator door slid open. Stepping into the car, I wriggled the tote's strap more securely onto my shoulder and pressed the button for the fifth floor.

"Mr. Dorfmeyer?"

My first knock had gone unanswered, as had my second, but my third knock, considerably more forceful than the first two, caused the door to Carl Dorfmeyer's suite to swing wide open.

I wasn't at all alarmed by this. The L-shaped living room I was looking into was brightly lit and the portion of it visible from the door was every bit as orderly as Dorfmeyer's office. Still, I didn't want to simply walk in. Somewhere in this suite there was a bedroom and a bathroom, and if the Big Kahuna was taking care of any sort of personal business, I had no intention of witnessing it.

I peeked to the other side of the door. There was a small dining area, and the folding door beyond that must have concealed a tiny kitchenette. That got me wondering, for a few seconds, about Dorfmeyer's eating habits. Did he occasionally rustle up dinner for himself? Something simple? Steak and eggs? A tuna melt? No. Probably not a tuna melt. That's one of my staples, and I didn't imagine Dorfmeyer and I would have much in common.

"Mr. Dorfmeyer?"

I took a couple steps into the suite, and became aware of a strong odor rather like the one put out by Casey Innis's cigars. Wondering about that, I took a deep breath. Yes. It was that same nasty smell.

I was letting the air out of my lungs when I heard the voices coming from the section of the living room that was out of my sight.

Aha. There were at least two people in the suite. Though the voices were faint, I made out a woman's tinkling laugh, followed by a comment from a man. A second later the woman began speaking, her voice pitched high for emphasis.

Lowering the tote to the floor and laying the other files on a chair, I headed toward the sound. When I rounded the living room's corner, however, I found myself alone, facing a diaphanous floor-to-ceiling curtain.

The happy voices continued. They were coming from the other side of the curtain, where there was obviously a terrace. I couldn't make out what the woman said, but it caused the man to break into hoarse laughter. If I was listening to Mr. Dorfmeyer and his secretary, Rose, they certainly had sides I hadn't seen.

The gauzy curtain shifted slightly, and a gust of cold wind found its way up my legs. Though it was hardly terrace weather, there might be a spectacular view. Or a romantic one. Wasn't it about time for a full moon?

Standing at the curtains, I called his name again. Again there was no answer. Pulling one of the curtains aside, I stepped through it. A large part of my mind was now occupied by the notion that I might be interrupting something interesting. I didn't shrink from this prospect. In fact, I embraced the idea as enthusiastically as those lovers—who could they be but Dorfmeyer and Rose?—would be embracing each other at this moment. They'd be embarrassed and break apart, perhaps with lame excuses. *C'est la vie.*

After that, just let him try his *bring your pad* routine on me, or her carry on about speed-building steno exercises.

The moon was almost full, and the entire terrace, which was narrow but longer than I'd expected, was aglow with a pale, lustrous light. It was cold, certainly, but there was clear beauty to the night. The light snow had stopped falling, but surfaces were dusted with flakes.

But where were the people? The voices had grown louder, but the terrace looked deserted. My initial glance, as I pushed the flimsy curtain away, revealed no corners, no hidden crannies.

At the terrace's far end—it must have stretched about sixteen feet along the side of the building—were three Ad-

irondack chairs. You must know the kind of chair I mean—
wide wooden slats, high backs. Two of them, huddled together near the terrace's iron railing, had been turned to
face the view to the east. The third chair was shoved against
the wall of the building, somewhat closer to me but in an
area even more bereft of light than the edge of the terrace.
I could see that this third chair was empty, but the almost
nonexistent light and the way they were arranged made it
impossible for me to be certain who, if anyone, occupied
the other two.

"Mr. Dorfmeyer!"

The voices continued. Still expecting the jolly couple to
poke their heads around the sides of the chairs, I moved
closer. I was a few feet from the chairs when the couple
got their laughter under control. I took a step nearer.

"Unbelievable," the man said, his voice suddenly crack-
ing.

"But true," said the woman faintly. "Now stay tuned
for a traffic update, and more about that accident on the
Brooklyn/Queens . . ."

It was a moment before I spotted the radio balanced on
the arm of one of the chairs. It was still another moment
before I digested the fact that my romantic couple were a
pair of radio commentators.

Both the chairs were empty. I stared down at them for a
moment, feeling a bit foolish, before turning away. I'd done
as much as I intended to do. If I put the files on the dining-
room table, Dorfmeyer would be certain to find them. There
was no point in my waiting around.

Unexpectedly, something firm but at the same time soft
grazed against the outside of my right ankle.

Why I always think *rodent* at times like this I'll never
know. There's probably a Freudian explanation, some rodent experience buried in my subconscious. For whatever
reason, I leaped to one side to escape the filthy thing. That
made matters worse. I landed against the iron railing, and
for a horrifying second felt myself tilting backward over it.

Even more afraid of a five-story free fall than I was of

whatever was on the terrace floor, I lurched forward frantically, at the same time trying to spot movement on the terrace floor so that I could avoid whatever was there.

Nothing moved, but something huge was on the floor between the third Adirondack chair and a big clay planter. My eyes had begun adjusting to the dark. There was a shoe. A pair of them, toes pointing up.

And was that . . . a leg?

"Mr. Dorfmeyer!"

He lay slumped in the corner, partly concealed by the chair.

A stroke or a heart attack. They were my first thoughts. Shoving the heavy chair aside, I crouched at his side. What do you do for a heart-attack victim? Immediate help was Dorfmeyer's best chance, and I was the only help around.

I held my hand in front of his nose trying to feel a breath of air. Nothing. A pulse? My fingers scrambled along the floor, reaching for his wrist. I grasped something on the floor beside him, a thing so cold that an icy shock wave traveled through my hand and up my arm when I lifted it.

The icy-cold thing was the barrel of a blue-black revolver with an ivory butt.

7

Ten p.m. East Side Medical Center.

Fluorescent lights glinted off the polished tile floor and stark white walls, giving the windowless waiting room a bright-as-sunlight appearance, although the straggly potted palms, strategically placed to create semiprivate seating areas, looked as if they had never seen the light of day. In deference to the season, a few poinsettias had been scattered around. The one nearest me, a pretty robust specimen, actually, had been used as a receptacle for a gum wrapper.

Even the most determined optimist would have had difficulty believing Carl Dorfmeyer was alive. Nevertheless, he, or better put, his earthly remains, had been taken by ambulance to the nearest hospital emergency room. I was taken there, too, by a grizzled, mustached NYPD sergeant whose stomach pooched against the patrol car's steering wheel. He'd left me in a waiting room with the instructions that I "take it easy" until a detective arrived to question me.

The curious life of a hospital waiting room buzzed around me as I tried, without much success, to follow his advice. Doctors, nurses, and orderlies pushed in through one swinging door and out through another, a faceless swarm in white jackets or pale green smocks. Sometimes they spoke to each other in passing, but what they said, about drips and IVs, admissions and remissions, was largely lost on me. Occasionally one of them paused to speak with the people who occupied the room's utilitarian chairs waiting for news, but this was done with voices low, so that only murmurs reached me. A public-address system erupted every few minutes, blaring out doctors' names, drowning out all other sounds.

Now and then one of the people who sat waiting for news rose and paced the length of the room, sometimes stopping at the vending machines in the corner near a public telephone, invariably peering through the small windows in the swinging doors, but never daring to breach them.

After waiting, uneasily, for more than a quarter hour, I grew impatient and paced the shiny floor and stared through the little windows, too. There was nothing to be seen but hallways and closed doors, empty gurneys and more medical people in pale green and white.

Moving on to the vending machines, I inserted some change into the one that dispensed coffee, hot chocolate, and chicken noodle soup. I don't have the vocabulary to convey to you the vileness of the liquid that splashed into the paper cup that tumbled into position under the spout, but I carried it back to my chair and sipped at it anyway.

I'd been waiting for about half an hour when a short, well-dressed African-American man walked hesitantly through the collection of struggling palms that set my little semiprivate area apart from others in the waiting room. The man, whose horn-rim glasses were perched near the end of his nose, peered into a small notebook and asked, "Miss Bonnie . . . Indermill?"

His words were so deliberate, each syllable so clearly articulated, that he might have been reading my name off an eye chart. When I responded yes, he introduced himself as Detective Reginald Givens.

Detective Givens asked, politely, whether he might join me, beginning this interview in an oddly genteel way. Certain that regardless of my response he had every intention of joining me, I nodded.

After removing his trench coat, folding it neatly over a chair arm, and balancing his brown felt hat on top of it, Detective Givens sat down across from me. He then cleared his throat, took an honest-to-God fountain pen from his jacket's inside pocket, unscrewed the top, looked across the small glass-topped coffee table separating us, and cleared his throat again.

After all this preparation, he got around to asking me questions. They poured out of him at about the speed that honey pours out of that little plastic bear that's been fossilizing in my refrigerator for as long as I can remember. It is no exaggeration when I say that the detective weighed every word that came out of his mouth, and wrote down most of the ones that came from mine.

By the time I'd explained about the personnel files and the mediocre evaluations in them, and explained why I'd taken them to Dorfmeyer's suite, which took what seemed an immeasurable amount of time, my emotional state had changed. The horror of finding the body had faded, replaced by almost uncontrollable impatience. All I could think about was speeding things up and getting done with this poky detective.

"Mr. Dorfmeyer wanted to see these files, even though he had already signed off on the evaluations?" Givens asked, repeating something I thought I'd made clear.

"Yes."

The detective nodded. "All right. Let's move on to something else. Did you happen to notice the time that you left your office building, Miss Indermill?"

"At about seven-twenty, I think. I was on overtime, so I was trying to keep track."

"Ah," he said. "And what time did you arrive at the Ivy League Club?"

"I'm not sure, but it probably took me ten or twelve minutes to walk there."

"What exactly happened then? You had the desk clerk call up to the deceased's suite?"

"No, because . . ."

When I'd explained what happened in the lobby of the Ivy League Club, Detective Givens looked at me long and hard before making any notes.

"And so you entered the deceased's suite unobserved? Is that correct?"

"Yes."

I sat quietly while he noted what I'd said. After that, he got to the subject of Dorfmeyer himself. By that time even my impatience was dulling. As I answered Givens's endless questions, I began to feel permanently numbed, as if all my senses had died.

"You told me that the deceased was not popular with your coworkers at Richards & Goode," the detective said, after consulting his notebook for about the hundredth time. "Could you explain to me exactly how you know that, Miss Indermill?"

"They told me."

I couldn't imagine why that answer gave him something to think about, but it did. While Detective Givens pondered, my body was tossed by the strongest wave of exhaustion I'd felt all night. My head dropped, and suddenly keeping my eyes open was a battle I was on the brink of losing. I blinked, trying to keep things around me in focus. My gaze fell to the few magazines strewn about the table between us. There was a *Travel & Leisure,* months old, but leisure never goes out of style, does it? On the cover, a beach in southern France beckoned.

Detective Givens asked, "Who told you that?"

I quickly jerked my head up, but a couple seconds passed

before I remembered what, specifically, we'd been talking about.

"Louise Gruber and Casey Innis in particular," I responded. "They're close friends. The three of us had lunch"—I paused—"yesterday." Had it been yesterday? I was losing track of time. "They both had a lot to say about Dorfmeyer."

"Mmm."

Givens wrote the names in his notepad, pausing in the process to ask, "Innis starts with an *I* or an *E*?"

"An *I*. Actually, there's something I have to tell you about Casey Innis. He smokes these cigars . . ."

The lingering odor in the hotel suite unfortunately had dissipated by the time the police had arrived. I'd mentioned it to one of them—the sergeant who later drove me to the hospital—but after sniffing the air, he had looked at me, shaken his head, and gone about his business, leaving me to wonder whether or not that bit of information would end up in his crime-scene report. Afraid that it wouldn't, I now described the lingering odor to Detective Givens in as much detail as I could. It was a unique and easily distinguishable odor, at least for me, I assured Givens. I'd first smelled it in the open air, and then I'd been smothered with it in a smoky restaurant. Later, I'd smelled it again in Casey's office.

Going on to talk about the gun—it had to be the one Casey had shown me the day before, didn't it? There couldn't be two floating around with that same elegant ivory butt—I became aware that my voice was developing a discernible quaver. Upset by that, I clutched my hands together. They were icy cold.

"I have to tell you something else," I said to Givens. "In Casey's office, when he showed us the gun, I kind of . . ." An almost desperate quality, a breathlessness, had entered my voice. I forced myself to continue. "I kind of . . . showed off. I aimed it at a picture of Carl Dorfmeyer that was taped to the back of Casey's door, and . . ."

"Yes?"

"I pretended to shoot Mr. Dorfmeyer."

Bang! Right between the eyes.

There was no noticeable change in Detective Givens's demeanor as he wrote down what I'd just said, but a terrible realization began toying at the edge of my mind. Unless Givens was even slower than he seemed, unless he was profoundly slow, he had to be considering me as a suspect in Carl Dorfmeyer's murder.

No one had seen me leave the office, and no one had seen me enter the hotel or Dorfmeyer's suite. How could I prove I'd only spent a few minutes there? I couldn't. What if the cold weather threw off the medical examiner's time-of-death estimate? What if the medical examiner decided that Dorfmeyer, having been *on ice,* to put it bluntly, could have been killed minutes before I called the police.

Worse, I'd handled the murder weapon after the murder, perhaps wiping away the murderer's prints with my own. And worse than that, I'd handled the gun the day before, in front of two witnesses, and done my stupid macho best to incriminate myself.

My rising anxiety took care of my fatigue. I was wide-awake now, heart thumping. The terrible realization no longer toyed with my mind. It jabbed hard.

That was the time, right then, for me to say something about my own shaky relationship with Carl Dorfmeyer. If Givens had only asked me how I got along with Dorfmeyer, I surely would have told him that the man had embarrassed me in public, and that he'd made me cry. Givens didn't ask, though, and for some reason which I'll never fully understand, I didn't tell.

Detective Givens had a habit of tugging at the skin around his chin. When I finally wound down, he took a few minutes to finish writing what I'd said, then stared at his notebook for several moments, tugging all the while. He must have been doing this for years, and though he was far from old—I figured he was no more than fifty—his jowls draped on either side of his face, bloodhoundlike. Considering the way I was feeling, that image wasn't a pleasant one to consider.

"And this individual who smokes the cigars—this Casey Innis—his file was in the stack you were bringing to the hotel suite?" Givens asked, repeating what I'd already told him.

"Yes."

While waiting for the detective's next question, I realized that my fingernails were digging into the flesh of my palms. Easing my fists, I took a long deep breath and rolled my shoulders.

"Can I get you some coffee?" the detective asked solicitously.

I nodded at my almost empty cup. "I had enough already, but thanks."

"All right, Miss Indermill," he said. "Then shall we continue? I'd like to talk a little more about those files."

There was that permission-seeking tone again. Such a polite, low-key man. Why didn't I trust him?

"You explained that Mr. Dorfmeyer wanted to give those employees minimal raises? Correct?"

"Yes."

"And two percent was the minimum being given?"

"Yes."

A bit of chin tugging followed. After a few seconds, Detective Givens asked me the same question I'd asked Tom, and myself, earlier: why was it necessary for Dorfmeyer to review their files for that purpose?

"You told me earlier that the deceased had already signed off on those reviews," Givens said. "Forgive me if I seem obtuse here, Miss Indermill, but couldn't Mr. Dorfmeyer simply instruct those employees' supervisors, or your payroll department, to give them the minimum? Why would a man in his position waste his time calculating percentages."

"I am only repeating what I was told by Tom Hurley."

"Oh yes. Mr. Hurley. The"—Givens thumbed back through his notes—"director of human resources. Hmm.

Tell me, Miss Indermill: why do *you* think that the deceased wanted those files?'' he asked, looking up again.

''Well,'' I said, ''he *was* called 'Dorfmeyer the Downsizer.' There was a reason for that.''

Givens's thoughtful nod indicated that he got my point, and that I didn't have to elaborate. However, in order to be sure that he knew everything that had happened, I continued.

''While I was pulling those files, I think someone got a look at the names on the list. It could have been Louise, and as I said, she and Casey are friendly. She might have called Casey and told him they were both on the list. For that matter,'' I added, ''Casey brags about going anywhere in the office he wants. He could have gone into the records room while I was getting a soda.''

Another thoughtful nod from Givens, this one accompanied by pursed lips. He believed me. Or did he? I couldn't guess. A moment or two later Givens stood up, collected his coat and hat, and told me I could go home. He asked me not to say anything about the lingering cigar odor I'd detected, or about the gun.

He also asked whether I had any plans to leave the city. It was a question; it wasn't a request, and it definitely wasn't a command. I remember being relieved by that.

As I shook my head, it occurred to me that I should mention Raymond and Noreen's party. Detective Givens hadn't said I *couldn't* leave town, though. He'd just asked if I planned to. In any event, visiting your relatives in New Jersey is hardly the same thing as jumping bail and heading for South America. I didn't mention the upcoming anniversary festivities.

I waited until the detective had disappeared through one of the swinging doors before I left the waiting room and followed glowing red exit signs to the street.

The dusting of snow had melted, and headlights shone in the damp pavement as cars passed the hospital entrance. The air felt colder than it had, and I turned my collar up and huddled into it as I tried to flag a cab. If I didn't find my scarf, I was going to have to buy another one.

On cold damp nights, cabs can be hard to find. After a few minutes I gave up trying to flag one on the side street and walked the half block to First Avenue. I was standing away from the glare of streetlights, between two parked cars, staring down First Avenue, when a now familiar voice reached me.

"What did you think of her story?" Givens was asking someone.

Face partly buried in my coat collar, I turned just enough to see the detective walk past. The grizzled, overweight sergeant was at his side.

"Can't tell," the sergeant answered. "At the scene of the crime she was talking about smelling that cigar smoke, but I didn't smell anything myself. I checked with the other officers on the scene. None of them noticed any smell, either."

"It might be true," Givens said, "or she might be trying to pin it on Innis. Can't tell yet. Has he been picked up?"

"Yeah. He's at the station now."

"It's his gun?"

"Looks that way."

Their voices had begun fading. I could just make out Givens's words. ". . . suspect it was an R&G homeboy who killed him"—and barely heard the sergeant's response—"Or maybe your homegirl back there."

That homegirl was me, and my situation was only going to get worse. Hadn't Dorfmeyer humiliated me in public? Made me cry? In New York City people have been hacked up with machetes for less than that. Just wait until the neat little detective found out that I'd had motivation.

Standing there in the cold, watching for a vacant cab, it occurred to me for the first time that perhaps Casey wasn't as dumb as I'd thought. If he *had* planned to kill Dorfmeyer, he might have been looking for someone to take the blame. He'd dangled his bait in front of me, and I'd taken it. *Bang! Right between the eyes!* I'd been the perfect dumb, hungry fish.

Finally a cab pulled over. It was a relatively new one. The backseat wasn't yet rump-sprung and the heater worked. On top of that, the driver spoke English and knew how to get to my neighborhood. Sometimes you do get a break.

Settling into the comfortable seat, feeling my body warming, I gave myself a pep talk. The police couldn't suspect me. Not really. Only a crazy person would shoot someone merely because they'd been embarrassed, and I wasn't crazy. Taking this line of thought further, it thus had to be obvious to him that I hadn't shot Carl Dorfmeyer. If I had been guilty I would have wiped my prints off the gun and hightailed it out of that suite without calling 911. Givens had to realize that I was merely a victim of circumstance.

I must have started to believe this logic, because the exhaustion I'd been holding at bay overpowered my anxiety. I dozed during the last few minutes of the ride home.

The only message on my answering machine that night was from Tom. I listened as I opened a can of food for Moses.

"Bonnie! Are you there? Guess not. It's about nine-thirty. I just heard about Carl. I can't believe it. You must be devastated. I'm so sorry to have involved you in this. I'm starting back to the city as soon as the kids are tucked into bed. I'll be at the office real early tomorrow. R&G's board of directors is already berserk. I should be at my hotel by midnight if you need to talk. Otherwise I'll see you tomorrow."

That was nice of Tom, but I'd talked about as much as I wanted to for one day.

Moses was madly hungry. I always leave dry food out for him, but it's not the same. He shoved his face into his blue plastic bowl before I finished spooning the tuna-and-turkey treat into it.

Though I hadn't eaten since lunch, nothing in my refrigerator appealed to me. After washing my face and brushing my teeth, I crawled into bed. The moment my head hit the pillow I was asleep.

8

THAT NIGHT THE EARTH WASN'T SHAKEN by a major quake or scorched by an erupting volcano. No dictator declared war on a neighboring country, famines were old news, and no basketball players or rock stars died of drug overdoses. Having little else to shout about, New York's morning papers gave Dorfmeyer's death front-page banner headlines.

The *Herald,* which can work itself into a frenzy over a fashion designer's divorce, outdid itself with its headline.

DORFMEYER THE DOWNSIZER MEETS DEFINITIVE DOWNSIZER: DEATH.

A shot between the eyes has ended the career of Carl Dorfmeyer, chief executive officer at Richards & Goode Corporation. The murder, which is believed to have occurred early yesterday evening, was reported by an R&G stenographer who said she had gone to the victim's suite to deliver files.

According to NYPD Detective Reginald Givens, it is believed that the murder weapon, a revolver, has been recovered and the gun's owner identified. When asked whether either the gun's owner or the stenographer was a suspect, Givens responded, "No comment."

As you might imagine, I was unnerved by the article. The "stenographer" had been identified as an R&G employee, so why not "the gun's owner"? Givens's "no comment" was even more unnerving. It was fine with me if he didn't want to comment about Casey, who was surely the murderer. But me? I was innocent.

Louise, who was poring over the scant details when I walked into the office, didn't appear to mind that she might be sharing her office with a murderer. She waved the paper at me excitedly.

"Was it you, Bonnie?"

"No! It wasn't me. How did you get such a ridiculous idea?"

"But it had to be you," she insisted.

Louise's eyes glistened and her excited smile left her incisors completely exposed. I'd never realized they were so long and vampirelike. She was just dying to sink them into something nice and meaty.

"It says that a stenographer from the office reported the murder. I've already talked to Rose," she added. "She was supposed to work last night, but her stomach was still bothering her. She told me she called Dorfmeyer and said she couldn't make it. It had to be you who found him, Bonnie. You're the only other stenographer he worked with here."

I was so relieved that Louise wasn't accusing me of murdering Dorfmeyer that I ignored the fact that she was accusing me of being a stenographer.

"You're right," I said. "I did discover the body."

"Wow! That must have been something! I would have been hysterical. Were you?"

"Not hysterical, but very upset."

"Did you actually . . . touch him?"

"Well, yes. I thought he might be alive."

"Oh my God! What did you do then?"

I was in no mood to discuss the details of the evening before with Louise. Detective Givens hadn't said anything about confidentiality except with respect to the gun and the smoky odor, but I stretched that into an overall information blackout.

"I called 911. That's all I can say, though. The police don't want me to discuss the case."

"Wow! Oh, wow! I understand," Louise said. "Police procedures. I'll bet you one thing, though: the killer was a disgruntled employee from right here!"

Another bet on the homeboys and girls.

I had every reason to agree with her, and so did the NYPD, but I merely shrugged, reasoning that if I completely dropped the subject, Louise would have no choice but to quiet down for a while. Well, occasionally my reasoning is off-kilter. Louise managed to control herself while I got settled at my desk. As I was waiting for my computer to warm up, though, I realized that she had left her desk and was standing behind me.

"Whoever killed him is my hero. Or heroine," she added softly. "The bastard was asking for it."

She spent most of the next hour whispering into her phone, and by coffee break, news of my part in the murder had spread through corporate headquarters. Not that anyone was saying that I had a part in the murder per se, but it was a given, confirmed by me, that I'd spent time alone in a hotel suite with Dorfmeyer's body—had actually touched the body—and that I'd called 911.

My celebrity status sprouted like a noxious weed through the always fertile office soil. As I walked through R&G's quiet corridors, I could almost feel the speculative vibrations. Wherever I paused I, as finder and toucher of the corpse, was a sounding board upon which employees tested their ideas. And though I hated even considering it, the possibility that I might have done the dirty deed myself didn't hurt my celebrity status. No one came right out and asked if I'd killed Carl Dorfmeyer, but any number of knowing, and even admiring glances were cast my way. I'd gone from possible *scab* to possible heroine of the workers' revolution.

The homeboy/homegirl theory was by far the most popular among R&G's employees, but there were a number of other notions floating around, too. Some of them were downright bizarre. The dour man from payroll caught me in the alcove where the fax machine was tucked away and said, "I wouldn't be surprised to learn that it was a team of paid assassins."

As I retrieved a fax from a tray, I shook my head doubtfully, and also with surprise. Wild imaginations turn up in the most unexpected places.

"... a downsized autoworker from Wisconsin," the dark-headed typist suggested when, trying to bring order to chaos—this was a memorably bad hair day—I borrowed her hair spray in the ladies room.

"... a hit man hired by a supervisor Dorfmeyer downsized on his last job," was a hypothesis a well-dressed woman from marketing pounded me with in the coffee room.

"Bullet between the eyes? Sounds like a Mafia hit to me," said a man I didn't know as I rummaged through the supply closet for pencils.

If speculation was rampant, grief was conspicuously absent. Sure, the company's board of directors may have been weeping over the rotten publicity and worrying about more to come, but none of the staff members I ran into were inclined to grieve for Dorfmeyer the Downsizer.

Louise put it most succinctly. "He got exactly what he deserved," she was saying into the phone when I walked back into the office. "The world is a better place without him. Whoever did it should get a prize."

She spoke more loudly than usual, probably trying to catch my interest. I ignored her, but it was obvious that the person on the other end of the line had agreed with Louise, because her next words were, "Not just a medal. Whoever did it deserves a million-dollar Christmas bonus! I just hope they get away with it."

She was staring at me as she spoke.

That was a turning point for me. I made a decision. I couldn't sit quietly waiting for the police to pin Dorfmeyer's murder on someone, because the someone they pinned it on might be me. Rather than letting that happen, I had to take an active part in finding the murderer. Not merely active. Proactive! That new word was one I'd discovered in many of the résumés I'd been perusing. Successful business types aren't just active anymore. They're proactive, and that was what I was going to be, too.

I may hate steno, but steno pads are another matter. Taking a blank one from my drawer, I made a few notes.

> *Casey. Suspect #1. Why murderer? Owns murder weapon. Smokes cigars with odor detected in suite. Motivation: may have seen his name on list. Why not murderer? Doesn't strike me as irrational; also, is looking for another job, which suggests self-preservation stronger impulse than revenge.*
>
> *Louise. Suspect #2. Why murderer? Tends to be irrational on some subjects, and admitted hating Dorfmeyer. Had watched my gun-handling exhibition closely enough to figure out how to do it herself. Motivation: may have seen her name on the list. Why not murderer?*

There, unable to think of any reason Louise should be discounted as a suspect, I paused. She didn't smoke cigars, true, but she might have taken one of Casey's and let it burn in Dorfmeyer's suite in the hope that Casey would be blamed for the murder.

I was jotting this down when Tom, whom I hadn't seen yet that day, called and asked me to drop by.

"Give me five minutes."

"Okay," he said. "That will give me a chance to make a quick call."

I made it to Tom's office in less than the promised five minutes. His door was open a crack. Pushing through without knocking, I caught him on the phone.

"You're an adult. It's not as if I forced you into—"

Glancing at me, he cut off his conversation. "I'll have to call you again. Yes," he added through clenched teeth. "I promise. Today."

He slammed down the receiver and glared at it. "I've been under siege since this thing started," he said after a moment.

I nodded sympathetically, though it hadn't sounded to me as if his conversation had had anything to do with Carl Dorfmeyer's murder.

"This is some mess, and I'm afraid it's not over," Tom said. "The higher-ups are keeping low profiles, so I've got to meet some detective in Dorfmeyer's office in a few minutes. Are you okay? You must have had a rotten night."

"It wasn't a lot of fun, but I'm all right now."

"Good. And thanks for showing up. In your situation a lot of people would have quit."

That shows how little Tom knew about my financial situation. Quitting simply was not an option.

"The directors are concerned about wild rumors. What are you hearing out among the troops? Anything interesting?"

In spite of the awful circumstances, a grin threatened to cross my face. Feeling guilty, I repressed it. "Oh, I've heard rumors about paid assassins and hit men. Someone even mentioned the Mafia."

Tom smiled, making me feel a bit less guilty. "Hmm. I like the paid assassin theory. Actually, I've been hearing talk about someone from out of Carl's past."

I nodded and said, "Could be," but having seen the gun that did the dirty deed, and having smelled that cigar-smoke residue, I was pretty sure that the murderer was someone out of Dorfmeyer's present.

"Think about it," Tom said. "Who would have hated Carl more than a downsized employee who's been out of work for a while? Someone in that position could build up a lot of anger."

Having no ready answer, I shrugged. Tom took that as a signal to continue. "Maybe this employee lost a job that his whole ego was tied up in. You know the kind of guy I mean, Bonnie? He's a braggart. He introduces himself to you at a party by telling you how important his job is."

And cheats on his expense account, and smokes smelly cigars. Yes, I knew exactly the kind of guy Tom was talking about.

"But now he's been out of work for a while," Tom said. "He's sent out dozens of résumés, and his ego is shot. Bills are running up. He may have a big mortgage and college-age kids. His wife is worried. She goes off to work every morning, and he spends the day brooding about what happened to his life. And one day, he . . . snaps."

Tom, whom I'd expected to provide an island of sanity in a sea of speculative lunacy, accompanied his mini-drama's finale with a snap of his fingers.

I said, "Maybe," as if his scenario struck me as feasible. It did, actually. The only problem I had with it was the ex-employee part.

Tom expanded on his theory, exploring how this ex-employee might have discovered where Dorfmeyer was staying, and how he—funny how, though a woman could easily have pulled that trigger, we both fell into that *he* thing—knew when Dorfmeyer would be returning to his suite.

Tom's theory was that this ex-employee had concealed himself somewhere on the street outside the Ivy League Club and waited for Dorfmeyer. "It would have been easy. There are lots of restaurants and shops he could have hidden in."

"And then he could have gotten into the club the same way I did—unnoticed. He was incredibly lucky to find Dorfmeyer alone, though," I added.

Tom appeared not to understand.

"Don't you see? When you talked to Dorfmeyer at about five-thirty, he was expecting Rose at his suite. She never went over there, though. Unless, of course, she did it herself! Do you think Rose might be lying about not—?"

"Rose got an excellent evaluation," Tom argued, "and she had been told that her increase would be the maximum. She wouldn't kill the man responsible for that."

I had to agree. Besides, my impression had been that Rose hadn't considered Dorfmeyer such a terrible boss.

Caught up in our *investigation* now, I asked Tom why he preferred the idea of an ex-employee of one of Carl Dorfmeyer's ex-employers to a current, angry R&G employee. "There are people here who really hated him. Why couldn't someone like Louise, or Casey Innis . . ."

I threw out the names carelessly, as if I hadn't already decided that one or the other, or perhaps the pair of them, was responsible for the murder.

"Why?" Tom raised his palms disarmingly. "Well, you can be certain Louise didn't do it. She left here at the same time I did. I gave her a lift to Grand Central in my cab. That was a make-nice-with-the-angry-worker gesture on my part," he added. "As for Casey, he could be a possibility, but where's the motivation? There's been a lot of talk about downsizing here, but so far it's only happened through attrition and the hiring freeze. No one has been fired."

"Yet."

"Yet," he agreed, which told me that I'd been on the right track about those personnel files.

"And speaking of firings, Tom," I said, "why exactly did Mr. Dorfmeyer want those files last night?"

Tom's gaze, always so forthright except when he felt guilty, flickered away from mine and sought refuge in a pile of papers on his desk. Reaching for those papers, he began flipping carelessly through them. It was an evasive tactic to give him time to decide on an answer.

"I told you," he said after a few seconds. "Those employees were getting minimum raises. Carl wanted to check the percentages.''

Tom stopped flipping the papers and took one green sheet from the stack. ''You've seen this, I'm sure.''

It was one of Louise's flyers about the union rally. I nodded.

''Hmm. I'll bet this is your roommate's doing. I'll also bet that she typed this on her R&G computer and copied it on R&G's copy machine using R&G paper. Right?''

I didn't say anything.

''Are you going to the rally?'' Tom asked. ''Maybe you should. You could fill me in on the details.''

I shrugged. ''It probably won't amount to much.''

''Just the same, if you do go I'd like to hear what happens.''

''Mm,'' I said noncommittally. Tom had shifted the subject away from the personnel files. I shifted it back. ''We were talking about why Dorfmeyer wanted those files, Tom. Your explanation doesn't seem logical to me.''

''Why not?''

''Because Dorfmeyer wouldn't think twice about giving a minimum raise to a mediocre employee, and he knew these were mediocre employees. He'd already signed off on their evaluations. Besides, even though he was a nitpicker, I can't see him spending his time checking percentages. I think he wanted those files because it had been decided that those employees were going to be let go. He probably wanted to review the files to make sure that R&G wasn't firing someone who might have grounds for a lawsuit.''

What I didn't add was that any reasonably savvy R&G employee who had seen that list would have come to the same conclusion.

Dropping Louise's flyer, Tom rubbed his eyes with his fingertips. ''You're right. Those employees were going to be let go after the holidays. They still are,'' he added. ''Dorfmeyer's death didn't change that. I didn't tell you the truth because this place is already thick with rumors. It's not that I don't trust you, Bonnie. I do. But you're friendly with Louise. I thought you might let something slip. And . . . it also occurred to me that . . .'' He hesitated, and his gaze again wavered.

''That?''

''Well, since I'm confessing, why not do it right? I was afraid you might refuse to deliver the files if you knew why Dorfmeyer really wanted them. I absolutely had to get to my son's game.''

Whoa! I'd fully expected the first part of Tom's *confession,* but that second admission was a surprise.

''That was a crummy thing to do to you,'' he said. ''I was only thinking of myself.''

Tom, eyes downcast and shoulders drooping, looked like a contrite little boy. He was good at that, and it may have often worked for him. People tend to forgive kids. I almost did myself. *It's nothing,* was on the tip of my tongue. I didn't say it, though, because the way things had turned out it wasn't nothing. It was a big something. Because Tom had used me, I had experienced the horror of discovering Dorfmeyer's body. And I may have now been a suspect in his murder.

As a boss, Tom may have been pleasant and low-key, and as an object of a short-term lust he may have looked good in a Speedo, but if it served his purpose he'd manipulate you and never look back. Not unless you forced him to. If he kept this up, he could be a big success in the corporate world.

Tom and I chatted for a few moments more, but our detective game was over. Mostly we talked about damage control. All calls from the press, in fact from any outsiders other than the usual job seekers, salesmen, and contractors, were to be referred to Tom.

''The board of directors has decided that I get to stand in the line of fire. I'm going to need a lot of help. I'm glad I can depend on you.''

After saying this, he grimaced and looked appropriately

overworked and put-upon. I pretended sympathy, but felt sure that Tom could take care of himself.

He had glanced at his watch. "I've got to get going."

We left his office together. I waited until he had disappeared down the corridor before sneaking back into the room.

Tom hadn't touched the telephone during our conversation, which meant that the call I'd interrupted was the last one he'd made. Hurrying around his desk, I picked up the receiver and pressed that little last-number-dialed button. It wasn't a shock to me when a 718 exchange, followed by a series of eights and two ones, appeared in the display. I replaced the receiver only after the woman who had been waiting for Tom's return call answered and asked eagerly, "Tom? Is that you?"

Victoria Cerutti was the "adult" who hadn't been "forced" into something by Tom. He could have been talking about her quitting her job, I suppose, but then why try to hide the conversation from me? If anything, wouldn't he want a witness?

Whatever was going on between the two of them, I had a feeling it had nothing to do with business.

Returning to my desk, I retrieved my personal steno pad and jotted my thoughts about Tom and Victoria Cerutti on a clean page. It was hard to imagine how whatever was going on could be related to Carl Dorfmeyer's murder, but you never can tell.

When I'd finished with that, I turned back to the notes about Louise. I briefly considered scratching out her name, but decided to leave things as they were. Grand Central is a labyrinth. Louise could have gotten out of that cab she'd shared with Tom, said good-bye, and gone off in any one of a dozen different directions. She could have headed straight out to the street, and straight to Carl Dorfmeyer's suite. And as she pulled that trigger, she could have been congratulating herself on having as good an alibi as Tom's.

• • •

Late that afternoon I finally had the opportunity to examine Tom's file. A few papers had to be filed in the little room in the file of a Mr. Jenkins. After taking the master key from Tom's desk while he was out of his office, I unlocked the inner records room. And what do you know? Right in front of Mr. Jenkins' file was Mr. Hurley's, just slightly misfiled. That, I reasoned, was why I hadn't found it when I'd pulled Casey's file the evening before. Placing the key on a narrow shelf near the cabinet, I pulled Tom's file.

He'd gone to the University of Pennsylvania and then to Cornell, I discovered, and had come to R&G from a company in Westchester that had gone out of business. One of his references, the former CEO of that company, had described Tom as "first-class." His salary was a healthy $125,000, and his benefits package pleasingly plump. As I'd figured—feared?—Elizabeth Hurley, next of kin in case of an accident, insurance beneficiary on a company policy, was clearly a wife in good standing.

And speaking of wives in good standing—

". . . and so if you and Sam will bring one hot vegetable that serves . . . oh, let me see now. The older kids are spending the night with their baby-sitter, so there'll be you and Sam, Mom and Dad, *my* mom and dad, Raymond and me, two couples from the neighborhood, another couple from . . ."

There I was, once again preparing to climb that ramp onto Noah's ark. This particular ark was located about thirty miles southwest of Manhattan, in the New Jersey subdivision where my brother and his wife, Noreen, live in blissful coupledom. While I'm sure that behind some of those suburban doors there are people leading unconventional lives, everything connected with Raymond and Noreen's house seems to come in conventional male-female pairings. From the his-and-hers towels in the master bathroom to the two cars in their driveway, one a masculine 4X4, the other a more ladylike Escort, to the guests at their upcoming fifteenth wedding-anniversary party.

Even their kids are evenly matched up. Tammy was followed by Raymond Junior, who was followed by Farrah,
who was followed by . . . Trevor! Noreen says she got that
from a *cutting edge* baby-name book, but it sounds to me
like something you'd call your collie.

The way I see things, the situation out there on the ark
is pure bedlam, but more about that later. The way that
Raymond and Noreen see things, I'm the odd woman out,
the Escort without the 4X4, the single woman who ruins
the dinner seating plan. I'm the one who, at their New
Year's Eve blowout a few years back, showed up dateless
and spent a good bit of the evening avoiding the male half
of a neighborhood couple. Except for those few moments
when he trapped me next to the Christmas tree and wriggled
his hips suggestively as "La Bamba" throbbed on the
stereo, I was successful. Noreen, however, witnessed what
she has come to call "the 'La Bamba' incident," and continues to believe that I had something to do with the couple's split-up, which I understand occurred only a few
weeks later.

I decided not to tell Noreen that Sam wouldn't be coming
to the anniversary party. It had been a long day, and I'd
already had more than enough aggravation. She'd get the
idea when I showed up without him, and with any luck
she'd be too involved hostessing to go into her *Alone
again? I don't understand it. Raymond? Don't you know
some nice man for your sister?* act.

Raymond, deep in his heart, probably wouldn't care
whether I show up alone or with a team of Navy SEALS.
He tends to be a go-along-get-along kind of guy, though,
and tends to go along with anything Noreen says. I expect
that rather than disagreeing with his wife, he would happily
see me married off to a whiskey-breathed geezer in white
shoes and maroon polyester slacks.

". . . anything but brussels sprouts," Noreen was saying.
"Are you able to do anything exciting with eggplant? I
know you don't often cook for company, but . . ."

Noreen's tone rankled me. She rankled me. She always

does. I felt like telling her that if I put my mind to it I could do any number of exciting things with eggplant including breaking one over her head. For the sake of peace in the family, I didn't.

"I'll do something with eggplant, Noreen. Or green beans or asparagus or—"

"You can't get decent asparagus this time of year. And don't use canned, whatever you do!"

"What about frozen?"

Before she could scream I said, "Just kidding, Noreen. Now could I speak to Raymond for a second?"

"Why?"

In addition to Noreen's many other attractive qualities, she is a little paranoid. I can't imagine what she thought I was going to tell Raymond that I hadn't told her, but I dutifully explained that I was working for Raymond's old friend.

"Well, that's interesting," she said, sounding not terribly interested at all, "but Raymond's still in the shower. Let me see if I can get him."

It wasn't that important that I speak to my brother, but before I could explain that to Noreen, she'd gone. While I waited for him to come on the line, I was treated to the sounds of Chez Indermill settling down for the evening meal: kids yelling, baby crying, television blasting. Bedlam.

"Hi, Bonnie. So Tom Hurley's a big shot at Richards & Goode?" my brother suddenly yelled over the background clamor. "It figures. He always was an . . ."

Before I'd even returned his greeting, much less discovered what he'd been about to say about Tom, a household crisis that involved an out-of-tune chorus of rising voices diverted him.

I'd committed a grave breach by not feeding Moses the moment I walked into my apartment. He was perched on my lap. I scratched his head and was rewarded with an impatient glare. A moment later Raymond's confused "Hello? Is anyone there?" traveled through the phone wire.

Raymond isn't stupid or crazy, but his home life is so chaotic that he has a hard time focusing on anything that doesn't involve an impending crisis.

"It's your sister, Raymond," I said, continuing to scratch Moses's head. "Remember? We were talking about Tom Hurley. He said to tell you hi."

"He did, did he? Old Tom Terrific. We all knew he'd be a big wheel somewhere someday. How much is he making, anyway? Got to be pretty good. Way into six figures, huh? One-fifty? Two hundred?"

There was touch of envy in his voice. I took care of that. "He's not a big wheel. At least not yet. He's a medium wheel."

"No kidding," Raymond said, sounding pleased by that tidbit. "I always figured Tom would make his first million before he was thirty. He was such an—"

The shriek of an angry child tore through the phone line. Raymond growled something—I couldn't tell what because he had muffled the mouthpiece—before returning to the line.

"I've got to go," he said.

"Okay, but you started to say something about Tom. What is it that, 'He was such an . . .'?"

"Huh? Oh. Yeah. Well, Tom and I were tight for a while. But what bothered me was, he was always an operator. Always looking for the next step up the ladder. Not that there's anything wrong with having ambition, but I'll tell you the truth, it annoyed me the way Tom—"

Tom what? Once again, whatever Raymond had been about to say was drowned out by a chorus of shrieking children. Within seconds, Noreen's voice had risen above it all.

"Raaay-mond! These kids are driving me crazy. I need help if we're . . ."

We all need help, but judging from Raymond's sign-off—"Got to go, Bonnie. See you next week. Wait. Noreen's saying someth—what? Oh. Noreen says 'slacks are okay, but no jeans.' "—the denizens of Chez Indermill wouldn't eat that night unless the man of the family stepped in and brought things under control.

I cradled the phone. Moses, quick to get the message, jumped from my lap. Following him into the kitchen, I opened his food. Sometimes when I'm a few minutes late dishing up dinner, Moses rubs against my legs, and if he's really overwrought he may butt my shin with his head. He never screams, though, and unless I try to fool him with the store-brand stuff, he always cleans his plate.

This time was no exception, and though I must be mistaken, the few small meows he directed toward me when he finally lifted his head out of his bowl sounded an awful lot like a "Thanks. You're a great cook."

You know, sometimes we women without husbands and children can feel left out of things, but there are other times when we have good reason to feel like pretty luxurious creatures. We may be missing some things, but we're sure being spared others.

9

IF MONDAY HAD BEEN WARM AND DRY, the planned rally might have attracted a handful of R&G's employees. However, a noontime flurry of snow made it an even bigger bust than I'd imagined possible. On the sidewalk outside of the building Louise paced, defiant and alone but for a couple of the ever-present smokers. When I pushed through one of the revolving doors, she was trying to press the green flyers into the hands of passing business types. From what I saw, she wasn't having much success.

Having just been rebuffed by a trio of young women who had dodged her the way they might dodge someone waving a fistful of religious pamphlets, Louise turned to me. Her face was red, with the cold or with anger or perhaps both.

"I can't believe it. Every rank-and-file R&G employee in the building should be out here supporting our cause. Just because Dorfmeyer's dead they think it's over, but it's not.'' Her voice rose sharply as she shifted her eyes to the smokers. "R&G will just get someone else to do the dirty work. Why don't you all join me? We workers need solidarity.''

She was so upset that she didn't seem to notice the melting snowflakes dampening her hair, or even to realize that her glasses were streaked with moisture. I darted onto the sidewalk, took her arm, and pulled her back into the shelter of the building overhang.

"Maybe you should give it up," I said.

"I can't. Somebody's got to take a stand against management's tyranny.''

Removing her glasses, Louise rubbed them against the damp wool of her coat. "It's so cold. I'd love to get inside to get warm. Bonnie? Would you take my place for a few . . . ?''

She thrust her fistful of water-spotted green flyers at me. I backed away. "No. Sorry. Why don't you come back upstairs with me.''

She shook her head defiantly. "I have an obligation to my fellow workers.''

"That may be," I said, "but the workers don't seem to feel the same obligation to you. Look around you, Louise. You're out here alone. No union rep, no workers. Maybe you should rethink this.''

"There's nothing to rethink," she snapped, "and if you're not with me, you're against me!''

The snow showed no sign of letting up, but Louise, with the determination of a fanatic, or a plain old lunatic, resumed her stand on the sidewalk.

I was standing among the smokers, still in the shelter of the building, when Casey, cigar and lighter in hand, pushed through the nearest revolving door. I hadn't seen him since Dorfmeyer's murder, and wondering how he was going to react to me, my shoulders tensed. I was the reason Casey had been picked up by the police, after all. He would have been questioned eventually anyway, of course, but as they say in the movies, I'd *fingered* him.

"Bonnie!"

He moved through the smokers, lighting up at the same time. The smell, floating through the cold air, reached me just before Casey did. One whiff and I knew I wasn't mistaken. It was the same odor I'd picked up in Dorfmeyer's suite. Just to be certain I scooted a little nearer. He didn't appear to notice and, being Casey, didn't bother blowing the smoke away from me, either.

"That was some awful business last week, wasn't it? How are you holding up?" I asked, trying to take a we're-in-this-together tack.

"Got to tell you," Casey responded. "Thursday night wasn't my idea of a good time. Givens—I always hated working with that joker—has me dragged out of my living room just when I'm settling down in front of the TV with a brew. Then he keeps me waiting at the precinct for over half an hour. And then he takes his sweet time asking his questions, the way he always does." Leaning closer, Casey added, "Just want you to know I've got nothing against you for telling him it was my gun. I'm just mad as hell at the jerk who stole it out of my desk. What a nerve!"

"It sure was," I said sympathetically. "When do you think it was taken?"

Casey shrugged. "The gun was there Thursday afternoon during coffee break. I know because I showed it to one of the guys from maintenance. What I figure is, somebody took it late in the day. Pisses me off! I mean, can you believe someone had the balls to go into my desk and steal my gun? And to add insult to injury, the jerk helped himself to a couple of my cigars, too. And you want to hear something interesting?" he asked, moving nearer still.

I nodded.

"From the questions Givens asked me, I got the idea that the murderer may have smoked one of them at the crime scene."

"You're kidding! That would take nerve."

"Yeah. There's probably no proof of that. No ashes or anything."

"Why do you say that?"

"I got a friend or two left on the force." Casey took a shallow draw on his cigar, then held the funky thing out at arm's length and gazed at it through half-shut eyes. "All I've got to say is, the cops better catch the murderer before I do. I'll kill him for messing with my property and then trying to pin Dorfmeyer's murder on me."

"Was your desk locked during the day?" I asked.

"Nah, but I never left my office without locking the door behind me. Not unless one of my guys was in the security room."

"But what if you left your door unlocked, and then the guy in the security room had to go somewhere? Or what if someone got hold of a key that would open your office?"

He blew a plume of gray smoke into the air, then gave me a sideways, vaguely smug look. "You're sounding like a cop, Bonnie, but I'll tell you what I've got to say about those possibilities. Ever since the powers-that-be moved us to the basement, I've been telling office services that we should get those surveillance cameras hooked up. They weren't in any hurry, though. They treat me like I'm a security guard or something instead of a manager. So their big-shot executive ends up getting killed with a stolen gun. Screw 'em! Maybe next time they'll listen to me."

Casey's logic was seriously flawed. Assuming that he himself wasn't the murderer, even if the surveillance cameras had been operating, it was unlikely that one of them would have been pointed at Casey's office at the moment the gun was taken. Nevertheless, that's how he was playing it. No apologies, and no guilt. If anything, he was a victim: gun stolen, advice ignored.

"Cops been upstairs yet? They've been crawling all over the basement since last Friday."

I shook my head. "Apparently they went through Dorfmeyer's office Friday afternoon, but I didn't see them. I haven't seen them today, either."

"You will, Bonnie." After taking a hard pull on the cigar, he added, his voice quieter, "You surely will."

That statement struck me as ominous, and possibly even intimidating. Considering the source, though, I wasn't surprised. Casey could hardly blame me for identifying the gun as his—he'd shown it to half of R&G's employees—but the lingering cigar smoke I'd detected was another matter. Apparently the police hadn't told him that I was the only one who had smelled the odor, but Casey might have figured that out for himself. If by some slim chance Casey was innocent of Dorfmeyer's murder, he could very well conclude that I was trying to frame him. Vague insinuations, the kind of insinuations that hint at inside information, would be an insidious way of striking back, harmless to him—he could always claim I'd misunderstood—but unnerving for me.

"Would you look at her. She's making a damned fool of herself." Casey was staring at Louise. A smile played at the corner of his mouth.

"She keeps this up she won't have to worry about being fired. They're going to have her hauled off in a straitjacket. Oh, no. Just take a look at her now! She actually expects me to get out there with her. Me. A manager!"

Louise was gesturing wildly, waving the now very damp flyers. "Casey! I know you're with the workers," she called. "You're one of us. Come on! Join the fight for . . ."

Whatever the fight was for was lost in the wail of an ambulance roaring up Sixth Avenue.

"She's insane," Casey mused as he ground out his cigar on the sidewalk. "Even if I wanted to, and I don't, I couldn't get involved in any of her union stuff. I'm management."

Not for long, I mused. And isn't it nice that when things seem fairly bleak, you can sometimes spot little rays of sunshine behind the clouds.

I'd already discovered that the curly-headed statistical typist wasn't immune from the dramatic impulses unleashed by Carl Dorfmeyer's murder. On Tuesday morning her gift for the theatrical soared. She burst through our office door just before break time and tossed back her mass of unruly hair. Her eyes were wild. Feral. How this woman spent her days typing numbers was a mystery.

She whispered, "They're up here again! I hear"—she glanced over her shoulder—"the gun's owner has been identified as Casey Innis! Maybe they're getting ready to arrest him."

She then disappeared from our doorway, so quickly it didn't seem unreasonable to suspect that they might be getting ready to arrest her.

I looked over at Louise. As usual, she was mumbling into the phone. If it hadn't been for her eyes, which were focused out the door and down the hall, I would have thought that the typist's performance hadn't affected her.

"I better make this short," she said to the person on the other end of the phone line. "I see them. They're near his office."

I moved nearer the office door and peeked out. There went Tom hurrying down the hall. Curious, I rushed back to my desk for my glasses, as an afterthought picking up a stack of résumés so that it might look as if I was actually working. I made it back to the door in time to see Detective Givens standing outside the office that had been Carl Dorfmeyer's.

Even from that distance I could see that his outfit was good enough to wear to a board of directors meeting if his investigation took him into that hallowed sphere. His gray tweed sports jacket draped just right, the crease in his pant legs was sharp, and his dark mahogany loafers gleamed under the lamp on Rose Morris's desk.

Casey and Tom were part of the detective's entourage, and while neither of them was dancing attendance, neither of them was quite in character, either. Tom, waiting at Dorfmeyer's office door, wore such a dead-serious expression that he could have been a model for a mask of tragedy. He wouldn't be playing any "whodunit" guessing games with the NYPD. And Casey, who I would have expected to be puffing himself up and trying to impress Givens, or perhaps influence him, hung back behind the younger of the uniformed cops.

When the procession moved into Dorfmeyer's office, Casey was the last to enter the room. Before he followed the others, he happened to turn in my direction. Realizing that I'd been watching him, he stared back. I was too far away to see everything that his look contained, but was there a vaguely contemptuous turn to his mouth? Unsettled, I immediately began going through the résumés in my hand. When I looked up again, Casey was gone.

As far as I was concerned, Casey had just about everything it had taken to kill Dorfmeyer: motivation, opportunity, gun. Cigar, even! He *was* the murderer. How could he not be? I wondered what he was feeling right then, standing in the dead man's office with the investigating detective. Guilt didn't seem to be a heavy part of Casey's emotional baggage, but what about fear? One way or another, fear can chew away at just about all of us. If I was right, Carl Dorfmeyer was dead because Casey had feared losing the job that was so closely attached to his ego. What Casey would fear now was discovery, imprisonment, and possibly even death. The electric chair hasn't been used recently in New York, but since the state reinstituted the death penalty, it has probably been tuned up and gotten its juice tested.

That cheerful thought brought me around to my own unfortunate situation. I hadn't heard from Detective Givens since our initial interview. Did that mean something? Maybe. Maybe it meant that the fear Givens had stirred up in me had been irrational. It stood to reason that the only suspect would be Casey. That being the case, why should Givens need to speak to me again?

"Bonnie?"

Startled by a tap on my shoulder, I turned quickly. Louise, who had been directly behind me, quickly backed away.

"You've been standing there forever," she said. "Is anything wrong?"

"No," I said sharply. "What makes you think anything's wrong?"

Louise raised her hands as if to keep me at bay. "Nothing, nothing. I was trying to be nice. Don't get angry."

Her expression seemed a bit odd. Cautious, and even apprehensive. Had I actually sounded so angry that she was frightened?

Sorry," I said, returning to my desk. "I'm still upset about all this."

A smile crossed her face. It may have been strained, but I was reminded of how attractive Louise could be when she wasn't harping about the oppressed workers.

"I understand, and if you should want to talk, remember that I'm here to listen," she said.

Now, there was a first! Granted I hardly knew Louise, but from the little I did know, being my confidante wasn't something that interested her. Not unless what I was confiding had something to do with bringing R&G's management to its knees.

I smiled and thanked her nevertheless, determined to take her gesture as nothing more or less than a friendly one. During the past two days I'd entertained far more paranoid thoughts than was healthy.

"This must be awful for Casey," I said.

"Why?" asked Louise. "Because Dorfmeyer was murdered with his gun? That's too bad, but Casey has accounted for all his time early Thursday evening."

"Thank goodness," I said as the surge of optimism I'd experienced just moments before drained away. "Where was he?"

"Well, he doesn't like this to get out—he thinks it's demeaning—but when Casey's department is short-staffed, Casey has to do security patrol. He was here in the office until his replacement got here at eight P.M."

"How can he prove that?" I asked. "The Ivy League Club is only a few minutes away. He could have told people he was going outside for a smoke . . ."

Louise was shaking her head. "Each security officer has

his own magnetic ID card. They use those cards to punch in at specific check-in points at specific times. You can imagine how crummy Casey feels about doing that," she added.

I felt pretty crummy about it myself.

"Not that anybody actually would have thought Casey was the murderer," Louise continued. "He's not the type."

"Mm. By the way," I said. "I'm sorry it snowed during your rally. That was rotten luck for you."

My attempt to be Louise's confidante met with little more success than her attempt to be mine. Her response, though not angry, was defensive.

"It wasn't *my* rally, or *my* rotten luck. The rally was for everyone's benefit. And the snow actually wasn't so bad. Some people stopped to talk with me, and one of the guys from technology told me he has a friend whose office was organized. What they did was . . ."

Within seconds she was on her soapbox. ". . . a strong voice at the forefront is what we need, a charismatic leader the workers will follow . . ."

After not too much of this, my mind began slipping away. It was brought back to full attention, though, when I heard the word "policeman" for the second time, and realized that for some reason a member of the NYPD was part of Louise's diatribe.

"A policeman?"

"One of the guys from yesterday afternoon. He was telling me that his mother's company is unionized. She's a receptionist at—"

"You met some cops yesterday?"

"Well, yes."

Up until that moment Louise had been staring at me in the fevered way she always did when she got on her soapbox, but suddenly her demon-possessed gaze wavered. "They have to talk to all of us, you know."

"When did you see the police? I obviously wasn't around," I added, trying to make my interest sound casual.

Louise responded in a rush, almost as if she was trying

to placate me. "There was a message waiting for me when I got back from the rally," she said. "I went to see Detective Givens just before leaving for the day. They're using a room on the lower level for interviews."

I turned back to the résumés I'd pretended to study earlier, and pretended to study them again. How strange. Yesterday afternoon Louise had known that she would be talking to the police, yet she hadn't once mentioned that to me, her officemate, not to mention the number-one witness in the case. And this morning, long after the fact, she hadn't mentioned it either. Why was that?

Louise might have been reading my mind when she added, "The whole interview was just routine, Bonnie. Nothing special about it. That's why I didn't mention it to you. You know what I mean?"

Actually, I didn't. An interview with an NYPD detective investigating a murder is hardly routine for most people. What I did know was that the same cautious look that had crossed Louise's face when she'd thought I was angry was back in place. And so was my paranoia. I'd never given Louise any reason to fear me, yet suddenly she was treating me as if I was a ticking time bomb. Funny how that hadn't started until she'd been interviewed by Detective Givens.

My second interview with Detective Givens took place later that afternoon. I was stopped while I was on my way out of the building for the day. I'd reached the downstairs lobby and was almost at the street door when the NYPD sergeant who had been with Givens the night Dorfmeyer was killed called out to me from the lobby security desk.

"Miss Indermill."

He had been talking to one of the building's security guards. When he knew he had my attention he held up his hand, indicating that I should wait. Within seconds he finished his conversation and lumbered across the lobby.

"Detective Givens asked me to find out if he could have a minute or two of your time. He apologizes if this is inconvenient, but . . ."

Now, this guy was about six-foot-two, and carrying about twenty pounds too much on his middle. His eyes were small, spaced close together, and his complexion swarthy. His mustache sprouted hedgelike under his nose, and his black hair, which grew low on his forehead like a gorilla's, shone from a major lube job. As he finished his spiel, I had the feeling that had he not been coached what I would have been hearing was, *Hey, lady! You in da gray coat. Gotta minute? Da boss wants to see you.*

Either way, there really was no choice for me. The sergeant and I both knew that. He headed for the elevator that went to the lower level without waiting for my response. I followed.

I can't claim that I felt good about the upcoming interview with Detective Givens, but I do recall that as I rode the elevator to the lower level, I felt confident. It would be a pleasure to get the dirty business of my sour relationship with Carl Dorfmeyer off my chest and be done with it. Givens knew that I wasn't guilty, but he also knew that I'd omitted something from my story. It had to be cleared up.

Detective Givens had set up shop not far from the security area, in a room much like Casey's office. Not being one for "roughing it," however, he'd added his own stamp of elegance. A leather blotter with a wide chrome border covered most of the desktop, the computer alongside the desk was a high-end 486, and the highbacked leather chair behind the desk looked more expensive than the one Dorfmeyer himself had occupied.

When I walked in, Givens rose from that chair—it dwarfed him, though I wouldn't have told him that— capped his fountain pen, and took my coat, which he hung over a coat hook behind the door with more care than it warranted.

"Please have a seat, Miss Indermill," he said, nodding toward the chair facing the desk. "I'm sorry about my timing. I realize it's late in the day. You probably have a dozen things you'd rather be doing right now."

A hundred. A thousand.

"It's no problem at all," I said.

The chair was directly under a ceiling vent that emitted a steady blast of cool air. As I waited for Givens to pick up his pen and unscrew the cap, the chilly breeze began finding its way down my spine. Givens reached into a desk drawer and took from it, of all things, a steno pad. For a discombobulating moment I thought it might be one of *my* steno pads. Was Givens going to have me read back Dorfmeyer's dictation? Or could he have gotten hold of my *murder notes* pad? Intellectually I knew that was impossible—the pad was safe in my tote bag—but between the cool air and the sight of that wretched pad, I was shivering by the time the detective spoke again.

"Let's see if we can get finished quickly."

He opened the steno pad. It was new. Not a mark in it. Not so much as a Gregg short form. I silently cursed myself for being such a mess.

"As I said, I'm sure you have more important things to do with your evenings," Givens continued.

Having experienced Givens's rate of speed before, it was just as well that the most important thing on my calendar for that evening was to open Moses's canned food. I nodded nevertheless, your average busy-as-a-bee Manhattan working woman.

"During our previous interview," Givens began, "you told me that the murder weapon looked very much like a gun Casey Innis had in his office. You described an incident during which Innis showed you and Louise Gruber that weapon. Are you aware that Innis's gun has now been positively identified as the murder weapon?"

I nodded very eagerly.

"You mentioned that you handled the gun, and I appreciate your candor about that. Now I'd like to clarify several other things, if you don't mind."

Givens folded his hands neatly on the desk in front of him. French cuffs peeked from beneath his beautifully tailored jacket. Certain that I knew what was coming, I nodded.

"Do you have access to an office master key?"

Surprise!

"No," I responded, shaking my head. "I borrow Tom Hurley's extra key when I need one."

Givens's neatly folded hands separated, and some jaw tugging followed. "That's the key that Hurley keeps in his desk drawer?"

"Yes."

The detective fixed me with an unnervingly serious look. "Yesterday, when I questioned Mr. Hurley in his office, that key was not in his desk. He said he did not recall seeing it since last Thursday evening. He further said that he gave you the master key Thursday so that you could do some work in a secure records room."

"That's right," I said, suddenly more agitated than I had been, "but I put the key back in Tom's desk before I left the office Thursday. Oh no!"

I clapped my hand to my mouth. Givens crooked an eyebrow.

"Friday afternoon I had to do some filing in that room. I took the key again, and forgot to put it back."

"Hmm," Givens said. "All right, then, Miss Indermill. Shall we move on to something else?"

Gladly.

"You neglected to mention something significant concerning your relationship with the deceased. I'm referring to an incident I understand occurred the day after you first handled the murder weapon. Do you know which incident I'm talking about, Miss Indermill?"

Could he be so naive that he'd believe I didn't? Feeling ridiculous and chastised, I mumbled, "Yes."

"Perhaps you'd be kind enough to relate your version of that particular episode to me. I believe it concerned some work you did for the deceased."

An unintentional sigh escaped me and seemed to fill the quiet little room with melancholy. "I wasn't trying to hide anything, Detective. It's just that I was so tired and—"

"That's all right," Givens said soothingly. "Just tell me

exactly what happened when you left Carl Dorfmeyer's office Thursday. I understand that the deceased had also left his office and was standing at his secretary's desk . . ."

Having given me that opening, Givens's voice trailed away. He already knew what had happened, of course. There had been half a dozen witnesses to the fill-in-the-blanks scene. What he wanted was my version of it. I obliged, leaving no blanks, and pausing frequently so that Givens could jot down what I'd said. I even backtracked to repeat what I'd said to Louise *before* going into Dorfmeyer's office: *I'd like to bring my machine gun,* I'd said, a remark that was right up there with *Bang! Right between the eyes* on the stupidity scale.

Givens had been tugging his jowls. When I stopped talking, he stopped tugging long enough to ask, poker-faced, if I actually had access to a machine gun.

"Of course not!"

He appeared to take my word for that, but I couldn't be sure.

"And the scene in the corridor with the deceased occurred at about what time?"

So much had happened over the past few days that I had to think before answering. "It happened in the morning. Early."

"Ah," Givens said. "Early in the morning on the day Carl Dorfmeyer was killed."

"Yes, but I have to explain something else."

"All right," he said.

"Even after Dorfmeyer embarrassed me, I didn't hate him. I was angry, but I got over it fast."

Givens's forehead creased.

"What I mean is, it was no big deal. I'm a temp. Carl Dorfmeyer wasn't important to me. Not on any serious level."

Nodding, the detective went back to writing notes while I, having nothing else to occupy myself with, went back to the pattern I'd been following on and off for several days. First I scared myself silly, and then I calmed myself down.

The fear came in a chilling blast of paranoia. By omitting something incriminating from my first talk with Givens, I'd demonstrated that I couldn't be believed. Why should Givens believe me now? He shouldn't, and he didn't. He probably thought that sometime before leaving the office Thursday evening, I'd let myself into Casey's office and stolen the gun. Hell! Givens probably even thought that I had a machine gun stashed somewhere. He figured that my story about the lingering cigar odor was a fiction I'd invented to shift police suspicion away from me and onto Casey.

Thoroughly frightened by then, I took a few deep breaths and told myself to be reasonable, and reason was the key to the calm that I soon talked myself into. No reasonable person—and Givens struck me as the soul of reason— would think I'd killed a man because he'd embarrassed me in an office situation. I mean, really! The idea was laughable!

And wasn't it obvious that Givens didn't consider me a suspect? *He didn't say anything about me having the right to have an attorney present,* I assured myself. *He didn't read me my Miranda rights. He's just trying to get his information straight. He may be slow moving, but he's got to have a lot of experience. Surely you're not the first innocent person who ever left anything important out of a statement.*

Looking up from the pad, Givens said, with even more deliberation than usual, "And there's nothing else you want to tell me, Miss Indermill?"

The paranoid part of me slipped immediately into overdrive, beating the reasonable part back down. This was a trick question thrown in to unnerve me. But maybe not. Maybe I'd really forgotten something. Something vital. The one and only thing that would clear me.

But what? I'd told all, hadn't I? Should I bring up my suspicion that Victoria Cerutti, a disgruntled former employee, had followed me home? I made a split-second decision not to. I had no proof, and it might seem to Givens

as if this, like the lingering cigar odor, was another ruse to
shift the blame away from myself.

I shook my head.

"All right. If you can give me one more second, Miss
Indermill, I'd like to ask if you recognize something."

He had opened the desk's top drawer. Taking out a clear
plastic folder, he laid it on the desk between us. In the
folder was a single sheet of notepaper on which two words
had been written with a thick black marker: COLLEGE, and
GRAD SCHOOL.

I recognized the handwriting, not to mention the thick
black marker.

"Mr. Dorfmeyer wrote that, I believe."

"You saw him write these words while you were in his
office?"

"No, but I recognize his . . . style."

Givens slipped the folder back into the drawer. "Do you
remember whether the deceased received any telephone
calls while you were in his office?"

"He didn't. The receptionist must have been holding his
calls."

Givens pushed back his chair and stood. "I thank you
for your time, Miss Indermill. And have a nice evening,"
he added as I slipped into my coat.

He sounded sincere; his smile looked sincere. I almost
headed for home feeling confident. However, after I stepped
into the corridor, I took a last glance at the detective. He
was back in the chair, dragging his fingers along the sides
of his face, staring down at the notes he'd just taken, and
. . . frowning. That frown stayed with me.

It was a good subway night. An A train was pulling in
as I walked onto the platform, and a corner seat waiting for
me. The car was heated and quiet, and the train ran fast
and smooth. I seemed to be having good transportation
karma. I was in my own private agony, though, and the
luxury of a good subway night was wasted on me. I spent
the entire ride agonizing over Detective Givens's frown and

that one unnerving question: *And there's nothing else you want to tell me, Miss Indermill?*

Taken at face value, it had been perfectly innocuous, as well as a natural close to an interrogation. So why was I having such a hard time taking the question at face value? Where had that strange feeling come from, that there was something more Givens had wanted from me? Was it just more paranoia, or had I really forgotten something vital?

Moses, having feasted on half a can of tuna-and-liver dinner, the thought of which makes my stomach clench, purred on the sofa beside me, fat and happy. My own dinner, Chinese carryout, though nominally more appetizing to me, remained untouched on the coffee table. General Ching's Chicken just wasn't enough to get my mind off of Detective Givens's question. Giving up on it finally, I picked up the phone and dialed Amanda and Tony LaMarca's number.

Amanda LaMarca, a mom of a little more than two weeks, is my closest friend, and Baby LaMarca, Emily Christina, the little princess herself, was soon to be my godchild. In truth, it was difficult to imagine myself in the role of godmother. I wasn't even sure what the role involved. Maybe when I got to know Emily Christina better— I'd only seen her once, and that glimpse of the dark-haired infant, asleep in her crib under her pink blanket, had been brief—I'd find myself growing into the part.

In any event, during the first week that Amanda and Emily Christina were home from the hospital, I'd called religiously every other day. Assuming godmothers should be good listeners, I'd allowed endless stories of four A.M. feedings and electric breast pumps to go uninterrupted. However, since I'd started at R&G, Amanda and I hadn't spoken. My fault, I told myself as I waited for an answer on the other end of the line. Obviously a new mom can't be expected to think of calling friends. It was up to me to keep our friendship alive.

That said, I was terribly disappointed when Amanda answered the phone. Yes, I cared about Amanda, about the way her world was suddenly better than ever, worse than ever, changed forever. The thing was, though, I didn't want to hear about it right then. What I wanted to do was talk to her husband, Tony. Tony, as I've mentioned, is an NYPD detective. He would know Reginald Givens, and if I was about to be arrested, Tony might know that, too.

When Amanda, speaking softly into the portable phone that she'd carried into the nursery, told of yet another sleepless night, I sympathized: "Oh, you poor thing." "How sweet," I said when she'd described what might have been a smile on Emily's tiny lips, and "Ohhh," I crooned when she explained that the expression actually had been caused by gas.

We went on this way, Amanda describing, me reacting, until Amanda suddenly said, "Ooops. She's waking up. Listen."

Amanda must have held the phone over the crib, because the next thing I heard, just audible above the phone's static, was the mewling of little Emily. Tony's voice followed, but he spoke too softly for me to make out what he was saying. A few seconds of what sounded like confused fumbling came next, and then Amanda's "I've got her."

More time passed, during which I experienced a sweeping wave of déjà vu. For years I'd been going through this with my brother and sister-in-law. Was this how it was going to be from now on with Amanda and Tony? Chaos?

Thinking I'd been forgotten, I was about to hang up when the phone abruptly came to life again.

"Is anyone there?"

"Tony? It's Bonnie."

"Oh. Bonnie. How are you?"

He sounded rushed, just like Raymond often sounds.

"I'm fine," I said. "What about you?"

Well, what came next was about what I had expected: a mixture of pleasures and complaints. No one was sleeping at the LaMarca house, but every groggy wide-awake moment had its joyful side. Emily had already lifted her head off the pillow. Emily seemed to recognize not only Mom but Dad, too. Emily was clearly precocious.

"... didn't spend much time with my other kids when they were babies," Tony said, "so I'm off for a while on FMLA. You heard of that? It stands for Family Medical Leave Act. I can stay home, get away from the job for a while, and still get paid."

Yes, yes. I cared. Tony deserved to enjoy his infant. But when he started off on a different tangent—one about the home movies he was making of Emily—I couldn't stand it anymore. Come on! The kid was barely moving at that point.

"Sounds wonderful," I said, interrupting, "but I wanted to ask you about someone on the force. Detective Reginald Givens. Do you know him?"

"Givens? Sure. Why do you ask?"

Tony hadn't removed himself so far from the job that Carl Dorfmeyer's murder was news to him. However, his profound lack of curiosity about the circumstances surrounding it was unusual. Describing what had happened, I left out some vital details. Most of them, in fact. Tony, a good detective, normally picks up on that sort of thing. This time, though, all he had to say when I'd finished telling my much-abbreviated story was, "Givens is a good man. He'll get it straightened out."

"You think so? He seems kind of . . . slow."

"Slow? Maybe Givens works slow, but he gets things right," Tony replied. "Ask anybody from the DA's office. The prosecutors love him. When he makes an arrest, they're just about guaranteed a win in court."

"Really?"

"Sure. Givens has the highest conviction rate in the city. Prosecutors call him 'the Exterminator,' because he's so good at getting the vermin off the street."

"He's never wrong?" I asked.

Here's what I mean about the condition Tony was in. Ordinarily he would have picked up on that question, or at least on the way my voice squeaked when I asked it. Instead of asking me what was bothering me, though, he chuckled. "Sure Givens is wrong sometimes, but the thing is, he's not wrong as often as most of us. Slow but sure. That's Givens."

We hung up a few minutes later, and for a while that evening I did feel better about things. If Givens generally came to the right conclusion—and according to Tony, he did—then he would realize that I was an innocent victim of circumstance. It wasn't until much later, when I was getting ready for bed, that Givens's question again fluttered through my mind.

And there's nothing else you want to tell me, Miss Indermill?

I fell asleep wondering what I'd forgotten.

10

By Wednesday Louise had developed a dreadful cold, complete with beet-red nose and watering eyes. That may have contributed to her mood, which started out disgruntled and went downhill from there. The first thing she said to me when she walked in that morning was, "They've stopped buying fresh flowers for the reception areas. We used to have gorgeous arrangements for Christmas. Now all we're getting are a few crummy fake candles. Did you notice?"

Settling behind her desk, she pried the lid off a cup of coffee. Before she could take a sip, though, a fit of sneezing overtook her, and following that there was a session of loud nose blowing.

"Yes, I noticed," I replied when things quieted down. I should have let it go at that, but I was engrossed in Tom's salary survey and without thinking added, "I knew it was going to happen."

"You knew? How?"

Eyes hard on me, Louise half rose. Her palms were flat on her desk and her elbows bent. Honest to God, if she'd wriggled her backside a little, she would have looked the way Moses does when he's about to attack a roach.

Trapped, I told the truth. "Dorfmeyer dictated the memo to me."

"And you didn't say anything?" she asked angrily. "You knew I was interested in anything he dictated that would affect the workers."

Disturbed by her tone, I responded sharply. "And what would you have done if I'd told you? Picketed Dorfmeyer's office, or maybe chained yourself to the flower delivery person?"

"The problem with you is, you don't care anything about the workers."

Louise's cold had added a croak to her voice, and that, coupled with her raised tone, caused her words to carry into the corridor. The man from payroll happened to be nearby. Probably surprised by the break in the hush that normally permeated the office, he poked his head through our open door.

"Anything wrong?"

Since Louise was poised as if she was ready to spring across her desk and rip out my throat, and I no doubt appeared ready to fight off her attack, his question was a natural one.

"No," she rasped hoarsely, keeping her eyes on me. "Everything's terrific. I love sharing an office with a management brownnoser."

Lowering herself back into her chair, Louise again blew her nose. After throwing the tissue violently into her trash can, she purposefully turned away from me.

I looked from Louise to the door, half expecting to share a silently expressive moment with the man in the doorway. You know: one of those moments when you and a near stranger roll your eyes in mutual understanding. *She's overwrought again,* our looks would say. It didn't work that way, though. The man from payroll didn't return my eye rolling. He merely glanced my way, blank-faced, looked at Louise again, and then walked off, leaving me wondering whether his sympathy was with me, or with Louise, or whether he thought we were both out of line.

That set the tone in our office for the early morning. Several times I tried to draw Louise out of her funk, but nothing I said pierced her anger. After a bit of this, the atmosphere in the office became uncomfortable enough for me that I began to think about apologizing. For what, though? Any number of times I thought over the entire sequence of events, from Dorfmeyer's dictating the no-more-flowers memo, to Louise's outburst. When I've done something wrong, I know it. This was one time that I felt guiltless, and an apology would have been disingenuous.

In the midst of this chill, Tom called me.

"I'm feeling like a prisoner in this place," he said. "How about bustin' out of here with me at noon for a long lunch."

I glanced toward Louise. She was typing something, and appeared to be paying no attention to me, but I lowered my voice to a near whisper anyway. There was no point in supplying her with additional fodder for hating my guts.

"Sure, as long as you're in no hurry for this salary survey."

"Hmm. Actually, I am in a hurry. Why don't you bring your notes along? That way we can talk a little business while we eat. There's a new restaurant at the Museum of Modern Art," he added. "Maybe we'll even take the time to look at a painting or two."

"Hey! Rank has its privileges," I said.

"So they tell me, but I haven't noticed any lately," Tom replied, sounding almost as disgruntled as my officemate.

We arranged to meet in Tom's office at 12:30. As we were hanging up, Louise went off to coffee break. She took her coat with her, which I figured meant she was going to join Casey in front of the building. She didn't say anything to me about joining her, and while I didn't miss being reminded about the workers I was oppressing by remaining at my desk, I did mind being shunned.

Louise's break that morning was longer than usual. To my relief, when she finally returned to the office, her mood had lifted somewhat. While hanging up her coat, she said, in a tone which, while not groveling, was civil, "I'm sorry for flying off the handle. It's just that everything's so . . ."

She completed that sentence with a disheartened grimace and a shrug. Then, spilling the considerable contents of a plastic shopping bag onto her desk, she began pawing through them. Instead of spending her break grumbling with R&G's other workers, Louise had spent it at the cold-cure counter in a nearby drugstore.

"It's okay," I said, adding as a pacifier, "when I have a cold I get cranky, too."

"It's not just my cold. It's . . . just that since the rally, I've been really depressed. If R&G's employees care about their jobs, they should have been out on the line with me, making a united statement, showing management that we're together in our struggle. I expect to be at R&G for many more years. . . ."

In which case she had to be delusional, but I wasn't about to get into that with her. Actually, I didn't want to get into any of this workers'-struggle business with Louise. I thrust my hand, palm up, at her. "Louise, maybe I liked it better when you weren't speaking to me."

She backed off immediately. "Oh, I'm not blaming you, Bonnie. You're just a temp."

Just a temp. That phrase is often intended as an insult, but I love it. It forgives a multitude of failings, both real and imaginary. The reality was, even if I'd been one of R&G's own, it would have taken the business end of a cattle prod to get me out there "on the line," but if Louise wanted to believe that only my temp status had kept me from joining her, that was okay.

Louise, looking down at the jumble of over-the-counter drugs on her desk, brightened a bit. "At least I can do something about my cold."

The drugstore had provided her with every conceivable cure, from pills to liquids to granular concoctions to be mixed into juice. She read from a couple labels: "If dizziness or sleeplessness occurs, discontinue use," warned one package. "May cause drowsiness," cautioned another. A green liquid in a plastic bottle apparently could cause both sleeplessness and drowsiness, and in some circumstances bring on a number of illnesses far scarier than a cold. The blood-red contents of another bottle elicited an appreciative "Oooh! Ten percent alcohol!" from my roommate.

"So depending on what you take, you're either going to be a nervous wreck or you're going to pass out," I said.

"Maybe I'll take them all at once," said Louise. "They can't make me feel any worse than I do now."

That was debatable, but as I'd discovered on the day we had lunch with Casey, Louise was open to a hit of something strong in the middle of the day. She shook two tablets from a bottle into her hand, popped them into her mouth, and washed them down with a swallow of what had to be very stale coffee. Following that, she unscrewed the cap from the bottle containing the ominous-looking green liquid. After downing a good-sized slug, she forced a smile.

"One way or the other, I won't be getting any work done around here. Not for R&G, and not for the workers either. I couldn't believe that not one of them joined me at the rally. They sure let me down. And Casey!"

"Casey?"

Louise gave out with an unpleasant back-of-the-throat noise. "After all the complaining he's done, did you see him out there on the line? No way! He's as big a coward as anybody else around here. Lots of talk but no action. A wimp!"

Attempting to stop her before she went off on a tangent, I made an offhand comment about people being afraid of endangering their jobs. This, however, was a subject about which Louise wasn't easily mollified.

"They're all cowards," she snapped back. "It's been

that way all along,'' she said. ''Remember me and Casey telling you about Victoria, and how she was so hot to get a lawyer and take R&G to court? You know what's come of that? Nothing. She hasn't done a thing, and she's not going to.''

''How do you know?'' I asked, wondering if Gladys Obus, attorney-at-law, had told Victoria she had no case.

''Victoria and I had lunch on Sunday. She told me there was no possibility she was going to sue. She's just''— Louise sighed unhappily—''dropped everything. It's like she doesn't care anymore. I mean, it can't be that Victoria's afraid of losing her job. She already quit. You know what she's doing now?''

I shook my head.

''She's working behind the concession counter at her cousin's bowling alley in Howard Beach. She's let herself go, and gained a little weight, too. The whole thing is unbelievable.''

Louise's words were coming slower and slower. Listening to her, watching her put her hand over her mouth lazily as she yawned, I made a bet with myself that her coffee break that afternoon would be a record breaker.

''Did Victoria say why she dropped everything?'' I asked nonchalantly.

''No,'' responded Louise, ''and she changed the subject every time I brought it up. Actually, she had started backing off even before she left here. At first I got mad at her, but then—well, Victoria's a friend. Not a real close friend, but a good work friend. She was always supportive to me and the other women at R&G. And now''—lifting her hand to cover her mouth, she yawned again—''the way things are looking, I might be able to do something supportive for her, even if she did wimp out on the workers.''

The gleeful smile that followed that statement wasn't forced. In fact, for a couple seconds Louise managed to look almost radiant. The drugs may have been on their way to creating havoc with her nerves, but they were rapidly taking care of her running nose and watery eyes, and perhaps of her bad mood, too. I'm not big on over-the-counter drugs, but this was an improvement.

"What can you do for Victoria?" I asked.

Louise's smile spread. "I didn't say anything to her because I'm not positive, but I may be able to find her a decent spot. If she wants to come back, that is."

"Here? You mean possibly to her old job?"

"Mmm. Maybe, or maybe a better one. I may have an 'in' with management," she added, her smile growing more cocky. "Victoria is top-notch when it comes to human resources."

Victoria's various evaluators hadn't thought so, but I was intrigued enough to pursue the subject. "What about the hiring freeze?"

Louise responded evasively. "There are exceptions to every rule."

What Louise was suggesting isn't unheard of, but even if R&G's management was willing to make an exception, given the circumstances under which Victoria had departed R&G, I couldn't imagine them taking her back. For that matter, I couldn't imagine Victoria wanting to come back. Still, in the business world strange things can happen.

"You can't say anything about this, Bonnie," Louise cautioned, growing serious. "I haven't mentioned this to anyone else except Casey. It's just an idea I've been kicking around."

Louise spent the remainder of the morning yawning, whispering into the telephone, and, at intervals that seemed far more frequent than necessary, slugging down one or another of those cold cures.

Tom and I lunched light. A salad for me, poached salmon for him. No cigars in sight, and no large bloody hunks of flesh, and since we really did spend time discussing the salary survey and looking over a chart I'd drafted, it seemed appropriate when Tom paid for the meal with his R&G credit card.

Throughout the meal I kept getting the feeling that Tom

had something to say to me that he wasn't saying. He
would start, say a few words—"You're doing such a good
job with this. There's—" . . . and then abruptly break off
and change the subject. I pretended not to notice, figuring
it probably wasn't worth noticing. Until ten days earlier, I
hadn't seen Tom in years, and back when I had seen him
more regularly, our conversations hadn't been on a particularly sophisticated level. Maybe this start-stop business
was a conversational quirk he'd developed to get him
through business lunches with women he scarcely knew.

After lunch we took a brief stroll around the museum's
second floor. It gave Tom a chance to show off a quality I
hadn't known he possessed. He knew about art. At least
some art. He proved that to me when we took a few minutes
to stroll through an exhibit of the late American artist Willem de Kooning's paintings. I recall part of Tom's lecture
as we paused in front of a big canvas that initially seemed
to me a hodgepodge of colorful brush strokes.

". . . and de Kooning was one of the few Abstract Expressionists to alter his style in his later creative years. His
earlier role model was Picasso, and so understandably his
earlier paintings were more aggressive. Here, you see that
he's influenced by Matisse's aesthetic sensuality as well as
Mondrian's clarity."

I was shaking my head when Tom glanced at me. I didn't
see what he saw on that canvas.

"You don't know how to see it," he responded. "De
Kooning's work is spare, yet at the same time animated.
Follow this line. You'll see a woman's head. And here
you're going to be able to see the shape of another woman's
back . . ." He accompanied this promise with a sweep of
his hand which followed, from a respectful distance, one
of the painter's sweeping curved brush strokes.

I'd seen de Kooning's work before, but he wasn't a favorite of mine. I'd never viewed the artist's work the way
Tom was now presenting it, though. Looking closely, following Tom's hand, I began to see those long curving brush
strokes as something more than a meaningless jumble of

color. I saw the lithe sensual figures dancing through space, the way they dance on a Matisse canvas. I saw them as clearly as I have sometimes seen the primary colors of a Mondrian on a stark white background. For a moment it took my breath away.

"You're full of surprises," I said, keeping to myself that I was thrilled by my minor artistic breakthrough.

Tom grinned. "You thought I was all occupational safety and salary surveys?"

"No, but I didn't know you knew art."

"I'll let you in on a secret." Leaning nearer, he whispered, "I don't."

His gaze had locked onto mine. Mischief seemed to flicker through his eyes, making me wonder what was coming next.

"It's all my wife's doing," he said after a moment as he straightened up. "Elizabeth's an art teacher. In graduate school she spent a lot of time focusing on the Abstract Expressionists. I happened to be hanging around with her at the time, and"—he shrugged carelessly—"I absorbed a lot of what she was studying. Like a sponge. As long as it happened in the U.S. during a certain period, I can talk art. I have no depth," he confessed, "but no one ever seems to notice."

"That's terrific, and think of how lucky you are that she wasn't an accounting major," I said. "Not many people would want to hear you on debits and credits."

Tom laughed. "I never thought about it that way, but I've always been glad that one of us is an 'arty' type. Two business majors could amount to one dull marriage."

"Is that what you were? A business major?"

"As an undergraduate at Penn. And then, to guarantee that everyone would think I was a complete geek, I got my master's in industrial relations."

I didn't think Tom was even a partial geek, but I let that slide by with nothing more than a smile. "I didn't realize there was such a thing."

"Well, there is. After that I didn't know what to do with

myself, but I was tired of school. Tired of being broke, too," he added. "Elizabeth and I were married by the time we both graduated. I decided to jump into the job market and see how things turned out."

If salary, status, and a happy family were good indicators, things hadn't turned out badly for Tom. Thinking about it, Tom himself hadn't turned out badly. He was interesting, attractive, and engaging. A week before I'd thought he was flirting, but reassessing things now, I changed my mind. Tom was very married, and his invitation at his hotel—*If you'd like, we can stop in here for a drink*—had been a friendly gesture and nothing more.

When it was time to leave, I paused at the information desk on the ground floor while Tom went ahead to retrieve our coats. Excited by my newfound *artistic* eye, I picked up a museum membership application and as an afterthought tucked a brochure outlining the exhibits for that month into my tote bag.

We took our time walking back to the office. The day was sunny and the temperature had inched up a few degrees. This change in the weather, and the nearing holidays, had brought people into the streets. As we turned the corner at Sixth Avenue and headed for R&G's main entrance, the smokers in front of the building came into view. It was the biggest group of them I'd seen. There must have been a dozen milling around. Above them, you could see a cloud of smoke trapped in front of the big wreath that had been hung over the building's main door.

"It's a good thing your roommate's not leafleting today," Tom said. "She might actually attract a few supporters."

"I feel kind of sorry for her. She's so . . . misguided."

"Misguided?" Tom responded. "She's a slacker, a complainer, and a troublemaker. She's lucky R&G's keeping her on through the holidays."

"You should tell her that she's being let go," I said. "That way she'll be able to start job hunting now."

"I did tell her."

Surprised to hear this, I asked Tom when he had done the dirty deed.

"This past Tuesday."

"Well, whatever you said to her didn't make much of an impression. She thinks she's going to be at R&G for many years."

Tom stopped short. "When did she say that?"

"This morning."

Taking my arm, Tom maneuvered me to the outer edge of the sidewalk, where a newspaper stand sheltered us from the sweep of pedestrians.

"Then Louise is not merely misguided, Bonnie. She's deranged. I met with her after that ridiculous rally and told her flat out that she was being let go. She already knows when her last day is, and the amount of severance pay she can expect. And it's a lot more than she deserves," he added.

I shook my head. "I'm only repeating what she told me this morning. She even said that she might get Victoria Cerutti to return."

"Return?" Tom asked when I broke off. "You mean to R&G?"

His voice had grown sharp.

I shook my head. "Please forget I mentioned it. Louise was just rambling. She was so full of cold medicine she was dopey."

"She's always dopey."

Yes, she was, but a streak of loyalty rising up from God knows where made me keep myself from agreeing.

Tom glanced at the clot of smokers in front of the building. "Guess we better run the gauntlet and get back to work, Bonnie, but there's one thing I'd like to mention. You can't tell anyone, though. A couple times during lunch I almost said something to you, but . . . well, I didn't. The thing is, this is very confidential."

I had started toward the building, but that warning drew me back to the curb, and to a most serious Tom.

"You've been doing an excellent job, Bonnie. Once we

get rid of Louise and a couple other pieces of deadwood in the administrative area, there could be a nice opening for you.'' He smiled. "No steno, I promise. The job would be far removed from that. I've talked to the board, and they've given me a tentative go-ahead. Would you be interested?''

For the second time in less than an hour, I had to take in a deep breath before I could speak. "Yes. Does that mean the hiring freeze is ending?'' I asked, wondering if Louise had gotten wind of that.

"No. It just means that there's going to be a short thaw. I'm hoping that everyone will get so used to seeing your face that they start thinking of you as one of us. That way, they won't notice that you stick around forever.''

If Louise stuck around forever, as she seemed to think she would, that wasn't likely to happen. Still, as Tom and I started toward the building, I thought, *It would be nice. . . .*

"So where's my girlfriend?'' Casey asked, hauling Louise's chair from behind her desk. "Haven't seen her all day.''

Girlfriend? I would have bet my paycheck that Casey wouldn't have recognized a girlfriend if a woman, risking anthrax or some other barnyard disease, had bitten him in a real sensitive place. Granted he had fathered children, something which requires some form of sexual joining, but despite his good looks Casey struck me as utterly unsexual. Looking at him as he postured near Louise's desk, I thought of weird biological happenings: osmosis, cell division. Maybe his children were the result of something along those lines.

He straddled the chair by slinging his leg high, sort of the way a cowboy might straddle his steed.

"I haven't seen her, but she wasn't feeling well this morning. She's probably resting in the sickroom.''

He glanced at his watch, calling my attention to his brass cuff links. They were shaped like full-sized bullets. What a man!

"It's close to three," he said. "She's got that same sickness she gets every afternoon."

"She's really sick this time," I said.

"Sure she is. You mind if I shut your door?"

Wondering what on earth he had in mind, I didn't respond.

"Law says you can smoke if you keep the office door shut, long as it doesn't bother anybody in the room."

"I'm afraid it would bother me," I said.

"Hmmph. Might have known." Rising, Casey shoved the chair back behind Louise's desk. "Tell Louise to call me when she gets back," he said as he started out of the room. "Tell her I want to hear a progress report on her latest wacky idea."

"You mean her idea about Victoria?"

Casey rolled his eyes. At last I'd found a compatriot to share my *Louise* problems with. Ugh. I'd rather have done without.

"Did she tell you how she plans to pull this trick off?" he asked.

I shook my head.

"Me neither. If you ask me, Louise is wacked. She's always been a little off-the-wall, but lately . . ."

He finished his sentence, and his visit to my office, with another roll of his eyes. Glad to see him go, I went back to my salary chart.

Computer input isn't particularly interesting, but I'm generally good enough at it that I can relax while I'm doing it. A few minutes after Casey left, though, as I was typing in the numbers and figuring out how to put in formulas, the scream of sirens from the street began disturbing my concentration. Sirens are nothing unusual in midtown Manhattan, but these went on and on, coming from a distance and growing in volume until they reached the street below. After a few minutes of this I began to wonder if there was a fire nearby. Stretching in my chair, I stared out the window. Things looked normal on the street, and in the air I saw no trace of smoke. Suddenly, though, another vehicle—an ambulance—sped past and rounded the corner, heading for the Sixth Avenue side of the building.

Hurrying to the set of windows farther from my desk, I looked down. Sixth Avenue was a mass of police cars and ambulances. I craned my neck trying to see straight down, but without my glasses I couldn't tell what the problem was. Figuring there'd been a multicar accident that would soon clear up, I started back to my desk.

Suddenly a scream from the corridor inside mingled with the howl of the sirens outside, creating a duet so eerie that the sound shocked me into stillness. When I finally moved nearer the office door, the thundering of footsteps reached me.

The usually quiet corridor had burst to life. Detective Givens was running in my direction, arms and legs pumping. Over his shoulder I saw his big sergeant, red-faced with exertion. Tom raced alongside him, jacket tail flying. It seemed as if the three of them planned to run me down. Heart pounding, I leaped out of the doorway. The men turned at the corner, though, and sped past my office.

Gathering my nerve, I walked into the corridor. The screams had trailed off. To my right, in the direction the three men had come from, Rose Morris bent solicitously over the curly-headed typist. The young woman, who was wearing her coat, was whimpering pitifully.

"She told me she was going to the sickroom," the typist cried, "but a few minutes ago out in the street I saw—"

She choked with sobs. At the same time, Detective Givens began pounding on the door of the first-aid room and shouting, "Is anyone in there?" Changing direction, I trotted up the corridor and stood beside Tom.

"Yeah, yeah!" came from inside the first-aid room. "Keep your shorts on!"

A lock tumbler clicked and the first-aid-room door flew open. A blue-gray haze of smoke whiffed into the corridor, followed by a belligerent Casey Innis.

"How long have you been in here?" Givens asked before the other man had a chance to say anything.

"Huh? I dunno. Five minutes. Maybe ten. Ducked in and decided to have a smoke. What's the . . ."

Givens fanned the air with his hand as he pushed past Casey. Turning, the big cop behind him glanced at me and Tom, and then stepped into position to block the room's door. Tom and I moved away at the same time.

"What's going on?" I asked Tom.

He didn't look at me, but in profile his skin was ashen. "A woman"—he breathed deep—"fell or jumped. From somewhere up here. She bounced off a taxi that had pulled to the curb, and then was run over by a delivery truck. Apparently the body's a terrible mess." Shuddering, he added, "Unidentified for now, but the typist from accounting saw the woman hit the taxi."

Tom's eyes shifted to the big cop. Lowering his voice, he added, "She thinks it's Louise."

"This morning, you and the deceased were overheard arguing . . ."

Sick of Givens's plodding questions, I broke in. "We didn't argue. Louise felt rotten and she let off some steam. She thought that I was being . . . unsupportive."

"Of?" Givens asked after a pause just long enough to make me want to screech with frustration.

"Of her damned cause! The tyranny of management, the oppression of the workers. The union thing." Closing my eyes, I took a long breath. "It wasn't just me she was angry at. She complained about her coworkers, especially Casey," I added, opening my eyes and meeting Givens's gaze.

"Tired of hearing about all that, were you?"

"Not so tired of hearing it that I pushed her out the window."

Drawing back in the leather chair and blinking, Givens did an impression of a man surprised—shocked!—by a suggestion. However, I'd been in the detective's *hot seat*— or that's what it would have been if the blast from the ceiling vent overhead hadn't been so chilling—for half an hour. To me his impression was as hackneyed as the worst of my stage performances. Givens may have been the DA's darling, but he was no Barrymore.

"I wasn't suggesting that, Miss Indermill," he said. "What I'm trying to ascertain is Miss Gruber's mental state when she went to the first-aid room."

He already had a pretty good idea about what her physical state had been. Upstairs, an hour earlier, he'd opened Louise's desk drawer and discovered her private pharmacy. The bottle containing the sleep-inducing green liquid was half-empty, and the bottle that had held the red liquid with the strong alcohol content had been drained.

"Her mental state was fine. Or it had been before lunch," I said, correcting myself. "As I told you, I didn't see Louise after lunch. When I got back to the office at about two-fifteen, she was gone."

Givens had personalized his basement office by putting a cluster of photos on his desk. Wife, two children. Tennis, basketball, track. He fit right in with the R&G family ideology. Straightening one of the photos, he asked, without looking at me, "And you weren't curious as to Miss Gruber's whereabouts?"

"I knew where Louise was. She spent fifteen or twenty minutes napping in the first-aid room every day after lunch."

"But this afternoon," Givens said, "her 'nap' went on much longer than usual. Is that correct?"

I nodded.

"Yet you never went to check on her."

I'd told him at least twice that I hadn't. If he believed me, why did he keep shoving the question at me?

"No," I said. "From the time I returned from lunch until the time you ran past my office, I was at my desk working on a salary survey. I didn't even leave my office to get a cup of coffee."

"And you say that Casey Innis joined you for a few minutes at about ten minutes until three."

"I'm not sure of the exact time, but that sounds right."

"Mr. Innis says he was with you for no more than two or three minutes."

"That's correct. He wanted to close the door and have a smoke, but I told him no."

"Mm-hmm. And he claims that after leaving your office he went to the men's room, and after that he went to check on Miss Gruber. Did you happen to notice which way Casey Innis turned when he left your office? Or did you see him pass your office a few minutes later?"

"No. I wasn't paying attention."

The issue here was obvious. How had Casey spent the four or five minutes between the time when he left my office and the time when Louise's body hit the sidewalk below? The men's room and the sickroom were in opposite directions, and a quick trip to the men's room would account for the lapsed time.

As Givens wrote something in his pad, his bloodhound features seemed droopier than usual, but they didn't give me a clue about what was going on in his head.

Casey was lying, I thought. I figured he'd gone straight from my office to the sickroom, where Louise was resting. He'd wanted to have a cigar, and she, with her self-destructive bent, had given in. "Okay," she'd said, "but open the window." That done, they'd started talking, and the talk had grown heated. Maybe Louise's rotten mood had returned. Maybe the drugs had made her more agitated. Maybe she'd gotten worked up enough to hurl that forbidden epithet at him. Wimp!

Casey was a big man, and Louise a slender woman in rocky shape. A flash of temper, the wrong word, an open window, a shove, and Louise was dead.

Casey had to be a psycho, pure and simple.

11

THE NEW SIDE-BY-SIDE REFRIGERATOR purred almost imperceptibly in its allotted space between the sink and the broom closet. All was right with the world.

I'm almost serious. There is something catching about the stupefying ordinariness of the life Raymond and Noreen share. Whenever I spend much time with them I start feeling pretty ordinary myself. Not stupefyingly ordinary, but ordinary within reasonable parameters. Though a murder investigation—perhaps two murder investigations—was swirling around me, I hadn't been at 215 Overbrook Terrace very long before all that unpleasantness faded to a dusty corner of my mind, and the world of measuring cups and meat thermometers took over.

As I've mentioned, my sister-in-law and I have a relationship that is, at best, bumpy. The fault is partly mine. The thing is, I'm never sure how to take Noreen, though by now I should know. Seriously. That's the way to take Noreen. Sometimes, unable to do that, I search behind her words for irony and double entendres. I never find them. The woman doesn't have a humorous bone in her body.

For example, here's what she said when she took four bottles of red wine from one of the kitchen cabinets.

"I'll open this Beaujolais Nouveau now so it can breathe a good long time. That way," she added, steaming into lecture mode like the junior-high home-ec teacher she should have been, "our wine will be everything it was meant to be."

I was stirring garlic and the juice from a lemon into the green-bean dish I'd decided on, and thinking that I'd achieved a small culinary triumph. Noreen, who until then had been carrying on over her lamb shanks, wasn't getting my full attention. I thought at first that I'd misunderstood her.

"So our wine can be what?"

"Everything it was meant to be."

No one could say that with a straight face, could they? Not about an inexpensive 1998 wine being opened in . . . 1998! Astounded by the ridiculousness of the statement, I stopped stirring to look at Noreen. She had to be putting me on!

A grin threatened to shatter the composure I'd shown for the last hour while helping with the anniversary dinner, a composure I'd maintained even when Noreen had sniffed at the sink drain and said, "Remind me to sweeten this."

She meant every preposterous syllable, I realized. Her lips offered no hint of a smile, and her forehead, generally as uncreased as a baby's bottom, showed faint but meaningful lines as she clumsily wielded the corkscrew.

Never mind that the wine, which many of us know and love, has a shelf life of about six months. Never mind that it surely had been all it was meant to be the moment the bottle was corked at the winery. Somewhere or other Noreen had heard that wine should breathe, and so hers would breathe long and hard.

Looking at her oh-so-serious face, I couldn't help what happened. To my credit it came out as a humble giggle, not as a full-blown guffaw.

"Of course you don't understand," Noreen said. "You don't often entertain. At least not formally."

I entertain plenty, and it's not always paper plates and jugs of Gallo, either, but rather than getting into a thing with Noreen, I got myself under control.

"You're right." Looking at the wine, I added, "Is that all you've got, though? Four bottles?"

If there's one thing Noreen hates even more than having her homemaking wisdom laughed at, it's having it openly criticized. She came back immediately and defensively.

"What do you mean? One bottle is good for at least five glasses, and we have six couples."

Having said that, she turned the full confidence of her pie-shaped face to me and added, "And you. That's thirteen guests. That comes to . . ."

Closing her eyes, she tried doing some calculating in her head. Failing, she opened her eyes again. "About a glass and a half each. Mom will only take a sip or two of hers."

"Do you plan to pour what Mom leaves into someone else's glass?"

"Of course not," Noreen snapped. "We'll be fine. None of us are heavy drinkers. At least not that I know of," she added pointedly.

I didn't pay much attention to that dig, mainly because I was still ruminating over the one that had preceded it.

And you, she'd said. A loose translation of that was: *The one without the man.*

By showing up uncoupled, I'd thrown the carefully orchestrated boy-girl-boy-girl seating arrangements into chaos. And who knew what, in my manless state, I might do as the evening progressed. Why, there might even be a repeat of—gasp!—the "La Bamba" incident. Marriages could tumble with me on the loose!

Feeling myself heating up, I turned my attention back to my green beans. Oh oh! During the last few seconds they'd reached the doneness line. My triumph was in danger of turning into a limp gray hash. Dots of perspiration breaking out across my forehead, I yanked the pot from the stove.

"These are done. Listen, Noreen. Just to be on the safe side, why don't I run to the liquor store and pick up a couple more bottles? My treat."

Giving the corkscrew a rest—she clearly doesn't get much practice with one—Noreen placed her hands on her hips. "I doubt if that's necessary, but if you want to waste your money . . ."

Muttering about borrowing Raymond's keys, I hurried from the kitchen, a manless boozy spendthrift making a break for freedom.

Raymond doesn't allow himself many personal luxuries, or maybe he isn't allowed them. One thing he does have, though, is a terrific car stereo. After putting on my glasses, I slipped a CD into the player and turned the volume loud. Wraparound Bruce Springsteen. When you're in New Jersey, you can't help but go with the Jersey boy.

Driving away from Raymond and Noreen's house, I glanced in the rearview mirror. My parents' car was pulling up at the curb from the other direction. I tapped the brake, wondering if I should give up on this idea. It would take me roughly half an hour to get to the liquor store and back, which meant that Noreen would have plenty of time to tell my mother about my latest transgression. For a moment Bruce and the E Street Band faded from my awareness, and the void was filled by Noreen's voice. How anyone can simultaneously convey both smugness and whininess is beyond me, but she manages.

Now, Mom, I imagined her saying, *I love Bonnie like a sister, and goodness knows I'm the soul of patience, but why does she always cause such problems when she comes to visit? To begin with she throws things into an awful disarray by showing up alone, when I've set the table for . . .*

I imagine a lot, but these scenes—Noreen ticking off my follies, and my mother, upset anew about my lifestyle, wringing her hands and wondering, aloud, what on earth is going to become of me—are not something I invented. I haven't been listening at keyholes, either. At 215 Overbrook Terrace the walls are fiberboard and the doors are hollow. Voices carry.

My foot was still on the brake. It was possible for me to stop Noreen before she got started on my mother. I could make a U-turn, hurry back, and stick to my mother the way Noreen's mashed potatoes stick to the roof of my mouth.

But then, what the hell! Life is short and I had the car keys. I lifted my foot from the brake and pressed the accelerator hard enough to send a baseball cap of Raymond's sailing from the dashboard to the passenger seat. It's not often that I get to drive fast and listen to Bruce full out at the same time. "Pink Cadillac" blasted from the speakers as I left the subdivision and headed toward the liquor store at the mall.

Noreen and Raymond's local mall—there is nothing in the area that could conceivably be called a "town"—isn't one of those behemoths flanked by department stores and acres of parking. It's—dare I say it?—a gussied-up strip mall, flanked by Taste of Mexico (called "Taste of Tourista" by Raymond) on one end, and A Stitch in Time, a craft shop where the window displays of crocheted afghans and embroidered pillows have kept me at bay for years, on the other. Between these oddly matched *bookends* are a midsized grocery store and a half dozen or so small shops, including Bo's Liquors.

I made a right turn into the parking lot, driving under a huge glittering star suspended over the lot's entrance. There were no parking spots near Bo's. After circling the lot a couple times, I pulled the Jeep into one of many vacant ones near the craft store, which goes to show you where the population of central New Jersey is spending its money these days.

As I'd expected, Bo's was doing a brisk business. I mulled over wine possibilities for a few minutes and then picked up three bottles of the same type Noreen had chosen.

She was sensitive enough to take any deviation as a slap at her taste.

There were several people ahead of me at the register. While I waited in line I stared out the big plate-glass window on the far side of the checkout counter. A thin but steady stream of shoppers passed, many toting white plastic bags from the grocery store to their cars, and some of them carrying smaller bags from the video rental store that adjoins Bo's.

I ordinarily wouldn't have paid particular attention to the young girl with the long russet ponytail—her jeans and denim jacket were de rigueur among the local teens and preteens. However, as she walked past Bo's, she turned toward the parking lot and called out loudly, "Mom! I'll meet you in the video store."

Initially all I saw was her back, but when she turned around, her attention was briefly captured by a display in Bo's window. It was then that I got a good look at her face. She had wide-set gray eyes, and her mouth, which was open, displayed a full complement of braces. If she wasn't the girl in the picture in Tom Hurley's office, she was her double. Erin. That was her name.

Realizing that I was looking at her, the girl clamped her lips together self-consciously and hurried away. I pushed my three bottles along the counter and then moved nearer the glass door. If the girl's mother—Tom's wife, Elizabeth—was here at this godforsaken little mall, Tom might be somewhere around, too.

We'd reached the time of year when night falls early, and daylight had all but disappeared, but the mall and parking lot were very well lit. No. Tom wasn't among the people on the sidewalk. I scanned the lot and didn't see him there either. In the direction the girl had called to, though, there was a navy-blue Audi with its trunk raised. Someone, momentarily concealed, was putting groceries into it. I continued staring. . . .

"Will that be it, miss?"

"Oh. Yes."

Turning back to business, I dug through my wallet and handed the cashier two twenties. While I waited for change, I again glanced out the door. As I did, the person who had been loading the trunk slammed it shut.

It was a woman, casually dressed. I squinted, hardly able to believe what I was seeing.

"Victoria."

I'd said the name aloud. The clerk attracted my attention once more by counting out my change.

"Sorry," I said, stuffing the money into my wallet. "I forgot something."

She was crossing the street in front of Bo's, coming closer, and the closer she came, the more certain I became that this woman who had just loaded groceries into the back of a blue Audi was the same woman who had followed me home.

I quickly stepped away from the counter, forgetting my wine. The clerk had put my bottles into a black bag. "I'll keep these here for you," he said as I ducked behind a rack of Chianti.

My thought-processing system was working hard, but not very well. What kind of a weird coincidence could this be? Tom Hurley's daughter, and Victoria, and me, all in this utterly undistinguished New Jersey mall at the same time? I knew what I was doing there. As for Tom's daughter . . . well, maybe the Hurleys were doing the same thing I was. They lived much farther north and on the other side of the Hudson, but maybe they had relatives in the area. But Victoria, too? She lived in Queens. This was impossible. Insane.

Nevertheless, it was the same woman. I knew that for certain when she walked past the liquor store. Peering through a space between the rows of bottles, I saw the same patrician features, the same mass of russet hair. The flared brown coat hadn't been hiding extra weight, I realized. This woman, who was now dressed in a short parka and jeans, was elegantly slim.

When she had disappeared from sight, I rushed to the

counter and grabbed my bag. The clerk, who was waiting on someone else, asked, "That's it?" but I was already half out the door and didn't respond. Peering up the sidewalk, I caught sight of the woman going into the video store.

This doesn't say a whole lot for my detecting ability, but it was only then that my confusion began to clear.

Tom Hurley's daughter had gone into the video store, where her mom was to meet her. A few minutes later, a woman of the right age and with hair almost the same color as the daughter's also had gone into the video store. The bottom-line reality had to be that unless Victoria Cerutti was stalking Tom Hurley's family, unless in the last couple minutes she had disposed of his wife and was now planning to snatch his daughter, and unless Victoria looked a lot like that daughter, the woman who had followed me home wasn't Victoria at all. She was Tom Hurley's wife, the ski-slope-schussing Elizabeth.

Damn! Things weren't just falling into place now. They were dropping like anvils. I had misinterpreted things totally. Victoria Cerutti hadn't followed me and she hadn't made those nighttime hang-up calls. Tom's wife, Elizabeth, had, and her reason had been as old as mankind, or at least as old as monogamous mankind. She suspected her husband was fooling around with another woman. Spotting me in his company, she decided to find out who I was, and then torture me.

I couldn't be certain when, but at some point on that evening when I'd run into Tom at the gym, Elizabeth Hurley had seen me with her husband. Perhaps she'd been waiting for him at his hotel. Why? I couldn't guess. Maybe she'd planned to surprise him. Maybe, missing her cute husband, she'd planned a romantic interlude. Or maybe she'd already suspected him of fooling around. Perhaps she'd been looking for evidence.

Elizabeth could have watched us get off the elevator and cross the lobby together. Seeing us pausing outside that shadowy bar, seeing Tom's hand on my back, and then seeing us traipse side by side out to the street—all that might have been devastating. Or it might have provided her with just what she wanted—proof.

It had been Elizabeth Hurley who had questioned the Codwallader sisters, surely. That was the only way she could have learned my name so that she could make those calls.

Where, I wondered, did Glenda Obus, attorney-at-law, come into this, if she came into it at all? Could it be that Glenda Obus was a divorce lawyer? If that was the case, might I be named in a divorce proceeding? That sure would give Noreen something to talk about!

I stood blocking traffic in the liquor store's setback entrance, wondering about all this and waiting for Tom's wife and daughter to leave the video store. After a couple minutes they emerged, the daughter first, the mother behind her. I leaned back to conceal myself, but it wasn't necessary. They were heading in the other direction, away from their car. I watched as they passed the card shop and the pizza parlor. There wasn't much else in that direction except—horrors!—A Stitch in Time.

Two young women, both pushing babies in strollers, passed me. Seizing the opportunity to see without being seen, I fell into step a few yards behind them. As I walked by the pizza parlor, I peeked between the young women. Elizabeth Hurley and her daughter were going into the craft shop.

They were safe from my prying eyes in there. The place is the size of a Manhattan kitchen. Besides, stitchery and macramé, in fact all of that handicraft stuff designed to keep the gentle sex from more robust pursuits, give me the willies.

In front of the pizza parlor I parted company with the young moms. Crossing the street, I unlocked the Jeep and climbed in. The sky was almost completely dark over the mall's roof, but a faint bit of day hung on. Pushing my glasses farther up my nose, I waited.

It wasn't too long before Elizabeth and Erin Hurley left

A Stitch in Time. A pink paper bag swung from Elizabeth's hand as she walked under the mall's bright lights. Maybe she planned to crochet some doilies or whip up a "Home, Sweet Home" sampler. If she was sufficiently upset with her husband, dementia might have set in.

I didn't start the Jeep until the Hurleys had reached the blue Audi and the car's lights had come on. Then I backed out of the parking slot and inched toward the lot's exit.

I really had no good reason to follow the Audi, except that its driver had followed me, and that I was in no hurry to get back to the anniversary festivities. Which, when I think about it, weren't very good reasons at all. Still, when the Audi turned left at the street, and it turned out we were going the same way, I figured, *Why not?* I wasn't even following, if you want to get technical.

I kept my distance as Elizabeth and Erin Hurley headed toward the development where Raymond and Noreen live, and when they turned into the development itself, I hung way back. I was sure Elizabeth Hurley hadn't seen me, but in case she was as paranoid as I was—and there was every indication that she was—it was best if she couldn't make out the Jeep's license plate. Otherwise she'd be able to trace the 4X4 to 215 Overbrook Terrace. And wouldn't that cause some stink there!

The Audi stayed on the development's perimeter road for a minute or two, passing Overbrook and several other streets. As it turned left on Hummingbird Lane, a third head appeared through the back window. I clicked my driving lights onto high beam. The head belonged to the basset hound. I let out a giggle.

Realizing that the blue car was slowing, I proceeded straight through the intersection and stopped about five feet past the corner behind a curbside postal box.

The Audi had pulled into a driveway three houses down the block. A young boy—that would be Eric—came out of the house and walked to the car. It was completely dark now, but a streetlight shone on Elizabeth Hurley and her daughter as they unloaded the trunk, and on the boy as he coaxed the basset hound into the house. A light shone on me, too, unfortunately, but unless Elizabeth had the night vision of an owl, she wouldn't be able to make out my face. To be certain, though, I retrieved Raymond's baseball cap from the seat and tucked my hair into it before getting out of the Jeep.

At the postal box, I made a big show of opening and slamming the chute door. The Audi's trunk was closed by the time I walked back to the Jeep, and as I slid into the driver's seat, a house door closed. Certain that Elizabeth and her children had gone inside, I swiveled in the seat and examined the house.

It was one of the ranch styles, more modest in size than Raymond and Noreen's split level. It stood out from its neighbors in several ways, the most immediately noticeable one being its lack of holiday decorations. In Raymond and Noreen's neighborhood there's no such thing as too much glitter, or for that matter bad taste, during the holidays. Up and down the streetlights twinkled and reindeer pulled sleighs across lawns. At Chez Indermill, lighted evergreens flanked the front door, and on the rooftop a plastic neon Santa toted a bag overflowing with toys. But at the ranch house Elizabeth and her children had gone into, there wasn't so much as a candle in a window.

Looking closer, I noticed a slightly bedraggled look about the house. The streetlight's glare showed a brownish, overgrown lawn, and even from a distance I could make out a green shutter hanging crooked at the house's side.

I released the emergency brake, intending to make a U and drive down Hummingbird, but as I pulled away from the curb, Elizabeth Hurley came through the front door. She tugged a chair behind her, which she climbed onto. Seconds later, after changing the lightbulb over the door, she stepped down. Almost immediately after she reentered the house, a yellow light flared at the house's front.

Afraid that as I drove past, Elizabeth might still be in the doorway, I headed straight back through the intersection.

Following Tom's wife had sure piqued my curiosity.

Who lived in that small white house Elizabeth and her daughter had carried groceries and videotapes into? There was no other car in the driveway, and the house had no garage where a second car might have been parked. Slim evidence, but it suggested to me that nobody was staying there but the Hurleys.

Had Tom and his family moved to central New Jersey without mentioning it? Was Tom in that ranch-style house right now with his wife and children?

Not likely. If he had been, wouldn't he have helped carry the groceries? At the very least, he would have changed the lightbulb on the front porch.

These thoughts meandered through my mind as I drove the few blocks to Raymond and Noreen's, and by the time I pulled into the driveway I would have bet the three bottles of wine on the seat beside me on one thing: Elizabeth Hurley had left her husband.

The reason she'd left him wasn't hard to figure out. She suspected that he was involved with another woman. Or maybe it went beyond suspicion. Maybe Elizabeth *knew* there was another woman, but she didn't know who that woman was. She'd made the mistake of pinpointing me as the other woman.

Taking this line of thought further, I knew that something had been going on between Tom Hurley and Victoria Cerutti. It could have been any number of things, of course, but my antennae told me it had to do with sex. Why else hide it? Why else the words I'd overheard him saying to Victoria? *You're an adult. It's not as if I forced you into . . .*

Into what? Call me a slut, but the only finish to that sentence that I could come up with was ''bed.'' My boss, Tom Terrific, had had an affair with a fellow employee, Victoria, and then dumped her. Distraught, she'd quit her job. Tom's wife, getting wind of her husband's cheating, had left him. Everybody was a loser. Victoria was working in a bowling alley, Elizabeth was living in a bedraggled house, and Tom . . .

What *had* Tom lost? His family, if my theory was correct, but how much did he care? During our lunch at the museum, had he been suffering inside as we'd discussed the salary survey? When he'd given me that inspired lesson on Willem de Kooning, had he been in emotional agony? I sure hadn't gotten that impression.

Walking up the driveway, I tried to convince myself that I could be mistaken about all this. If I wasn't mistaken, then Tom, the man who had just offered me a decent job, was more than a mere manipulator of human beings. He was a real scumbag!

That thought, coupled with Noreen's "Well! At last!" when I entered the living room, was enough to ruin my appetite for those lamb shanks, if I'd ever had one.

12

THE ANNIVERSARY DINNER WAS A SUC-
cess, though by dessert—a much admired
orange custard with raspberry sauce—the
carefully orchestrated seating arrangement was in a shambles. The women had
gravitated to one end of the table, the men
to the other.

From the women's end came ". . . and
then you add a half teaspoon of finely
grated lemon zest . . ." while from the
men's I heard, ". . . never knew he was a
state trooper until those lights started
flashing . . ."

This wasn't the dining room at San Simeon. Raymond
and Noreen's table had been lengthened with two card tables. One of them wobbled alarmingly; the other one would
have if it hadn't been shoved up against the wall. I was
fortunate to be at the sturdy middle table, with a conversational choice of how-I-talked-my-way-out-of-a-ticket or
lemon zest. I can do a brief stint of either, though if you

ever catch me grating a lemon peel, please put me out of my misery, but endurance is my downfall. I'd already said everything I had to say about recipes, which isn't much, and related my experience behind the wheel of an ex-boyfriend's Mustang. That was a pretty good story to begin with, and of course I'd embellished it, but enough is enough.

It was nine o'clock, not late, but if I didn't leave soon, I wouldn't be able to get the last bus into Manhattan. My other choice was to spend the night on Noreen and Raymond's sofabed. Owing to Noreen's housekeeping methods, that was a fate only marginally more attractive than spending the night as a guest of the Spanish Inquisition.

I can't understand it. Here is a woman who sprays air freshener with such abandon that a visit to her bathroom can demolish your sinuses, yet over the years so many spills have been allowed to sink into the sofabed that the once off-white upholstery—remember when Haitian cotton was the rage?—looks like it did hard time as Jackson Pollock's drip cloth.

So I wouldn't have minded if Noreen or Raymond had started making noises about moving to the living room for coffee. According to dinner-party etiquette, once the move to the living room is completed, the guests are free to start talking about their long rides home and their baby-sitters' curfews. From there, the move to the door isn't far off.

From the look of things, though, the move to the living room wasn't going to happen for a while. I suppose the blame, or the credit for that, is partly mine. The wine—need I mention that all of it was gone, and that even my mother had exceeded the minimum Noreen had allotted her?—had loosened things up. Raymond, normally rather reserved, was waving his hands as he described some brouhaha involving himself, a Teaneck cop, and a truck driver. My father, caught up in the drama, was gesturing madly with a fork while the man beside him was trying to interrupt by slapping the rickety card table with his hand and bellowing, "But let me tell you . . ."

At the other end of the table Noreen the Kitchen Queen held court. She hadn't downed enough of that Beaujolais Nouveau to get loose and giggly—there probably wasn't that much Beaujolais Nouveau in the entire county—but she was slightly more animated than usual, and the rosy tip of her nose stood out from the bland paleness of the rest of her face. To my disgust, every woman present, with one exception, me, seemed to be in her thrall as she explained how to tell when your custard has set.

Did they really care? I was sure my mother didn't. Mom's never been a gourmet cook, and I suspect that these days, if my father wasn't around she'd happily live on those frozen dinners in the plastic trays with three little sections and one big one.

Somewhere in the midst of the custard discussion, it occurred to me that if I wasn't going to be going home that night, there was something I might accomplish. Chances were slim, but I had no more traffic-cop stories to contribute and there wasn't a chance in hell that I would be able to shed any light on the subject of custard.

"Why don't we all take a walk?" I blurted. "It's not too cold. We could look at the Christmas lights."

A couple of eyebrows went up. Noreen's jaw went down. You'd think I'd suggested a trip to the biker bar out on the state highway.

"You can go ahead if you want, Bonnie," she said in that holier-than-thou voice she uses when I'm especially out of line, "but I don't think that the rest of us . . ."

It didn't seem a bad idea to me, the bunch of us, or some of the bunch, strolling the neighborhood's quiet streets. As ringleader, I could steer us past that white ranch-style house three blocks away. What that would accomplish I didn't know, but a group of strolling, chatting suburbanites was probably less likely to raise Elizabeth Hurley's paranoia level than one lone woman skulking around in front of her house.

My idea was trounced, and not only by Noreen, either.

The subdivision's residents may jog, but they don't take walks.

Having recovered, Noreen finally sounded the move-into-the-living-room signal, adding that she'd made some almond biscotti to accompany the coffee. Lots of ''ooohs'' followed her announcement, but I didn't join the chorus. I'd become rather worked up about the prospect of my after-dinner walk. I might not learn one thing more about Elizabeth, but if I was outside I wouldn't be inside with Noreen and what was certain to be a good long lecture about crushing almonds. It was another break for freedom.

The evening had grown quite chilly, actually, and I walked quickly. Almost directly overhead, the moon was a sliver of light, and the sky was so dark I could pick out the constellations. Several times I was caught in a passing car's headlights, and once I paused as a man pulled a car out of a driveway. Otherwise, I felt that I walked through the quiet streets unnoticed. I was more at ease than I am on dark streets in New York City, and more at ease than I can imagine feeling in the country. Although all sorts of hell may be going on behind the subdivision's closed doors, it seldom if ever spills into the streets. The houses' neat and familiar facades always suggest that all is well, whether it is or not.

I turned down Hummingbird Lane and slowed my pace.

At the third house in from the corner, the yellow bulb burned brightly over the front door. The blinds were all closed, but lights were on in two of the rooms at the side. I walked past slowly, memorizing the address: 134 Hummingbird Lane. The lawn was in even worse shape than I'd realized. A border of evergreen shrubs against the front was dying, and what remained of the grass was brown.

The reason for this became clear when I walked past the driveway. Several feet in from the sidewalk a piece of plastic, about 12 by 15 inches, with a pole attached, lay face-down on the brownish grass. A hole in the dirt near the end of the pole indicated that until recently the sign had stood erect.

I glanced at the house to be sure no one was observing me, then stepped onto the lawn and flipped the sign over.

FOR RENT, it read. Under that, in smaller letters, was the name of a real estate company, Warniers, and a phone number. No area code was mentioned, which meant that it was the local one, but the exchange wasn't Noreen and Raymond's.

I didn't trust my memory with seven digits, and I didn't have a pencil with me. I lifted the entire sign and pole. They weighed almost nothing, but the pole was cumbersome. I snapped it off easily, tossed it onto the lawn, and continued on my way with the sign tucked under my arm. The notion that I might be giving the neighborhood's residents a touch of petty vandalism to carry on about wasn't lost on me. Returning to 215 Overbrook, I felt pretty high-spirited.

Shadows moved behind Raymond and Noreen's living-room curtains. The anniversary festivities hadn't broken up, which meant that sneaking into the house with that sign under my arm was impossible. I walked up the driveway and then across the grass, to the side of the house where an overgrown rhododendron bush threatened to block the window of the bedroom shared by Raymond Junior and the baby, Trevor. Crouching in the damp grass, I pushed the rhododendron's branches aside and slid the sign against the wall. Raymond and Noreen are usually awake by seven A.M., which meant I'd have to get out there real early with a pencil and paper. That was easily enough done, though. Their sofabed's sagging springs encourage early rising.

Feeling proud of my evening's work, I scurried out of the dense cover of the bush in a crouch. Before I was upright, though, a wayward branch caught on my jacket arm, broke loose, and snapped hard against the bedroom window. A second later a light went on in the boys' room and my sister-in-law's voice reached me.

"Raymond! Someone's trying to kidnap Trevor!"

Still half-crouched, I hurried around to the front of the house. I straightened just in time to meet the menfolk as they poured out the front door ready for battle. Raymond had a baseball bat over his shoulder, my father carried a long flashlight, and the male guests, though empty-handed, were puffed up like gamecocks. In the doorway behind them the womenfolk had gathered, Noreen at the front of the pack. Trevor, looking confused by the sudden outburst of activity, squirmed in her arms.

Raymond, who looked almost as confused as his infant son, lowered the bat to the ground.

"Were you out back just now, Bonnie? Noreen was checking on Trevor. She thought there was someone out there."

"Out back? Oh, yes. I cut across from over there."

I waved my arm vaguely toward the next block, meaning to convey that I'd taken a shortcut through their neighbor's yard. No one could construe that as criminal, even if it did seem odd.

My brother has a healthy tolerance for strange behavior. Perhaps he didn't even find it odd that his sister would roam the neighbor's yard in the dark. All he said was, "Phew. We thought we had a prowler."

Noreen, far less tolerant, wasn't about to let me off the hook that easily. As I made my way through the now sub-dued merrymakers, I caught her giving my mother one of her famous pinched-mouth Bonnie-is-impossible! looks.

By six-thirty the next morning the phone number from that sign was jotted in the steno book in my tote bag, the sign itself was in a neighbor's trash can, and I was drinking coffee with one hand and feeding Trevor with the other. He's a happy baby when he's dry and full of mashed bananas, and we exchanged some pretty interesting baby talk.

It wasn't long before Raymond and Noreen got out of bed, and minutes after that the gum-popping teenage baby-sitter returned the other children. A big breakfast followed soon after. Noreen called it *Sunday brunch,* and to make up for my unorthodox behavior the night before, I did the same, but the bacon, eggs, and toast, not to mention the fact that it was on the table by 8:30 A.M., made it look like breakfast to me. Whatever it was, I polished off a lot of it.

While Noreen cleaned up after breakfast, I did the good-aunt thing and entertained the three older kids in the den. By "entertain" I mean we settled on the unmade sofabed and watched cartoons. Soon, though, I tired of cartoons and rooted through my tote for something to read. My murder-clue steno pad seemed inappropriate, so for lack of anything else, I pulled out the brochure I'd picked up when Tom and I had visited the museum.

The description of the Willem de Kooning exhibit was only three paragraphs long. Mildly obsessed by de Kooning after my recent artistic breakthrough, I read it carefully. And when I'd finished, sort of surprised by what I'd read, I reread it.

How odd! Every key idea that Tom had conveyed to me was contained in those three paragraphs. Thinking back over what he'd said, I realized that there wasn't one deviation. Not only in the ideas, but in the language. Not only were Picasso, Matisse, and Mondrian mentioned in this short write-up, but the adjectives—"aggressive," "spare," "animated"—were the exact ones Tom had used.

Yes, there is a party line in most areas of study, but how could both Tom and the expert who had written this brief description have chosen the same exact language? It was impossible. It was also impossible that Elizabeth, a high-school art teacher, had anything to do with writing the description. In the unlikely event that she had, wouldn't he have mentioned it to me as we strolled through that exhibit?

The only other explanation I came up with seemed almost as impossible. Tom was spending a lot of time in Manhattan these days. Could it be that he had read the description before taking me to the museum, and had decided to impress me with his knowledge?

I already suspected that Tom had been lying about his relationships with his family and with Victoria Cerutti, but at least there was some logic behind those lies. Tom's personal life was his business. But to lie about art expertise to someone who couldn't have cared less carried lying into an entirely new sphere. It was weird. Scary.

I extricated myself from 215 Overbrook and climbed into the Jeep with Raymond shortly after ten A.M.

Though I don't often admit it, I suspect that Noreen is a good wife for my brother. She reins his wilder impulses and keeps him on the straight track. Who knows? Left to his own devices, Raymond might usurp my crown as the family's black sheep. Noreen hasn't tamed him completely, though, even after fifteen years of marriage. When she and the kids aren't in the Jeep, Raymond drives just like he did when he was eighteen and roaring around suburban New Jersey in a red Camaro with yellow flames painted on its hood.

Okay, so I'm not the most conservative driver on earth, but Raymond leaves me in the dust. Riding with him is harrowing, and his Jeep's suspension makes it worse. We'd no sooner turned off Overbrook Terrace than I had an urge to fold myself into the airline crash position.

"So, how about that Tom Hurley?" he said affably as he took the turn at the end of the development's perimeter road on two wheels.

My fingers clutched the binding on the seat. "How about him?"

"It sounds like he's got it made."

Raymond's mind was obviously on Tom's job. When I responded with a noncommittal "Mmm," I had Tom's home life in mind.

"Yeah," Raymond said, undeterred by my lukewarm reaction. "That guy always did know how to look out for number one. Bet he's making six figures now. Right?"

"Low."

"Like one-twenty? Or more?"

When anything goes wrong at 215 Overbrook Drive, I'm generally able to convince myself that it's Noreen's doing, but Raymond isn't a complete innocent. Occasionally he displays a surprising jealous streak. No, he doesn't suspect Noreen of carrying on with deliverymen or anything like that. Though Raymond loves Noreen, by now he must realize that even the most desperate UPS guy would hesitate to take a spin around the block with her.

What Raymond is jealous of is other men of about his age and background who *have it made*. That's one of Raymond's favorite expressions. By his standards, having it made means that the other man wears good suits to work, does his work in a decent office, and gets a six-figure income for doing that work. These are very personal standards, when you think about them. They have more to do with what Raymond thinks he might have achieved if he hadn't gone to work at Baker's Garage right out of high school than with any realistic measure of success. He would never say that a surgeon or even a zillion-dollar-a-year basketball forward had it made. They're not of his world. A Tom Hurley, though? Absolutely.

"Tom makes a little more than one-twenty, but when you consider his commute, and the hours he puts in, you're doing better than he is."

That didn't mollify my brother one bit. Lifting a hand from the steering wheel, where in my opinion, it was critically needed, he scratched the side of his head and said softly, "Damn. I always wondered what would have happened if—"

I interrupted. "There's a red light!"

"I see it."

We came to a tire-screaming stop. "What I was saying is," he continued, "if I'd gotten a scholarship and gone away to college the way Tom did—"

"If you'd gone away to college, you wouldn't have been able to spend as much time stupping Noreen in the backseat of your Camaro."

The light turned green. Raymond grinned self-consciously as he jackrabbited through the intersection and made the turn into the bus station. "Yeah. There is that.

But I'll tell you one thing, Bonnie. I wouldn't have screwed things up. I wouldn't have flunked out,'' he added, pulling to the curb.

The one-story bus station is too small and suburban to be truly seedy, but it does aspire. The gray tile floor is pocked with blobs of blackened gum and the two wooden benches are scarred with graffiti and burn marks. If there are stray drunks in the vicinity, those benches send out a homing signal. *Come to me,* they broadcast over central New Jersey, and by God, it works. I've often spent my waiting time leaning against a wall listening to the wet snoring noises coming from the benches' soused occupants.

"You going to be all right here?"

Raymond's always in a hurry to get somewhere, but he always asks me that when he drops me at the station. I always give him the same answer: "You should see the one in Manhattan."

Now, though, I wanted a few seconds more of his time. "What did you mean by that remark that you 'wouldn't have flunked out'?"

My brother seemed surprised that I'd asked.

"Just what I said. I would have graduated. And after that, I might even have gone to business school or something." He smiled. "You never can tell."

"No, you can't, Raymond, but that's not what I mean. When you were talking about Tom Hurley and his scholarship, I got the idea that you thought Tom had flunked out."

"I don't just think it," he responded. "That's exactly what happened. Tom flunked out of Penn. Or something."

"Or something?"

Raymond shrugged. "Tom and I weren't close anymore when it happened, and since he never moved back here, I don't know all the details. Actually, the way I heard it, he didn't actually flunk out. He got thrown out of Penn."

I was shaking my head. "That's ridiculous. He graduated from Penn, and then he went to graduate school."

"Maybe so. I'm only repeating what the rumors were.

I'm not trying to make you think any less of him," Raymond added. "I've got good memories of the guy, even if he was a smooth operator who always got the prettiest girls."

"Did he? I never paid attention."

"You were older. Tom always knew how to 'get over' where women were concerned. You know what I mean? He had a line a mile long. And it always worked. He dated girls who looked like models. I heard that while he was at Penn he was going out with a runner-up in the Miss New Jersey contest. Of course by then I was engaged to Noreen . . ."

Now, that must have been a comfort.

". . . so what did it matter to me?"

From the way Raymond sounded, it must have mattered at least a little, but he wasn't about to tread into that territory.

The bus heading for New York City pulled into the parking lot behind us. After kissing Raymond on the cheek, I opened the Jeep's door and reached for my tote bag on the backseat.

"If you really want to know everything . . ." Raymond began.

Wanting to know everything he was willing to tell, I hesitated in the Jeep's open door.

"There was a rumor going around that Tom was thrown out of college for cheating."

I watched Raymond speed away, then walked into the bus station's waiting room. It was too early for drunks, or for much of anybody else. At one side of the long room a gray-haired woman passed the time with a book of crossword puzzles, and several seats away from her a young couple spoke in low voices.

I had a five-minute wait before my bus was due to leave, and since the phone booth in a dimly lit corner of the station was unoccupied, I used that time to tap into my home answering machine.

First came a message Amanda had left the afternoon before. Nothing special, she said. Just wanted to chat.

That was nice, if unusual, in these Emily-intensive times.

Following Amanda's message there was one from Sam. "Maybe we can talk?"

Hearing Sam's voice, I became unexpectedly misty-eyed. Before I had a chance to dissect that emotion, though, the machine moved on to a message from Mike.

"It's me again," he'd said. "I'd still like to get together with you."

Maybe later that evening, I said to myself as the machine skipped to the next message.

"Hey, Bonnie. It's Tom Hurley. We're having a quiet Saturday night out here in the Chappaqua boondocks. I finally got a chance to tell Elizabeth all about what happened with Dorfmeyer. She thinks R&G has made you suffer enough. She wouldn't let me come to the dinner table until I picked up this phone and made that job offer official."

Huh?

"Don't take me too seriously," Tom had continued. "I've had a couple beers. And so has Elizabeth! Just the same, on Monday let's talk about your future with R&G. What I have in mind is an HR position at the manager level."

Was I having aural hallucinations? From Tom's call, you'd have thought that he and his wife had been in the same house in Chappaqua, New York, the night before. They hadn't been, though, unless I'd been having visual hallucinations and the woman I'd been spying on wasn't Tom's wife, Elizabeth.

I was still trying to make sense of Tom's message when the last message on my machine began playing back. It was Amanda once again. This time, however, she sounded anxious, whispering "Bonnie? Please pick up. This is important. Tony heard that some piece of your clothing was found on Mr. Dorfmeyer at the crime scene. I don't know what it was, but you may have a problem. This is no laughing matter, Bonnie."

No laughing matter? I could have guaranteed Amanda I found it even less amusing than she did.

What piece of my clothing could it have been? I'd left Dorfmeyer's suite dressed exactly the way I'd arrived there.

I didn't see the bus pull up, and realized it was there only when the young couple and the middle-aged woman filed past me and out the station door. Hoisting my tote up on my shoulder, I followed them onto the half-empty bus.

13

AS THE BUS SPED NORTH ON THE TURN-
pike, Amanda's words echoed in my
mind.

*... some piece of your clothing was
found on Mr. Dorfmeyer at the crime
scene.*

Anyone who has ever taken a journalism class knows those five important *W*
questions—who, what, when, where,
why—plus how. This wasn't Journalism
101, though. ''Who?'' wouldn't be
known until the other questions had been
answered.

When traffic is light, the trip into Manhattan takes only
forty-five minutes, but a lot of heavy thinking can be done
in that short time. I had a double seat to myself. Rummag-
ing through my tote on the seat beside me, I pulled out my
steno pad and began adding to my notes. The first thing I
wrote was the word ''What?'' as in ''What piece of my
clothing?''

Taking dictation from Dorfmeyer was just that—dictation. There wasn't a hint of funny stuff. I hadn't walked out of his office minus a blouse or even a shoe. I hadn't misplaced anything near his secretary's desk either, or anywhere else on the thirty-seventh floor.

The one item of clothing I had misplaced at R&G was my knit scarf. It had disappeared somewhere between the lower level and the lobby elevator, but it was still the only probable answer to the question "What?" I jotted down *Scarf.*

"Where?" on Carl Dorfmeyer this scarf of mine had been found might have given me a few giggly moments if the situation had been different, but my mood was far from giggly. I tried to visualize the moment I'd discovered Dorfmeyer's body but wasn't able to pull together a fully coherent picture. I'd been upset, and the light had been very bad. Certain only that my scarf hadn't been covering Dorfmeyer's chest or face, I momentarily put "Where?" aside.

"How?" That was an important one. Had Dorfmeyer, with his fat income and all the goodies that come with a big job, found my scarf on the lobby floor? Had he then been so taken with it that he'd made it a part of his at-home wardrobe? Had he carried it to his suite and wrapped its unraveling strands around his neck at night to warm him when he walked onto his terrace?

No way. Carl Dorfmeyer, coming across my scarf on the lobby floor, probably would have removed it from his path with a swift kick. There was only one way that my scarf would have ended up "on" him and that was through someone else's intervention. Someone either had put that scarf on Dorfmeyer, or had forced him to put it on himself. Next to the word "How?" I wrote, "The killer put it there."

"When?" had the scarf been put on Dorfmeyer? Easy. Just before he was shot.

"Why?" Nothing hard about that question. The person who murdered Carl Dorfmeyer had put my scarf on the victim so that I'd be blamed for the murder. The ancillary

"Why?"—which was "Why me?"—was another grim one. Did someone hate me that much? I didn't think so. I'd simply been available, complete with missing scarf, rudimentary gun know-how, and motive. The question "Why me?" was answered with a paraphrase of the answer people give when asked why they climb Everest: *Because I was there.*

As the bus pulled into the line of traffic waiting to enter the Lincoln Tunnel, I went back to the big question: "Who?"

I eliminated the obvious ones first. The scent of Casey's cigar had been in the suite, and he'd had a motive. At this point, though, I had to face reality. Casey's alibi had satisfied the NYPD's most meticulous detective, so the answer to "Who?" wasn't "Casey."

Louise was another one with plenty of motivation, and she had been a little nuts, too. The alibi Tom had provided for her—a cab ride to Grand Central—hadn't been foolproof. As I'd said, Louise could easily have circled back to Dorfmeyer's hotel. But Louise was now dead, too, from a fall that I couldn't believe was an accident.

If I assumed that the same person who killed Dorfmeyer had then killed Louise, and that that person wasn't Casey . . .

An outsider?

As far as theories about Dorfmeyer's murder went, there were always the paid assassins and the disgruntled ex-employees, but why on earth would they have chosen to put my scarf, or anything else of mine, on Dorfmeyer? For that matter, how would they have gotten hold of my scarf, known it was mine, known I had a motive, and known about Casey's gun?

All this pondering led me back full circle to the ugly notion that had started tugging at my mind the evening before, the notion that had been growing stronger ever since I'd tapped into my answering machine less than an hour earlier.

The bus entered the dimly lit tunnel. I lifted the pencil

away from the steno pad until the interior lights came on. Then I wrote, after the question "Who?" in big capital letters—

TOM HURLEY

Tom Terrific. The man with the fake college degree, if Raymond was right. The man with the fake loving wife and children. Hell! Even the basset hound probably hated his guts.

Tom had murdered Carl Dorfmeyer and had set me up to take the blame.

I figured that Tom had noticed my scarf hanging with my coat on the back of the office door. It wasn't overly bright, but it was unique enough to catch his eye. He'd later found the scarf somewhere—maybe on the floor on the lower level, maybe over a doorknob where an earlier discoverer had hung it.

By that time Tom would already have planned to kill Dorfmeyer. Another "Why?"—but Raymond had an answer. Tom had been thrown out of Penn, yet his résumé indicated he'd graduated. If Dorfmeyer had discovered that . . .

He had! My heart leaped with a sudden realization. Dorfmeyer had learned about Tom's college record. That would explain the cryptic words on that piece of paper that Givens had shown me: *College. Grad school.*

Somehow Tom had gotten wind of this, and had decided that the one sure way to hang on to his job was to kill Carl Dorfmeyer. Tom had known about my scene with Dorfmeyer, and through the office grapevine he'd learned that I knew how to handle a gun. He'd figured that my scarf would add the perfect convincing touch to the crime scene.

And hadn't it, though? There he was, free as a bird and snug as a bug in Chappaqua, even if he was minus wife, kids, and basset hound, and here I was, facing what my best friend had described as *no laughing matter.*

Interesting, wasn't it, that when I learned that Tom was Louise's alibi, I'd jumped on the fact that he could be mistaken, yet overlooked the fact that the reverse was also true.

Louise was Tom's alibi. What if, after parting company at Grand Central, she'd caught sight of Tom leaving the station and heading in the direction of Dorfmeyer's hotel? That might explain why Louise had been so cocky about her "in" with management when she talked about Victoria returning to R&G. Louise's "in" could have been the knowledge that Tom's alibi was garbage.

That would also explain why Louise was now dead. I'd told Tom enough to raise his suspicions. He'd confronted Louise in the sickroom, and learned that what he feared was true. After that—well, it's a long drop from the thirty-seventh floor to the street.

This was all conjecture, of course, and there were still unanswered questions, but as the bus pulled into the labyrinth of tunnels beneath the Port Authority Bus Terminal, I felt as if the pieces were falling into place.

By the time I emerged from the subway onto 181st Street and Fort Washington Avenue, the noonday sun was glinting through the dark clouds marching across the sky. Bad weather was anticipated, but right then, the glare off shop windows and the roofs of parked cars was so bright that I put on my sunglasses before heading for my apartment building.

As I've mentioned, my building is on a corner at the bottom of a long, curving hill. Beyond that hill is the West Side Highway, and past that, a stretch of Riverside Park. From several points on the curving hill, and from the promontory overlooking the highway, the Hudson River is visible, and I suppose that in Raymond and Noreen's subdivision the stretch might have been called "Overriver" or possibly "Overpark." They wouldn't have called it "Overhighway."

In any event, when I reach the middle of the hill I have an unbroken view not only of the Hudson but of my apartment building's front steps, and once I'm fifty feet or so away, I can even see clearly through the glass street doors into the building's vestibule.

As soon as I spotted the first man, I got a bad feeling.

He was leaning against the wall just inside the doors. From there he would have a clear view up the street if he was waiting for a friend or for a cab. That didn't seem likely to me, though. Not the way that the man was dressed. Inside that vestibule, a vent from the basement laundry room warms the air until it feels like a sauna regardless of the season, yet this man wore an unbuttoned plaid shirt over a sweatshirt. The flannel shirt's collar was up and the sweatshirt's hood was pulled over the man's head. Nothing showed of his face except his dark glasses.

I slowed my pace. The man's running shoes were bright white. His hands were tucked inside the plaid shirt. He might easily have concealed a box cutter there, so he could cut my throat if the contents of my wallet were too meager. His entire being almost screamed *street punk*. Only his well-padded stomach, straining against the front of his gray sweatshirt, seemed out of place.

He wasn't one of my neighbors. I know all of them, at least by sight, and I recognize a lot of their friends, too. Though I wouldn't trust some of them with my credit cards, I don't think any of them would be inclined to attack me in the vestibule. In any event, not at noon.

That was the weird thing. It was the middle of the day. Why had my antennae gone up? So what if there was a chubby punk in my vestibule? There were dozens of people on the street. Ordinarily I'd have walked into my building and slipped through the inner door to the lobby, making sure the punk didn't follow me. And if he'd tried to, I'd have yelled for George the super.

Glancing farther down the street, my eye was caught by a black kid at the far end of the block. He was dressed in a bright white parka that stood out against the graying sky. He was lounging against a parked car, and though he was some distance from me, it seemed that his eyes were focused on my building's vestibule

A gypsy cab, thinking I was waiting for a ride, pulled nearer me. Crouching as if I intended to get into it, I took the opportunity to examine the first man more closely.

He must have been feeling the heat from that laundry-room vent. As I watched, he pushed the hood off his face and wiped at his forehead with the back of his hand. His other hand tugged at the plaid shirt's collar.

He was a cop! An NYPD sergeant, to be precise. He was the big-bellied, big-mustached sergeant who had been with Detective Givens the night Carl Dorfmeyer was killed, and who had later escorted me to Givens's office in the basement of R&G's corporate headquarters.

Unnerved, I waved the cab away and sidestepped into the little shop that offers aromatherapy.

They don't do much business, and I have neighbors who swear they're a cover for a drug cartel. I doubt it. I just think that essential oils, balm of hyacinth, and New-Age music haven't found their niche in upper Washington Heights.

Under the watchful gaze of the dark-eyed female clerk, I sniffed at the delicious-smelling little bottles that sat on mirrored counters. As I ran my hand over the cushioned portion of the back-rub chair, she mumbled as if certain she'd be rebuffed, "Can I help you?"

Had the cop noticed me? Cops, rather. The black kid had to be one, too. Had either of them seen me go into the shop? If they had, they would wait. For a while, anyway. Then they'd come to the shop.

The clerk was young. Not much more than a teenager. Her eyes were dull with boredom. I looked quickly around the shop. Behind the counter with the cash register was a curtained-off back area. A rest room, probably, and . . .

"Do you have a back door?" I asked.

That brought a hint of life to her eyes. "Yeah, but it's just for employees."

"This ex-boyfriend of mine—" My eyes flickered nervously to the street. "He's been following me."

The girl caught on immediately. Straightening, she crossed the small space and stared out onto the street.

"Which one is he?"

"You can't see him from here," I said.

She looked back at me. "Did he see you come in here?"

"No, but if he was to start looking, and find me here, well . . ." I looked helplessly at all the pretty little bottles filling the mirrored shelves.

"I'll let you out the back," the clerk said, quickly moving away from the window. "The alley gate's unlocked."

"Thanks."

I followed the young woman through the curtain into a narrow space crowded with cartons. She pressed a bar on the shop's heavy back door, and I stepped into an alley lined with trash cans. The door closed behind me before I could say thanks.

The wrought-iron gate was closed, but the latch turned easily, letting me out onto Fort Washington.

Now what? What was I doing, anyway? A city bus roared past, leaving me in its trail of fumes, as I stood there trying to get my head together.

The cops weren't staking out my apartment building, incognito, because Givens wanted merely to question me again. It didn't work like that. I didn't think it did, anyway. Not that I was thinking too sensibly, but if questioning had been Givens's only goal, wouldn't he have dropped by my apartment, perhaps even calling in advance?

Givens wanted to arrest me. That hulking cop in that stupid punk disguise planned to put handcuffs on me, read me my Miranda rights, haul me downtown, and throw me into a holding cell.

Would Givens listen to my theory about Tom Hurley? Of course he'd listen. He'd take a few notes, and pull on his jowls, and then he'd have me returned to my cell and start polishing up the case against me. Givens the Exterminator, getting another bit of vermin off the street.

Sure I might be wrong about all this, but intuition kept telling me I was right, and when your teeth have started chattering with fear, you have nothing else to go on but intuition.

How long would the cops wait at my building? Did they

know I'd been to Raymond and Noreen's? Of course they did. Amanda had known about the anniversary dinner. She would have told Tony, and . . .

Oh God, no! The cops would contact my family.

"She was on the ten-oh-eight bus," my astounded brother would say to the cops who looked utterly out of place standing on the doorstep at 215 Overbrook. And I could just hear Noreen. "Not that I think Bonnie's guilty, but I knew that someday the way she was living was going to catch up with her." My father would be stoic, while my mother would wring her hands and, prodded by Noreen's self-righteous blathering, weep as she collapsed under the weight of my supposed crime.

More than anything else, I think it was that vision of my family's reaction that got me moving. The idea of an arraignment before a judge, the idea of a trial, of a prison cell, they all frightened me. But the idea of Noreen's *I always knew* and of my Mom's tears was worse than frightening. It was unthinkable.

I had to clear myself. I'd suspected that would be the case when I started keeping my steno book of notes. Why else had I started being "proactive"? Well—I patted my tote, and was reassured by the feeling of the coiled-wire binding pressing into the tote's side—the time had come.

The thing for me to do first—the only sensible first step, really—was to contact Tony. And then second . . .

Second? What I'd do second could wait until after I saw how what I'd decided to do first turned out.

There was a pay phone on 181st Street, around the corner and down the block from where I stood, but that would put me within spotting distance of the cop in my vestibule. He probably wouldn't recognize me—he'd never seen me in slacks and my red parka—but then again, he might have gotten tired of standing around. For all I knew, he could be patrolling the street between the phone booth and my apartment building right now.

There was always the A train. The steps leading to my station were right there on 181st Street, but there was an-

other entrance farther up Fort Washington. The bus stop
was there, too, but buses are poky. While I may have been
confused about how I was going to clear myself, I wanted
to do it quickly.

Just as I was about to head for the farther subway entrance, a blue-and-white police car prepared to round the
corner from 181st Street. I turned, pulled open the wrought-
iron gate, and stepped into the alley. When I looked back,
the cruiser was passing my hiding spot, heading north on
Fort Washington.

The sight of a police car on a neighborhood street isn't
unusual. They probably hadn't been looking for me. Not
specifically, anyway. Still, they'd probably heard about me.
The pending arrest of a murder suspect in their own precinct, especially a white, middle-class female suspect,
would spread through the precinct grapevine quickly.

The wind had picked up, and I became the center of a
whorl of blowing dust when I once again left the alley.
Stepping between two parked cars, I stuck out my arm. A
gypsy cab obligingly pulled over. I needed to go only as
far as a safe phone booth, but as I climbed into the cab,
another blue-and-white police car appeared at the edge of
my vision. It stopped at the other side of the intersection
near the subway entrance.

The cab-driver was waiting for my instructions. One of
the cops stepped out of the patrol car and walked into the
diner on the corner. They weren't interested in me, but my
anxiety level had reached a new high.

"Midtown," I said.

The cabbie pulled into traffic but was stopped immediately by a red light at the intersection. A blast of static came
from his two-way radio. Picking up the microphone, he
responded in rapid-fire Spanish. His eyes flickered back at
me through the rearview mirror. I tensed, ready to jump
from the cab and run.

The light changed and the cabbie drove on easily. We
passed the idling patrol car and headed toward the West
Side Highway. And just in case a blast came through that

radio warning the cabbie about a local white woman, a murder suspect, on the run, I built a little wall of fiction around myself.

Smiling at the cabbie's reflection in the mirror, I said, "Saks Fifth Avenue. Christmas shopping."

As we merged into traffic on the West Side Highway, something very important occurred to me. Moses. I'd left enough food to last him through breakfast, but what about dinner? The poor guy.

As you might imagine, Christmas shopping was the last thing on my mind. Still, Saks wasn't a bad destination. I made a flimsy pretense of entering the store, but once the driver pulled off, I marched back outside, crossed Fifth Avenue, and walked into Rockefeller Center. It offered shelter, a ladies' room, and phone booths.

The ladies' room on the concourse level was first. After taking care of the necessary, I wiped my face with a damp paper towel and combed my hair, while the room's sharp-featured matron pushed a mop around me and muttered under her breath.

I didn't look bad. A little pale, perhaps, but the red parka seemed to brighten my complexion. The blustery wind had made my hair frizzy, but a stranger, seeing me, wouldn't have thought I looked particularly desperate. That could change, though, I thought as I dropped some change into the matron's tip plate. Enough of this fugitive stuff could turn me into a wild-eyed desperado.

Phone booths are scattered all around Rockefeller Center. I dialed the LaMarcas' number from a booth near the ladies' room, and got the beep-beep of a busy line.

Scooping my quarter from the slot, I dialed George, my super. He picked up the phone on the first ring.

"Hello?"

"George. It's Bonnie Indermill. I may not be able to get home this evening. Could you please feed Moses?"

"Not coming home tonight?" he responded, sounding oddly disturbed about that.

"Maybe not, but could you—"

"Aw, you should try to get home. Where are you, anyway?"

Why did George care? He'd never cared before. I couldn't recall him ever once asking where I was, or where I'd been. He'd just gone about feeding Moses with hopes of a bigger Christmas tip.

"I'll try," I said, "but you'll feed him?"

"Sure, sure. But you just try to get home to that cat of yours. Okay?"

"Okay."

I hung up, so flooded with anxiety that my knees were quaking. To that point I guess I'd held out some slim hope that the cops didn't really plan to arrest me, that Givens merely wanted to chat one more time. George had confirmed my worst fear. From the way he'd responded to my simple request, I knew that the cops had spoken to him, had asked him where I was, when I'd be home. They may or may not have told him they planned to arrest me, but he'd gotten that idea. George may not do much about graffiti on the building's front, but he likes the tenants to have a veneer of respectability. The idea of a fugitive tenant at large would upset him no end.

Afraid to stand in one place for long, or simply unable to, I moved to a booth on the main floor and tried Tony and Amanda's number again.

Beep. Beep.

A Rockefeller Center security officer in an olive-green uniform walked by me, turned, and passed me again. What did that mean? Was I starting to look more desperate? Had he heard about a woman on the run, suspected of murder?

Once the guard was out of sight, I dialed Tony's precinct. "I saw him earlier today," the desk clerk told me, "but not in a while. He may have gone home. Want to leave a message in case he comes back?"

"Yes. You could tell him that Bonnie called." After cradling the phone, I took the stairs back down to the concourse level.

Rockefeller Center offers more than shelter, phones, and a ladies' room. For the Manhattanite it represents a ground zero for subway transportation. The trains on the Concourse level fan out in all directions, and if they don't happen to go exactly where you want to go, they'll get you to a good connection quickly.

The train I thought at the time would be my salvation was the F train to Queens. It was arriving as I pushed through the turnstile. I ran, making it through the doors just as they were closing.

The LaMarcas live "close in," as Amanda is fond of telling me. What she means is that she, resident of Queens, can be in midtown Manhattan more quickly than can I, resident of Manhattan. "Three quick stops to your five," she says, adding, "Jackson Heights is almost next door to Bloomingdale's."

I counter with, "But the F is such a cattle car during rush hour," but Amanda, refusing to give up the last vestige of her life as a "player" on the Manhattan scene, merely smiles and says, "And the F runs every five minutes."

There she's right, and for once I was glad to admit it.

This being Sunday, the car was only half-full. People read newspapers and books, adjusted packages and children on their laps. In the seat beside me a teenage boy read a comic book, while across the aisle two middle-aged women and a man, all in somber dark clothing, talked in hushed tones.

Nobody paid any attention to me. Nobody would, unless I did something exceptionally strange. This was a New York City subway, where any behavior short of the truly berserk tends to be ignored.

It wasn't long before the conductor's voice rasped through the train's loudspeaker system. "Jackson Heights. Roosevelt Avenue."

I followed some of my fellow riders, including the two women and their male companion, from the train. Almost immediately I spotted a transit cop in the station.

Late at night, when you're stuck in a car with a screaming crazy or with a gang of kids who keep eyeing your handbag, how many of these guys do you think you see? Not many.

This one seemed hyperalert, his eyes shifting up and down the platform, focusing briefly on the people passing him. Not wanting to catch his eye, I stared straight ahead and remained in the midst of the departing passengers. Once I was out on the street, I headed for the LaMarcas' house. The middle-aged threesome walked ahead of me until the first corner, where they turned. I glanced down that block as I passed it. There was something going on at a local church, and the usually quiet sidewalk teemed with darkly clothed pedestrians. It was a funeral. Parked in front of the church, amid several black limousines, there was a big black hearse.

I continued on to the next block, where the LaMarcas live, and turned. I can't remember whether I was disappointed or relieved when their driveway came into view and I saw that Tony's car wasn't there.

14

AMANDA WAS LOOKING AS UNDONE AS I felt. Her usually sleek black hair was pulled into a messy ponytail, and her outfit—baggy gray sweats and pink bedroom slippers—was most un-Amanda-like.

In some situations, when she's not completely sure of herself, Amanda still can manage a pretty cool act. Those situations, however, usually involve social niceties. Choosing the correct fork, even at the most formal dinner party, is hardly in the same league as greeting a suspected murderer at your front door.

When, upon seeing me, she said, "I don't believe this. Tell me I'm seeing things," and clamped her forearm over her eyes, my notions about a warm and fuzzy welcome fled.

"You're not seeing things, Amanda. Tony's car isn't here," I added. "When's he getting home?"

As she lowered her arm, her eyes met mine briefly, and

then darted nervously to the street. "I'm not sure. He had some things to do at the precinct."

The LaMarcas' block is tree-lined, but the trees had lost their leaves. Standing on the front stoop, under the bare branches of the maple tree that is usually so lush, I felt completely exposed.

I shifted on my feet. "Are you going to let me in and give me a cup of coffee?"

For a second it seemed as if she actually might refuse, but finally she stepped hesitantly out of the doorway. "There's an infant here," she said as I walked past her.

And what did that mean? Did Amanda think I was going to cause a shoot-out or something? Or that her infant daughter might become the centerpiece in a siege? A bit of black humor found its way to the tip of my tongue, but I kept quiet. The merest suggestion that I might shield myself from a hail of police bullets with Emily Christina's tiny body was sure to put an end to her tenuous hospitality.

"How is the little sweetheart?"

I tossed my parka on the sofa and made my way through the babyland the LaMarcas' living room had been turned into. How many apparatuses does a baby need to contain it, anyway? Right now Emily Christina, at her basically immobile age, didn't need much at all, but would she really ever need the thing that sat on the floor and rocked, and the thing that hung in the doorway and bounced, and the thing that rolled across the floor? Honest to God, there was already a device available to accommodate every position the kid might possibly assume during her first couple years.

"She's fine. She's lifting her head by herself now."

"So you told me." I gave my friend a serious look. "Why don't you try to reach Tony?"

She jumped on that suggestion—"Oh, yes"—and as soon as we had pushed through the swinging kitchen door, she grabbed the wall phone. She called the precinct first, but Tony was gone. A minute later, she reached him in his car.

"Bonnie's here," she announced with no preamble. After listening to her husband for a second, she handed me the phone.

"Hi, Tony," I said. "Looks like I'm in some mess."

"Mm . . ."

There was a world of meaning packed into that "Mm."

"I think Givens wants to charge me with murder."

"We'll work things out," Tony said. "You wait there. I'll come and get you."

"And take me where? Are you going to turn me in?" I asked, my voice rising.

He didn't answer, and at that instant whatever glint of hope might have remained alive in me—*They couldn't arrest me for murder. Not me. An innocent*—died. They did plan to arrest me. Tony's silence was making that clear.

"I didn't kill anyone," I said.

"Of course you didn't."

Did he really believe me? I couldn't tell.

"I know who the murderer is, Tony, but proving it is going to be hard. He's slick."

"That's all right," Tony reassured me. "We'll work on it, Bonnie. I swear. We're going to straighten things out. You just wait there with Amanda. Okay?"

"Sure," I promised, and at the time I meant it. What were my other choices? Putting myself into Tony's competent hands sounded preferable to life on the run. I hadn't been running long, but already it struck me as a generally icky way to live.

I've spent so much time in the LaMarcas' kitchen that one of the stools at the counter seems like my own. This time, however, the seat was heaped with neatly folded pastel-colored baby outfits. After hanging my tote over the backdoor knob, I moved the baby clothes into a wicker basket half-filled with laundry warm from the dryer. A flannel-lined denim jacket of Tony's waited there for Amanda's housewifely touch.

"I was starting to fold clothes," she said. "Let me put on the coffee."

Amanda, usually so confident in the kitchen, fumbled

with the bag of coffee as she opened it, sending dark grains spilling to the floor. Trying to wipe them up, she cracked her elbow into the stove.

"Can I help?"

"No."

Her voice was quite a lot brighter than it should have been. I took a onesie from the top of the heap of folded baby clothes. Under other circumstances I might have had something to say about the tiny brown bears floating on a sky-blue background, but all I could do was stare at them.

"I found that one on sale," said Amanda. "It's probably supposed to be for a little boy, but honestly, Bonnie! You wouldn't believe how many outfits she goes through. I'm doing at least one load of laundry every day, and the amounts of soap and fabric softener . . ."

Amanda's words were pouring out in what I recognized as a rush of anxiety. She was falling apart, and I was the reason. I put the onesie on the counter and, as the expression goes, cut to the chase. Looking at her, I said, "You're acting as if you're entertaining a homicidal maniac in your kitchen."

That took care of the laundry chitchat. Amanda stopped mid-sentence and gaped at me as if such an idea had never occurred to her.

"I've never for one minute thought you did it. Even when Reggie said—"

"Who?"

Amanda's gaze shifted from mine. She began focusing on preparing the coffee so intently you'd have thought it wouldn't drip into the carafe without her undivided attention.

"Amanda? Who is Reggie, and what do you mean by 'Even when Reggie'?"

"Oh, you know Reggie," she said lightly as she took two mugs from a cabinet. "Reggie Givens. Yesterday he and his wife dropped by to see Emily . . ."

This was unbelievable. Not only was my nemesis dropping in on my best friends, and to see my goddaughter, but . . .

"You call him Reggie?" I asked, appalled by the idea. "You're on a nickname basis with the man who's trying to put me in prison?"

Amanda responded defensively. "Everyone calls him Reggie."

"I don't! I call him Detective Givens."

"Well, in your situation that's understandable."

She filled our mugs, put them on the counter, and slid onto the stool across from me, but she still didn't meet my eyes. Trying to sound as if I wasn't close to hysteria, I said, "Let's drop the subject."

"Okay," Amanda replied with obvious relief. "Want to hear what Dr. Spock has to say about—"

"I meant let's drop the subject of what we call Reginald Givens. You started to say that *Reggie* said . . ."

I let my voice trail off, hoping that Amanda would pick up the line. When, instead, she began straightening the little blue onesie, I nudged.

"What did Reggie say about me, Amanda?"

"Well, he didn't say *anything* to me," she replied, "but I happened to overhear . . ."

Givens hadn't spent his entire visit admiring Emily Christina, Amanda told me. After a few minutes of that, he'd suggested to Tony that they "talk business."

"They came back here to the kitchen while Reggie's wife and I stayed in the living room. I could tell that Emily was getting hungry, though, and after a few minutes I started to come in here to heat a bottle. I stopped when I heard Reggie say, 'Your friend Bonnie's guilty as hell.' "

Those had been Reginald Givens's exact words. Tony's, in response, had been, "I don't believe it."

"How did Tony say that?" I asked. "I mean, did he say it like he *really* didn't believe it, or like he was having a hard time coming to grips with it?"

"Like he didn't really believe it, of course," said Amanda.

She went on, telling me how she had remained outside the kitchen door, listening to Givens make his case. Seems it was a good one. I had motivation, opportunity, and an office key that gave me access to someone else's gun. My prints were the only ones on the gun. That I might have explained away, but how was I going to explain the fact that a scarf, identified as mine by several R&G employees, was resting under the dead man's body?

Amanda, having finished this recounting, peered at me over the top of her coffee mug. She wanted to know how I explained that scarf, too.

"I lost it at the office the day before Carl Dorfmeyer was killed," I said, answering her unasked question. "Obviously the killer found it and decided he could use it to pin the murder on me."

"Oh, I see," Amanda said with a quick nod.

She was my best friend, and she wanted to believe me, but I couldn't tell if she really did or not.

It wasn't too long before we heard a car pulling into the driveway. Tony was home. Amanda, all nerves, ran from the kitchen and out the front door.

I'll never know why I didn't just sit there quietly. Maybe it was my intuition, which was in high gear that day. For some reason, though, I went back into the living room, parted a curtain, and looked out onto the street.

Tony and Amanda were standing on the far side of his car, staring down the block as if waiting for someone. She said something to him that I couldn't hear, but her expression was angry. After a minute a plain black sedan with two occupants in the front seat approached the house. As the sedan drew nearer, I recognized Reginald Givens in the passenger seat.

If Tony had shown up alone, I probably would have done just as I'd promised. I would have let him drive me to the precinct, let him book and fingerprint me, and take me to a holding cell. Seeing Givens, though, I snapped.

Reacting without thinking, I raced back into the kitchen and grabbed my tote. When I flung open the door that leads to the LaMarcas' backyard, a cold gust of wind hit me in the face. My parka was back in the living room. With no time to spare, I grabbed Tony's old denim jacket from the laundry basket and hurried through the door.

There was only one direction I could go from there that wouldn't bring me to the front of the house. It wasn't an especially scenic route, but it was more appealing to me right then than a trip to jail with Detective Givens. I headed into a neighbor's yard through a narrow opening in the ramshackle wood fence that separates the properties, and skirted around the back of a storage shed. From there I made my way through a hedge and fought past a barrier of trash cans, finally ending up in the courtyard of a small apartment building one street over. An icy-cold rain began falling as I trotted down the driveway. Completely exposed then, I walked as quickly as possible until I reached the church where the funeral service I'd noticed earlier was being held.

The service had ended a few minutes before, and the sidewalk outside was crowded with people in dark coats. As I moved in among them, the casket was borne through the church door by six pallbearers.

I remained at a respectful distance. My slacks—gray wool—and crepe-soled loafers were all right, but my too large denim jacket didn't fit in. The rain started coming down harder. An elderly woman standing beside me unfurled a big black umbrella.

"He was a wonderful man," she said in slightly accented English.

I nodded. "He'll be missed." It was time for me to move on, but before I'd taken a step, the woman reached for my arm.

"Are you going to the subway? I am, too. Get under here with me," she offered. "It's big enough for both of us."

Oh, that generous woman. Maybe Tony and the other cops were still searching the house by the time she and I reached the subway station—according to Amanda, they searched it long and hard—but maybe they were already in their cars looking for me. If they were, what they saw through the now heavy rain were two people sharing an umbrella, hurrying toward shelter.

It was almost three P.M. when the F train brought me back to Rockefeller Center. The subway station was teeming with people now, and no one paid me any attention when I switched to a train bound for Manhattan's West Side.

During the short ride back from Queens I'd made myself a mental "to do" list. It didn't amount to much, this list. My options, as I saw them, were limited.

I left the train at Columbus Circle and bought myself a three-dollar umbrella on the street. Hungry by then, I stopped in the first café I came to on Broadway. It was a lavish-looking place, and very brightly lit. I got as far as the sign that read PLEASE WAIT TO BE SEATED but changed my mind when a smiling hostess came my way. She was decked out for the holidays with a big red bow in her hair and dangling earrings shaped like bells. That was too much good cheer for me. I hurried back outside.

Farther up Broadway I found a hole-in-the-wall coffee shop. Frank's, it was called. The counterman didn't look up from the griddle when I opened the door, but a sleepy-eyed woman in a sweatshirt and black jeans who was nursing a cup of coffee waved an arm carelessly.

"Sit anywhere."

This was more like it, but what really drew me in was the pay phone on one of the walls. Among the "to do's" on my list were a couple of calls. Closing the door behind me, I walked to a small booth at the restaurant's rear and sat with my back to the street. Light flickered from a shot fluorescent bulb on the ceiling as I looked over the menu. A radio played from behind the counter. Someone was talking about the Middle East.

"Grilled cheese on rye, and an order of french fries," I said as the waitress poured me a cup of coffee. This was hardly the time to concern myself with cholesterol.

While my lunch was frying up, I went to the pay phone.

Everything I know about tracing phone calls comes from the movies and it may all be a bunch of hooey, but I had to assume that the police would bug the phones of anyone they thought I might contact. Three minutes after I dialed—it's always three minutes in the movies—technicians would pinpoint my location, and two minutes after that a SWAT team would swoop down on me. And there I'd go in a blaze of bullets.

There was no chance, however, that they would have bugged the phones of a real-estate company in central New Jersey.

Opening my wallet, I fingered the phone card that I seldom use. It presented me with another quandary. Could the police trace calls made with a phone card in three minutes? Maybe, but the movies hadn't caught onto that yet. In any event, I had to start somewhere.

Using my card, I got the number for Warniers Real Estate and dialed them. My call was answered by an annoyingly chipper man.

"Warniers," he said happily. "How may I help you?"

"I'm calling from the Sears Credit Card Division. A Ms. Elizabeth Hurley has applied for credit here. She's listed your firm as her landlord."

"That's not quite correct," he said playfully. "Warniers is the agent for the owners of the home Ms. Hurley rents."

"Ah," I said. "That's on Hummingbird Lane?"

"It certainly is. A nice property. I showed Ms. Hurley the house myself."

"And Ms. Hurley has lived there . . . ?"

"Not long. She rented the house last month. I believe she and her children moved in two weeks ago."

"So you couldn't tell me anything about Ms. Hurley's creditworthiness?"

"I can tell you that she put down a first and a last month's rent, and a security deposit. And that the credit check we ran on her didn't indicate any problems. Besides," he added with a chuckle, "anyone willing to teach math to junior-high kids has my vote of confidence.''

Math, and not art? Had Tom even lied about that?

I chuckled along with the man from Warniers. ''Oh, I couldn't agree more. And Ms. Hurley's previous address was in Chappaqua, New York?''

''Yes.''

''Thank you very much,'' I said. ''You've been a big help.''

''Glad to be of assistance. And if you're ever looking to rent in central New Jersey, remember Warniers. Best selection of houses, condos—you name it, we've got it.''

I told the man I'd definitely keep Warniers in mind and said good-bye.

My lunch was ready, so I returned to my table. Slathering the fries with ketchup, I dug in. My own troubles weighed so heavily on my mind that the newscast on the radio was little more than background noise.

''. . . all on the national front. Locally, the firefighter hospitalized after fighting a three-alarm fire in Brooklyn is expected to recover fully. Good news. And earlier today in Queens . . .''

I had a ketchup-soaked french fry at my lips, but making sense of those words, I froze.

''. . . the botched robbery of a candy store led to the arrest of two juveniles suspected of committing a rash of robberies in the area. And on the weather front, it's raining. We're showing temperatures dropping into the mid to low thirties late this afternoon, with increasing winds and a fifty percent possibility of wet snow tonight. Now back to the Top Forty . . .''

Nothing about me? That was amazing. Even in New York City, a woman running from a homicide arrest is news, and I'd been running for a couple hours now.

A wild stab of hope seized me. I popped the french fry into my mouth. Maybe Tony had convinced Detective Givens that he was wrong about me. Or maybe Tom, awash with guilt, had confessed. Maybe . . .

Maybe pigs really were flying over Manhattan. There

was only one reason I hadn't made the news. Someone with some influence was keeping my escape quiet. Tony. Good old Tony. When this was all over, assuming I wasn't making license plates for the state of New York, I owed him one.

I finished lunch and downed another cup of coffee, then paid my bill. After putting a tip on the table, I counted the money remaining in my wallet. A twenty, a ten, and a couple singles. Whatever I did from then on, it had to be done cheaply.

Before leaving the restaurant, I made another call, this one to the LaMarcas' home. Tony answered.

"It's me," I said.

"Bonnie! Where are you? I'll come get you."

"You and Reggie?" I asked sarcastically.

"Givens is on the case. I can't ignore him," Tony responded. "He's gone now, I promise. Where are you? I've been able to keep things quiet, but that's not going to go on forever. You're going to have to trust me to work things out."

Once again I was almost persuaded. Tony would take care of things for me. Good old Tony.

"Can you put Amanda on for a second?" I asked.

"Sure. Here you go."

She must have been hanging over the phone because she was on in an instant. "Bonnie. You shouldn't have run. Where are you?"

I'd turned so that I could watch the front of Frank's Restaurant. No SWAT team so far, but I was too nervous to stay there much longer.

"I'm with an old friend. You don't know him," I added. "No one knows him."

"You've got to let Tony help you. Give me the address and—"

"Answer yes or no, Amanda. Is your phone tapped?"

"Uh . . ."

That was a yes. I had to move quickly. "Does Tony really believe I'm innocent."

"Yes," she said emphatically.

"And does he actually think he can clear things?"

That question was answered with silence.

"Okay," I said. "Tell Tony that if I haven't cleared things up myself by morning, I'll turn myself in to him."

There was some scrambling on the other end of the line, but by the time Tony said, "Please tell me where can I pick you up, Bonnie," I was already cradling the phone. For the time being I was best off working alone.

Leaving the coffee shop, I walked north on Broadway. Mid-afternoon, but it was growing darker. Nightfall was about an hour away. Where would I go then? With so little money in my wallet I couldn't even afford the kind of flea-bag hotel so beloved by detective novelists. Sam's house was out, too. Sam would welcome me, of course, but his next step, assuming the police weren't already watching his house, would be to call Tony. It's not in Sam's nature to harbor a fugitive. The same was true of my parents. As for Raymond and Noreen's place, get real!

There was someone else, though. The "old friend" I'd mentioned to Amanda hadn't been a total figment of my imagination. Mike was living nearby, and though I'd doubt-less mentioned him to Amanda once or twice, that had been a long time ago. She didn't know he was in New York. Mike's earlier phone messages, when he'd left his name and number, had been erased from my machine, which meant that the police would have no way of identifying the anonymous "me" who had left a message over the week-end.

I continued up Broadway until I reached Seventy-ninth Street, and then walked the two blocks to the Hudson riverfront.

The Seventy-ninth Street Boat Basin, which I have strolled past many times, is secured with a locked gate. I called Mike from a booth on the corner.

"It's Bonnie."

"Hey! Glad to hear your—"

"Want some company?"

If Mike said no, I planned to hang up and move on. Without access to a car, the most important thing on my "to do" list was going to take hours.

"Now?"

"I can be at the gate in five minutes."

"Sure. I hope you're not expecting anything too elegant, because—"

"Just meet me at the gate."

Mike's short and has a hint of a stomach. His face is more cute than handsome, and he often wears a hat of one kind or another to conceal the fact that his sandy-brown hair is thinning. When he unlocked the gate for me, a silly-looking tweed hat with a red feather tucked into its narrow brim covered his bald spot. I didn't remark upon that, as I normally might have, or even give my old friend a kiss on the cheek. I just wanted to get past the guard standing near a shelter just inside the gate. Why had I never noticed that the boat basin was guarded by a watchful human being? Probably because I'd never been on the run before.

Mike tipped his hat to the guard, a ruddy-faced man who gave a lazy salute in response. "Afternoon, Captain Mike."

"Afternoon, Bob. This is my friend Bonnie—"

I cut Mike off by grabbing his arm and marching him away from the guardhouse.

"Nice to see you, Bonnie," he said, ducking under my umbrella. "You're looking a little . . . rushed."

I was looking frantic and I knew it. "You said your boat's at the south end?"

The guest from hell, I released Mike's arm and took off down the walkway without waiting for his confirmation.

"Yeah. I'm on E dock," Mike responded, trotting to catch up. "There are five piers in all, and about eighty households. A lot of the boats are empty now. During the winter people go south. I'm by myself down at the end of E dock."

"Mm," I responded, and Mike, assuming that was a sign

of interest, told me more about the neighborhood as we headed for his floating home.

He explained how a series of steel ice barriers at the north end of the marina kept ice on the river from crushing the houseboats in the winter, and how the northernmost pier, Pier A, acted as a wave barrier of sorts.

"Of course," he added, "whenever a barge or freighter goes by, the waves eventually reach us. The boats bob around a bit more than usual, but then they settle down until the next time."

If you've seen houseboats only in magazines, or all shiny and new at boat shows, you might be surprised at the reality of what years on a river can do. What once was glossy paint peels, and massive fiberglass patches cover once pristine hulls. All the whites are either gray or yellow, and anything wood is warped into odd shapes. Near the boats' bottoms—that's the keel, Mike said—lines and bumpers are all covered with heavy marine growth.

Mike and I kept moving, passing every conceivable type and size of floating home. He pointed out white trellis shading some decks that would offer climbing room to plants in warmer weather. On some boats there were Colonial cornices, on others fake Greek columns. Almost all of them had weather vanes and TV antennas. "I hear that in the summer some people have vegetable gardens in window boxes," he told me.

Four-foot-wide walkways, made of two-by-sixes with one inch gaps in between the boards, connected the houseboats' moorings to the piers, and on each narrow walkway several white fiberglass boxes marked FIRE HOSE BOX had been installed to take care of smoking in bed gone awry.

Mike's description of his own temporary home had been right on target. The *Little Brown Jug* was mind-bogglingly ugly. Its brown metal front, which was pocked with rivets, curved like an old mobile home's, and both the side window and the door beside it were slightly askew, as if they had been installed by an amateur following instructions from a do-it-yourself kit. The narrow deck that surrounded the "house" part of this floating home on the Hudson was a hit-or-miss assortment of metal sheets and wood planks.

Mike jumped onto the boat and opened the door. "Welcome to paradise," he said. "I got some insulation the other day. It's not bad in here now except when the wind picks up."

I walked past him into the small space that served as living/dining/bedroom, and looked around.

Mike was right. It wasn't elegant. The narrow daybed was covered with a brown-and-yellow-plaid blanket that no respectable horse would have worn, and the small dining table's wood surface was scarred with overlapping fade rings. There was no Reginald Givens, though. It had that going for it.

Closing the door behind him, Mike offered me a cup of coffee.

"I've had more than enough coffee."

I'd thought that I was okay, that I was handling this awful mess pretty well. Unexpectedly, though, a feeling of complete futility devastated me. My situation was hopeless. There was nothing I could do about it. I'd only made things worse by running.

My back was to Mike. He didn't know that my eyes were brimming with tears until he touched my shoulder. A sob burst from me.

"Uh-oh," Mike said. "This must be serious. An affair of the heart?"

The phrase, so odd coming from Mike, and so wrong, almost cured my tears. I sputtered, "I wish," and within seconds regained control of myself. A few minutes later, sitting at that scarred table, I spilled out the basics of my problem.

Mike, no stranger to trouble with the law, nevertheless was left wide-eyed with astonishment. "Wow. This is serious. What do you plan to do? Head for the Caribbean? That worked for me for a while. I could put you in touch with a few people. There's an island off the coast of Venezuela—"

"That's not an option," I said. "At least not right now. What I want to do when I leave here is go to Queens. Way out in Queens near Kennedy Airport," I added.

He shrugged. "Caribbean, Queens—almost the same thing."

"There's a woman who lives in Howard Beach who might have information that would help me clear myself. It's going to take me forever to get there by subway, though, and I don't even know if a subway would get me near her house. What I actually need to do is borrow a car. And," I added, feeling like a beggar, "I'd like to know that I have a place to spend—"

Mike interrupted. "So you didn't really kill the guy?"

"No way! I'm not even really a fugitive yet," I added defensively. "So far I'm just evading arrest."

"Take it easy," Mike said. "I was kidding."

"I'd just like to be sure that I have a place to stay tonight if I'm desperate. I'm not the *sleeping out* type. I don't have any money, and I was hoping you might have some floor space."

Pushing back his chair, Mike rose. "I wouldn't mind you using my car, and staying here. Ordinarily I'd welcome it," he said, pacing the short span between the table and the bed, "but I've got a date tonight, and besides that, well . . ."

He turned and faced me, and seeing the reluctance that showed on his face, I realized I'd made a mistake. Mike didn't feel any loyalty to me, and with good reason. We'd had a short-term romance, and after that we'd talked on the phone once or twice, but he didn't owe me a thing.

"The problem is," he continued, "I've just gotten myself out of one bunch of trouble. I don't want to risk getting into another. I know that you're innocent," he added, "but I'm still on probation. Aiding and abetting is a crime."

"I shouldn't have tried to involve you. That's what comes from muddled thinking." Rising, I moved to the door.

"Please don't go off angry at me, Bonnie. Try to understand. I *can* give you some money. I'd have to get to a cash machine, but . . .''

He might go out and call the police and turn you in, a voice at the back of my mind whispered. It was a crazy, baseless thought, but for a few seconds my stomach churned with anxiety and I wanted desperately to get away.

As I grabbed the doorknob, I shook my head. "I'm too distraught to be angry." To prove I meant it, I closed the door softly behind me as I left.

I made my way up the dock, so profoundly disheartened that I was scarcely aware of my surroundings. The reality was I had been depending on Mike. I'm not a solitary type. Sure I live alone, but for me it's good to have people around most of the time. When times are bad—and they don't get much worse than the time I was having—I might play hermit for a while, but the hermit's life doesn't suit me for very long. I want someone reasonably sensible to share things with. I want this person either to validate my ideas or to say flat out, *You're nuts. What you've got to do is* . . . and then convince me.

Once on solid ground—not emotionally but physically; I'd reached Riverside Drive—I headed back in the direction of the IRT station, mentally running through my "to do" list as I walked. It hadn't changed significantly since the last time I'd run through it. I still had to find Victoria Cerutti, get her to tell me what was going on between her and Tom Hurley, and from what she said, try to piece together enough evidence to shift the blame for Dorfmeyer's murder onto Tom. The only difference now was that I had to do it by subway.

"Yo! Myrtle!"

The shout from a passing car was loud enough to shock me out of my musing. On the other side of West End Avenue in front of a florist shop, a dinged-up white Ford pulled partly into a loading zone. The driver lowered his window far enough to stick his head out. He was wearing a black watch cap pulled low over his ears and preposterously dark glasses when you consider that daylight was almost completely gone.

"Myrtle! Want a ride?"

An elderly couple who had been walking a few feet ahead of me rounded the corner and disappeared. I glanced behind me. About twenty feet back a man stood under an awning trying to flag a cab. That was it for company on the sidewalk.

The man in the white Ford was looking directly at me. Did he think I was someone else? Lowering the window farther, he stuck his arm out and gestured with it.

I took a step forward, then stopped. The man slipped off the glasses. "Come on, Myrtle. I can't wait all day."

It was Mike. As I hurried across the street, my eyes were caught by a turquoise sticker on the car's rear bumper. I'D RATHER BE ON MY BOAT.

I climbed into the passenger seat, uncertain whether I should be grateful or anxious. "What's with this 'Myrtle' stuff?"

Mike slipped the dark glasses back onto his nose. "You can't expect me to be shouting 'Hey, Bonnie' in the middle of the street with the cops looking for you. Myrtle seemed about right."

"Thanks. It's always been a favorite name of mine. You changed your mind?"

He nodded. "A couple of friends helped me when I was on the run, but one or two others turned me down. They had good reasons for refusing, but regardless, I'm not friends with them anymore. I want to stay friends with you."

"I'm glad to hear that."

"This isn't a permanent solution," Mike added. "I'll help you out this afternoon, and you can stay at my place tonight, but one way or another it's got to be settled by tomorrow."

"What about your date tonight?"

"She's an investment banker. I don't think my place would impress her. And if things get to the point where we're looking for some privacy, which they probably won't, we'll go to her place.''

"Thank you," I said. "If I haven't cleared things up by tomorrow morning, I'll turn myself in and never mention your name.''

I settled into the worn seat. The car smelled like mold and fish. The windows were dirty and the floor littered with old newspapers. The heater was starting to warm the interior though and for now I had a companion. Things were looking up.

"Just don't do anything to get us into trouble," Mike said. "If you do, I'm going to claim that you took me hostage. And listen, if there's a reward and it looks like you're going to go down, we might work things out so that I end up collecting. I'll be glad to invest your half for you while you serve your time.''

Mike was grinning broadly, but I wasn't sure he was kidding.

15

HOWARD BEACH ISN'T FAR FROM KEN-
nedy Airport, and airport-bound traffic on
the Southern Parkway was heavy. Mike
drove carefully, doing nothing to distin-
guish the battered Ford from the clot of
other vehicles moving through the light
rain. At an especially slow point, he
glanced at me.

"Ignoring the fact that this Victoria
woman might not be willing to talk to
you, what makes you think she's going to
have anything to tell you that's relevant
to your . . . difficulties?"

I'd given Mike a sketch of my suspicions about Tom
Hurley and Victoria Cerutti. After the roar of a departing
jet had faded, I went into more detail.

"Victoria has called Tom at work two times that I know
of. He hasn't liked it. What does that say to you?"

"It could say a lot of things. It could say that she wants
her old job back. It could say that she's harassing Hurley

for the pure hell of it because he took the job she thought she deserved."

"It could," I agreed, "but then why would he be so secretive about her calls? Tom's good at his job, and he puts everything in writing. If Victoria was calling him for a reason that had anything to do with business, he would have put a note in her file."

"So you think what's going on might be—"

I completed Mike's sentence using his earlier words: "An affair of the heart. Everything points that way," I continued. "Victoria planned to stay at her job, but then quit abruptly. She'd talked about bringing a lawsuit, but it never happened. And now she's working in her cousin's bowling alley."

"It could be she decided twelve years at any job is enough. Maybe she decided that a lawsuit is too much trouble. Maybe . . ." Mike lifted his shoulders. "Maybe Victoria decided to get a life that didn't involve corporate America."

"Then she wouldn't have been calling Tom. Think about this. Victoria's a plain-looking single woman in her thirties who's been taking care of aging parents. She runs into an attractive, urbane man on the loose." My voice had grown in fervor until I sounded like some hyped-up attorney pleading a shabby case.

"And this attractive urbane man is swept away by her many charms," said Mike, calmly playing the devil's advocate.

"I'm getting to that," I said. "Tom's wife is very attractive. From what my brother told me, his high-school girlfriends were the prettiest girls in the class, and his college girlfriend made the Miss New Jersey finals."

Mike's face lit with mischief. "There's a sure sign of beauty. Was she Miss Discount Outlet or Miss Truckstop?"

I was too involved in defending my case to concern myself with defending New Jersey's undeserved bad reputation. "What I'm suggesting is that Tom Hurley wouldn't have had anything to do with Victoria Cerutti unless he had to.''

''Assuming he did have something to do with her, Bonnie, which we don't know for certain.''

Mike hadn't seen Tom's expression when I'd interrupted his phone conversation with Victoria, and he hadn't heard the eagerness in Victoria's voice when she'd thought Tom was calling her back. I had, and though there are a lot of things in this world I don't know, I do know something about *affairs of the heart.*

''I know for certain,'' I insisted.

''Okay,'' Mike said, giving in on that point. ''Assume you're right. The two of them got involved for whatever reason. Then he dumped her. So what? Victoria might have lost her head with this creep, but what makes you so sure she's going to spill her unhappy guts to you?''

''Because she's known to be supportive of other women, and Tom Hurley is hurting a whole bunch of us.''

''Ah,'' said Mike. ''The sisterhood is beautiful, and it's a sure thing. But...'' He looked at me across the front seat, his expression unusually serious. ''If you don't get anything out of Victoria, you *will* call your friend Tony in the morning. You can't keep running,'' he added, driving in his point. ''I speak from experience.''

For a guy who had had his own problems with the law, Mike was sure turning out to be a police booster.

''That's my plan,'' I said.

Turning away, I stared out at the flat landscape of southern Queens.

Howard Beach is set apart from other Queens neighborhoods by tidal basins on two sides and Jamaica Bay on the south. It struck me as an anomaly among New York City neighborhoods, which generally flow one into another and where you have to crane your neck to see house tops. Here most of the buildings were low, and merely by shifting my eyes, I could see an endless stretch of stormy gray sky.

A shopping district was located along a wide main thoroughfare. In addition to the usual dry cleaner and pizza parlor, there was a fish restaurant complete with a neon jolly angler in hip boots hauling in his catch over the front door. Next to that, lo and behold, was Manny's Bowling Alley.

"You think that's the one?" Mike asked as we drove past.

"How many could there be?"

He responded defensively. "Hey! Nothing wrong with bowling. I'm a tenpin man myself, but duckpins will do in a pinch. What's your preference?"

"The little ones, but bowling's not my game."

"What is?"

I shook my head. "I'm not sure, but it's not bowling."

From the sound of Mike's sigh, you would have thought that I'd pierced his fondest hope.

Using the street map as a guide, we turned onto one of the residential streets that branch off the main drag. I'm not certain why, but the block-after-block-after-block of smallish houses with smallish yards we passed surprised me. I'd seen similar developments, of course, but I hadn't seen them in New York City. As we traversed the wide orderly streets, I felt almost as if we had driven into alien territory. Come to think of it, that's the same way I feel approaching Raymond and Noreen's place.

The Ceruttis' block was a long stretch of white houses, separated from each other by driveways. Almost without exception, each tiny front lawn was surrounded by a chain-link fence.

I peered at house numbers through the rain-dotted window as Mike drove slowly along.

"There it is," I said finally.

"Sure is," responded Mike.

The Ceruttis' house stood out from its immediate neighbors in one distinct way. Under the front bay window, tucked into a neatly tended garden and lit by a spotlight that shone through the darkening evening, was a statue of the Madonna and Child.

It wasn't the only religious statue that I'd noticed in the last few minutes, but it was the biggest and the brightest, too. The folds of the Virgin's sky-blue gown had an iridescent sheen. So, for that matter did her complexion, which in color wasn't all that far from the lipstick my friends and I wore in the tenth grade. Kiss Me Pink.

"You may be wrong about the *affair of the heart*," Mike said, his eyes on the Madonna's flushed and glowing face.

As I stared at the statue gleaming under the spotlight's yellow radiance, my confidence, which hadn't been all that strong to begin with, wilted.

Mike pulled to the curb—the dozens of empty parking spots added to the foreign feel of the neighborhood—and after giving him a nervous look, and seeing his reassuring nod, I got out of the car.

With every step I took up the sidewalk toward the house, I grew more unsure of myself. When I climbed the three steps to the front stoop, my eyes were drawn to the Madonna's face. Her placid pink smile was frozen into place, but I could have sworn her eyes followed me. This was giving me the willies. By the time I pressed the doorbell and heard the chime from inside the house, I was on the verge of turning, running back to the car, and telling Mike that on further consideration an island off Venezuela's coast sounded damned good.

When the bell stopped chiming the house seemed deathly quiet. After a moment I heard a shuffling noise from inside and then the scraping sound of something being pulled across the floor. After all this came a click, indicating that a tiny peephole in the door had opened.

There was a heavy screen door between me and the peephole. I couldn't see a thing, not even the flicker of an eye. Still, I knew someone was looking at me.

"Yes?"

I honest to God couldn't tell if the voice belonged to a man or a woman. All I would have bet was it belonged to someone very old and, judging from what I detected as a second syllable on the word—"yes-a"—foreign-born. Stretching on my toes to put my face level with the peephole, I said, "I'd like to speak with Victoria Cerutti. Is she at home?"   .

Well-intentioned strangers don't pay unannounced house calls in New York City. It just doesn't happen. Push-in robbers, con men—they pay unexpected house calls. As I might have expected, the person on the other side of the door was skeptical.

"Whose'a callin'?"

The voice belonged to a woman. Hoping she might be as susceptible to charm as I was certain Victoria Cerutti had been, I smiled cheerfully.

"I'm a friend of Tom Hurley's."

"Who?"

"Tom Hurley," I said more loudly.

The peephole clicked shut. The shuffling and scraping on the other side of the door resumed. Glancing up at the second-story window, I saw a curtain move. That made me even more uncomfortable. For all I knew the mention of Tom Hurley's name could earn me a bucket of scalding water on my head.

Without warning, the inside door opened, revealing a dimly lit hall. The screen stayed firmly in place, but some of the hottest air I'd felt in days gushed through it. It was so warm I turned my head away. When I looked back, an elderly woman had moved so close to the screen that her nose almost pressed into it.

"No need to yell. Victoria don't have nothing to do with that man." Turning her face to the side, she said the name Tom Hurley with such vehemence that it could have been the most vile curse imaginable.

In spite of the broiler-level temperature inside, the old woman had a wool throw bundled around her shoulders. She may at one time have been of medium height, but the years had bowed her to the point where she had to roll her eyes to the top of their sockets to look straight ahead. Her head seemed strangely oversized, but that probably was because her body had shrunken. By her feet was the wooden stepstool she'd used to raise herself to the level of the peephole.

I bent my knees to bring myself closer to the woman's face. "Is she at home? I'd like to ask her about that myself."

"Vicky's at work," she responded. "Anyway, she don't need to talk to nobody. Everything's taken care of. She went to see the priest."

It wasn't elation that I felt hearing that, or even vindication. It was a profound sadness. For Victoria, for Elizabeth, for myself. All the women who had thought Tom was so terrific. And perhaps also for Louise, who had thought she could cut a deal.

"Thank you," I said to the old woman.

I hurried down the sidewalk and into the car.

"So?" asked Mike. "Did they lay out the welcome mat?"

"Let's go to the bowling alley. I'm not only right about Victoria and Tom. I may be . . . extra right!"

"Extra right?" Tilting his head, Mike stared at me. "You think they're getting married?"

"Fat chance."

"Then what—?"

"Louise said that Victoria's gained weight. Her mom just told me she went to see the priest," I said. "Think about that."

"Hmm." Mike pulled into the street. "I hope this Manny at the bowling alley's not one of those musclebound guys who hits first and asks questions later."

It had to be Victoria behind the dark wooden counter of a bar-concession stand. As Mike examined a list of prices posted near the shoe-rental booth, I watched her from the corner of my eye.

She was draining ketchup from big containers into those little red squeeze bottles that always feel greasy. When she finished with one, she would wipe it clean of drips and place it on the counter next to a yellow squeeze bottle and a pair of salt-and-pepper shakers. As she did this she remained blank-eyed, but then it wasn't exactly a managerial-type task, and since all the stools in front of the counter were empty, she didn't have to fake an interest in anything.

With the help of Louise, Casey, and that anonymous HR type who'd first interviewed Victoria for R&G, I'd fashioned an awful-looking creature with a mop of unruly hair. The reality wasn't nearly so startling. Victoria's hair was on the "big" side, and her features were neither delicate nor patrician, but she looked perfectly all right by most reasonable standards.

Tom Hurley's standards, though, weren't reasonable. The road from a Miss New Jersey contestant to a woman with big hair and a sallow complexion is a long one, and not one Tom would have traveled unless circumstances demanded it.

"So? Are we going to play a game?" Mike asked. "There's a free lane."

There were several of them. For all I know, bowling enthusiasts may be thick on the ground, but on that particular Sunday afternoon in that particular bowling alley, fewer than a dozen of them were in evidence.

The few alleys in use were at the other end of the building, away from the concession stand. The mostly female players appeared to belong to a league. Yellow shirts versus red shirts. I actually felt a familiar tug. The rumbling balls, the tumbling pins, the shouts and groans that invariably followed briefly transported me back to a time when my father had belonged to a league. I don't recall exactly how old I was, but as kids, Raymond and I had loved going to the games. I recalled how grown up I'd felt the first time I stretched my fingers into those holes and tossed the ball down an alley. It went into the gutter, but everyone clapped anyway. Life should always be so easy.

Looking at the concession stand, I shook my head. "You can play a game by yourself. I've got business."

"I can't play a game by myself," Mike countered.

"Then practice."

"For what? Maybe I should wait in the car in case we have to make a quick getaway."

Leaving him to his own devices, I went to the concession stand and hoisted myself onto one of the stools. From there I could see Victoria below the waist. The tunic top she wore fell loosely to well below her hips. It almost, but not quite, concealed her middle. In front there was a definite bulge, and to me it looked a little high up for your run-of-the-mill belly fat.

Glancing at me, she raised a dark eyebrow in question. I shifted my eyes to a menu posted on the wall and tried to piece together a strategy. *Hi. Your unborn baby's father is a murderer* . . . That was an attention-grabbing introduction. *Hi. I'm running from the police because I've been set up* . . . They say the truth will set you free, but if Victoria was even marginally intelligent, her reaction to that would be to pick up the phone and dial 911. The reality was, no matter how I approached her, this thing could play out very badly for me.

Still uncertain about how to begin, I looked at her across the counter. "Victoria? Can I get a black coffee?"

"Sure. Have we met?"

"No," I said. "When's your baby due?"

This nervy question was met first by stunned silence, and then by a response that stunned me. Growing pale, Victoria backed as far from me as the narrow space behind the counter would allow.

"You've got to be Elizabeth," she said softly. "I can't believe Tom told you about me. Oh my God!"

Oh my God was right! Victoria had handed me a role I hadn't rehearsed. My mind immediately was pounded by a hailstorm of ideas. I could play the pitiful scorned woman. Or the vengeful one. Yes! Take the offensive. Call her a home wrecker. Threaten . . .

The truth is, I never was much of an actress. A few seconds of considering these over-the-top possibilities and my frazzled nerves were already worse. Stage fright is a fearsome thing, and not something I was willing to risk. On the other hand, here was the opening I'd needed.

"I just want to talk, Victoria," I said. "You're not to blame for what happened. Tom is what he is. We've both learned that."

For a moment she seemed confused. One of her heavy black eyebrows lifted. "So you and Tom aren't together anymore? I didn't know whether or not to believe him."

"No," I said. "We're not together. For my own peace of mind, though, I'd like to know how things happened."

She was a proper penitent, beginning with tears and apologies, and I was a proper sad-but-wiser injured party. In some way I think she actually got some pleasure out of it. By *it* I don't mean her brief affair with Tom—although that had doubtless given her fleeting pleasure—but our meeting. Her contrition might have a cleansing effect, at least for a short time.

Did I experience any guilt during this scene, which was played out on a curved red leatherette bench at the end of one of the empty alleys? Yes. I'm not much better at manipulation than I am at being a fugitive. Perhaps my view that Victoria got something out of it is mere self-justification, but like Tom Hurley, I did what the situation demanded of me.

"Everyone who interviewed him was impressed," Victoria said about Tom. "When it came time to check his references, his previous employer was out of business. You know that, of course," she added, "but Tom had given us the names of the company's former CEO and also of a vice-president. They had fabulous things to say about your husband."

"I can imagine," I said, not adding that Tom might have gotten friends to play those particular roles.

Victoria went on. "We also wrote to Tom's college and graduate school, but it takes schools forever to get back to you and R&G hired him without waiting for their responses.

"At first I resented Tom so much that I considered bringing a discrimination suit against the company. Tom knew about that—Louise never could keep her mouth shut—but he was very nice to me anyway."

"You heard that Louise is dead?"

She pushed a stray lock of hair off her face. "Yes," she said sadly. "A mutual friend from R&G called me. What an awful accident. I understand Louise had taken a knockout dose of drugs before she fell. She always tended to overdo that kind of thing."

"Mm-hmm," I responded. "Anyway, you were talking about how nice Tom was."

"Oh, yes. Tom was so nice that after a while I started thinking that it wouldn't be bad working for him. He was a lot easier to get along with than our former boss."

"Tom can be a very charming man."

Flushing, Victoria shifted her gaze away from mine. "Anyhow, a few weeks after he started, I got a letter from the University of Pennsylvania. It said that Tom never graduated, so I called Cornell to double-check on his master's degree. They'd never heard of Tom at all."

She'd been staring at the pins at the end of the alley, but she turned abruptly to look at me. Again there was that questioning tilt at the end of one dark eyebrow.

"Tom's a world-class liar."

"Tell me about it!" she said, her voice cutting through the crash of falling tenpins. "Anyway, by that time I kind of liked him. Not the way you're thinking," she added hastily, "but I didn't want to see him out in the street. He was so nice to me. Almost . . . flirting. I can't explain it . . ."

"You don't have to."

"But I couldn't ignore the school thing, either. I told Tom there was something we should discuss, but not in the office. So he suggested we meet after work at a bar in his hotel. I don't usually drink much but—"she grimaced, perhaps at the thought of the drinks, or perhaps at the thought of what had followed—"you know how it is."

"Oh yes," I said sympathetically.

One thing had led to another. Over the first drink in that dim little bar, Victoria had told Tom what she discovered. He, in turn, had defended himself by explaining how desperately he'd needed the job at R&G. Poor man. He'd been pushed to the financial edge by his soon-to-be-ex-wife's—my!—out-of-control spending.

Over the second drink, Victoria had been sympathetic and Tom contrite. Over the third drink, he'd told her how lonely he was, and had also said that the way the little candle on the table flickered in her eyes was mesmerizing. You can guess how the rest of the evening had gone.

The affair had continued for several weeks, until Victoria discovered that she was in an unfortunate *predicament,* as she called it. Tom, informed of this predicament, had not reacted the way Victoria had hoped. Nothing was said about love, much less marriage.

"Tom told me that the two of you had had some problems, but that you were getting back together. He said he'd pay for an abortion." Eyes clouding with tears, Victoria added, "There was no way I could do that."

"How awful for you," I said.

"It was devastating. I quit my job, of course. I couldn't possibly stay there. The humiliation would have been unbearable. At first I thought there was a chance Tom would leave you," she continued. "I kept calling him, but he always brushed me off. Finally I faced reality. Tom didn't want me. He never had. He'd just tried to get me into a situation where I'd keep my mouth shut."

"He couldn't have known you were going to get pregnant," I said.

"No, but Tom must have figured that I'd be less likely to tell any tales if I'd been sleeping with him. And he probably was right. If I hadn't gotten pregnant, maybe he would have been able to end things more . . . gently. Or maybe our relationship would just have fizzled out. Either way, I probably would have been too embarrassed to say anything about his college record. The way things happened, though, I was so hurt and so angry that . . .''

Victoria had called Carl Dorfmeyer and told him what she had discovered about Tom's falsified school record. She wasn't sure what had happened next, and neither was I, but if I were Carl Dorfmeyer, I would have pulled Tom's file. If he had, that would explain why Tom's file had been missing the first time I'd looked for it. It would also explain why Tom had become so agitated that afternoon in the records room when he'd gotten Dorfmeyer's call.

Victoria went on to tell me that after exposing Tom's lie to Dorfmeyer, she felt a touch of shame. ''That's when I went to talk to our priest. And then, finally, I told my parents about my *predicament*.'' She glanced at her stomach, then lifted her shoulders in a way that suggested a lightened spirit. ''Now I'm getting on with my life. Everything's going to be fine.''

Staring up the bowling alley, I asked offhandedly, ''Victoria? Did you ever think that Tom might have killed Carl Dorfmeyer?''

Her response was quick and emphatic. ''No! Tom has his faults, but I could never be involved with someone who would murder another human being. My judgment isn't that bad. And neither is yours, Elizabeth.'' Leaning closer, she put her hand over mine. ''If that's been bothering you, put your mind at rest.''

A nice sentiment, but my mind wasn't going to rest until Tom Hurley was behind bars and I was cleared.

16

THE HOUSEBOAT SWAYED CONTINU-
ously, and the thumping of its bumpers
into the wood pilings was ceaseless.
Above my head light rain pattered on the
fiberglass roof. A freighter going up the
river in the night sounded its horn. Its
low, powerful noise shuddered the sides
of the boat, echoed off the New Jersey
Palisades for a moment, then stopped.

Trying to think of a way to prove Tom
guilty had proved fruitless, and my
thoughts had turned briefly to the direc-
tion of "escape to an island." How bad would life be as a
fugitive? Lonely, scary, broke, and basically crummy. Still,
if I looked on the bright side, there wouldn't be any more
dinners at Raymond and Noreen's house.

It wasn't going to happen, though. In my soul I knew
that. I'm not good fugitive material.

The alternative, which I would face in the morning, was
a call to Tony from a phone booth somewhere far from

Mike's houseboat. Tony would arrive soon after I made that call, and after that I might get to strut my stuff doing the infamous *perp walk*. How would I feel, climbing the precinct steps in handcuffs with photographers shouting and shoving cameras at me? "Hey, Bonnie, say hello to your mother." *Flash*. They get the picture. You go to a holding cell.

And then would come the trial. Me and some bargain-basement lawyer against the DA and Givens the Exterminator. I wouldn't have a chance. Mom would pray for my soul when I went to prison, lighting candles and weeping. She and Dad would visit every weekend, at least for a while, and so would Raymond. Noreen would keep her distance, and maybe even take back her maiden name.

And what if I got the death penalty? During an especially bleak moment, I wondered how it felt when you'd had your last supper and they strapped you into that electric chair.

I'd never really thought much about dying, but when I had . . .

One of my favorite stories is one I heard about an elderly, wealthy bon vivant. She was having a wonderful dinner with her friends, and had just finished the main course when she suddenly felt ill. Fighting off her illness, she grappled for the dinner bell. The maid, who had been standing attentively at the edge of the dining room, rushed to her side. "Madam? What can I do for you" she asked. "I think I'm dying," the elderly woman replied. "Please hurry up with the dessert." Sure enough the woman died that night, but not until after dessert. To me that sounds like the ideal way to go.

The foghorn sounded again. Pulling a curtain aside, I peeked out the window at the blackness of the river. The combination of rain and fog was so thick the freighter was invisible but for its lights, which looked like fuzzy yellow blobs. Letting my imagination run wild, I pictured a sea monster with yellow reptilian eyes, quietly swimming around in the foggy night looking for prey.

I let the curtain fall back into place. There was nothing but cold, wet, muffled darkness out there.

The room was lit by a single shaded lamp. In addition to the tiny kitchenette, where a hefty Swiss army knife served as knife, bottle opener, and corkscrew, there was a tiny bathroom with a shower hose. A *bathette,* perhaps. Mike had explained that the small oil furnace tucked into a corner was supplied from a barge that made the monthly rounds, and that electricity supplied to a utility cable plugged into an outlet on the dock powered the stove and dehumidifier. The phone lines came through that same cable. All the comforts of home.

My nutritious, well-balanced, career-girl-on-the-go dinner had consisted of a Cup•A•Soup, two turkey hot dogs with ketchup (the vegetable!), half a dozen Oreo cookies, and a soda. Not as good as that elderly gourmet's, but better than nothing. After dinner I'd showered, washed my underwear in the tiny sink, and then inventoried the houseboat. My best *finds* were a portable Walkman-type cassette player, a clean set of long underwear, and wool socks—not stylish but so warm. R&G's basement felt like the Sahara compared with this place, and I had to slip Tony's jacket on over the long underwear before I felt cozy.

Mike's tapes, including some blanks, were lined up neatly on the bookshelf. I picked out the Rolling Stones' *Some Girls,* put it in and pressed play. ''Miss You'' bounced into the headphones. I settled into the daybed and listened to Mick go on about walking in Central Park after dark, and people thinking he was crazy.

I could identify.

When the tape was finished, I popped it out and returned it to the shelf. I was about to put the tape recorder aside when a weird idea hit me. Unwrapping one of the blank tapes, I put it in the recorder and pressed play and record.

''Testing one two three, this is Bonnie Indermill on the run.'' I rewound the tape and listened to my voice. Sounded authentically gritty. Some wiseass news commentator had recently quipped that these days the first thing following a felony trial was a book tour. I wasn't sure I had the makings of a ''tell-all'' in me, but if by some fluke I wasn't found guilty, I was going to have to earn a living. Even Adele at Pro-Team Temps has some standards. She wouldn't touch me after a murder trial.

I dictated a few protestations of innocence into the recorder before clicking the thing off and slipping it into the jacket's pocket. It was about ten o'clock, and I had begun to feel as if I might actually be able to sleep. After brushing my teeth with Mike's toothbrush, I crawled under the brown plaid coverlet and blanket, jacket and all, and switched off the lamp. The last sounds I heard before falling asleep were the rain pattering on the roof and the houseboat pounding into the pilings.

In my dream I was at work in R&G's records room when the wall phone started ringing. I picked it up, but there was no one on the line. The phone kept ringing. Someone told me I'd broken it. ''You could be fired for that,'' Tom's voice said. The phone's hand piece had disappeared. I was trying to find it when I woke abruptly.

The phone in the boat was ringing.

The cabin was almost pitch-black. Leaping up, I felt my way to the bookcase and grabbed the receiver. Whoever was on the other end may have hung up, but there was no dial tone. Could it be Mike trying to reach—

A tap on the cabin's door.

''Bonnie.''

A whispered voice from outside the cabin.

''Bonnie Indermill. It's me. Tom. Open up.''

He knocked harder. The phone was still in my hand, but I realized with a chill that it was dead.

''Bonnie, please. I've got to talk to you. It's cold and raining out here. Please let me in.''

Wide-awake now, I quietly moved away from the door until I stood next to the sink. There were two windows on the other side of the cabin. I could open one and sneak out, and possibly jump onto the deserted boat next door and hide until he left. I pulled my loafers from under the bed and was struggling to get them on over the wool socks when the doorknob rattled.

"Bonnie, I know you're in there."

The knob rattled again, louder. "The guard told me that your friend went out. Looks like your neighbors are away, too. You might as well let me in. Otherwise . . ."

Thump. The floor vibrated as he kicked the door.

"Bonnie. You know we have things to discuss. The cops questioned me today. I got the idea that you told one of them you know who the murderer is. Let's talk about this like the civilized people we are."

Something in me went dead calm. Tom had killed at least once and perhaps twice. He wouldn't hesitate to add me to his list of victims. Running my hand along the counter, I found the Swiss army knife and pulled open its serrated blade.

Holding tight to the knife, I tiptoed across the swaying floor and braced against a window. As I tried to raise it, the door crashed open, letting a gray light into the room.

Tom charged straight at me. Unprepared, unable to aim my blow, I stabbed down at his side as he reached to grab me. I felt the knife strike and released it. Tom clutched at the top of his leg through his trench coat. Spinning sideways, I kicked him as hard as I could manage with a crepe-soled loafer. He grunted and went down hard. As I ran out into the night, I heard him say, "You've really trapped yourself, Bonnie. Nobody's going to believe you now."

The night was filled with noise, but I moved carefully and quietly on the wood planks. Crossing the walkway, I climbed onto the deserted boat's shadowy deck. At the stern, beside a big coil of rope, a partly inflated blue plastic float with a mesh center leaned against a rotting deck chair. An empty soda can nearby clacked rhythmically against the houseboat's wall. Pulling the float to the wall, I crawled in behind it and stepped against the can to keep it from rolling.

The fog stood thick and damp. Peering through the mesh, I watched it silently hanging in the yellow glow of the shore lights. The rain continued falling, droplets making tiny circles as they hit the water's surface.

The cold rain had started soaking through the jacket and dripping into my shoes. I adjusted the blue float and crouched lower, quaking with cold and fear. Were those footsteps I heard, or waves slapping on wood? I swung my eyes around the corner. Lights shone from inside a boat a few slips away. Even in the winter there were lots of people living in the marina. Did I dare cry out for help? If I did, would I be heard with water slapping into boats, lines creaking, and bulkheads clanging?

I remained quiet. Tom, the accomplished liar, would have too good a story. He'd somehow figured out where I was. A good friend, he'd come out here to talk some sense into me. And I'd stabbed him, proving just how homicidal a maniac I was.

Tom was right. I was trapped now.

I sat still, at first shivering with the cold, but then growing oddly warm. I recall thinking that if I sat here long enough, hunched inside the damp jacket, I'd feel better. There was no reason to move. He wouldn't find me here.

"Bonnie."

A whisper.

Tom was on the move. I held my breath and listened.

Suddenly I saw him through my blue mesh shield. He was a dark, hunched shape on the walkway at the deserted boat's side.

"Bonnie. I know you're here. Come on out. It's okay. I won't hurt you."

I had to get away. Head for the opposite side of the boat and run for it. I started to move out from behind the float, but a wave of frigid cold swept over me. I started shaking violently. Hypothermia. If I didn't get somewhere warm in a hurry I'd pass out.

Frantic, I looked for a way to divert Tom. The recorder in my pocket poked into my hip, but it was too valuable to use as a projectile. Noiselessly moving the float aside, I grabbed the soda can and flung it hard. It clattered onto the finger pier just behind Tom. He turned away from me.

"Bonnie. You can't imagine how sorry I am."

Tom limped as he took a step, dragging his injured leg. One of his leather-soled shoes skidded across the rain-slick surface. I took the recorder from my pocket and flipped on the record button.

"I didn't realize that you'd be blamed for shooting Dorfmeyer. I planned things so that Casey would be blamed. We can still work things out, though. We're smart people. We'll put our heads together and brainstorm. There's sure to be a way to get us both out of this."

Returning the recorder to my pocket, I snuck from my hiding place, crept from the boat, and followed Tom down the walkway. He stepped onto the finger pier slowly and deliberately, and clutched at one of the pilings for support. When he took another step forward, he stumbled. Collapsing, Tom rolled onto his side near one of the white firehose boxes. Through the falling rain I saw him grasp his leg. His breaths were deep and rasping.

Uncertain how much the tape had picked up, fearing it wasn't enough, I drew nearer. Tom's chest was heaving and his eyes were closed. Thinking he might be near death and that I might miss a confession that would save me, I took a step that brought me almost to his feet.

His eyes opened, startling me. When he rose on an elbow, a smile played at his lips. "On the other hand, maybe you're not as smart as I thought."

I started backing away, but Tom shifted his good leg into my foot. Thrown off balance, I fell against the fire-hose box. My knuckles scraped over the rough hose. Desperate for a weapon, I grabbed the hose, pulled it from the box, and twisted the faucet. The fierce stream of water made the hose jump. I hung on, tucking the lurching tube under my arm. With my free hand I dug the recorder from my pocket.

Tom was almost on his feet when I gave him the first icy blast of water.

"So you admit you killed Dorfmeyer," I said.

The stream of water hit Tom in the chest and forced him

to the edge of the dock. His bad leg slipped below the barrier chain. I trained the spray away from him and into the water.

"There was no other way, Bonnie. He'd found something on my résumé that wasn't accurate. It was no big deal, but Dorfmeyer was going to fire me anyway, even though I was doing a good job. I had no choice. I have a family to support," he added, struggling to pull his bad leg onto the pier.

"And you tried to frame Casey?"

"Casey's worthless," he said. "The fool set himself up, showing everyone that gun."

"Then why plant my scarf on Dorfmeyer's body?"

"I found it behind Casey's door. I didn't know it was yours."

Tom had pulled his leg back onto the pier and risen into a crouch. I was about five feet away from him when he lunged. Aiming the hose, I sprayed him full in the face. He was still full of fight. After faltering briefly, he leaped at me again. I dodged him and hammered his head with the hose's brass nozzle as he tumbled past.

Tom fell into the water between the boats. Surfacing within seconds, he splashed wildly, struggling for air as he fought for a handhold on the walkway's slippery planks. I turned the hose away and went after him. Where was that security guard, anyway?

"How did you find me?" I asked.

He spat out a mouthful of water. "Come on, Bonnie. You've got to let me out. I'll die in this water."

I trained the hose inches away from where his hand clutched at the planks.

"When the police questioned me today, one of them said that you were staying with an old friend nobody knew about. I remembered that address you'd written on the EEOC poster. Your old friend who'd been out of the country. Figured I'd give it a shot."

Furious, I gave him a shot in the face with the spray. "How did you get in here?"

"Bribed the guard," he gasped.

"Oh no he didn't!"

A man's voice came from behind me.

"He said he was your husband. Suspected you of fooling around, but I didn't trust the slick bastard. When I went to call Mike's boat, though, the line was dead."

All at once lights were everywhere and the ruddy-faced guard was taking the hose from my hand. Before I realized what was happening, three burly cops stepped past me and hauled Tom out of the water while a fourth handed me a blanket.

"I like your interrogation technique there," the cop near me said. "Where'd you learn how to do that?"

I pulled the blanket around my shoulders. "Dale Carnegie."

The cop bent to look at something on the pier. I followed his gaze, and saw the cable that supplied electricity and phone service to Mike's boat. The plug had been pulled free of the outlet, and lay in a puddle of water.

"Dale Carnegie? Well, whatever works," the cop said as he straightened. "C'mon. Let's get you dried off before you catch your death out here."

Just before I burst into tears, I turned off the recorder and put it in my pocket.

EPILOGUE

I WAS ARRESTED ANYWAY. THIS IS NEW York. You can't run away from the cops, even if they subsequently hear someone else confess. Everything has to be official.

Mike, who showed up as I was being escorted into a police car, called the lawyer who had cut a deal for him. When that lawyer heard the tape, he went ballistic and sent a copy to a reporter at *The New York Record*. The entire transcript appeared in the *Record* the next morning, and after that the police bent over backward to make life nice for me until I was officially cleared.

Amanda got to the precinct where I'd been held before I had to appear before a judge, and brought me a change of clothes from my apartment. Emily was with her. The kid will never remember that she visited her godmother in jail, but it is kind of a hoot, isn't it?

I was released before noon that day. A boisterous crowd

of photographers greeted me when I walked out the court-house door.

"Bonn-ie! Bonn-ie! Hey, Bonnie! Look this way. Bonnie! You're beautiful. Let's have a picture for the mayor."

There was a call from the mayor that afternoon, and then a talk-show interview. In the days immediately following, a couple people stopped me in the street and said they were proud to live in the same city as I did—*me*? On top of that, an agent—he said he was from Hollywood—called to discuss a possible movie deal.

Now, two weeks later, it looks as if my fifteen minutes of fame is over. In the time that has passed, a sex scandal involving some United Nations delegates has captured the city's attention, supplanting the public appetite for news about the death of Dorfmeyer the Downsizer. The Holly-wood agent, if that's what he really was, hasn't returned my last phone call.

Victoria Cerutti passed on her fifteen minutes of fame. The reporters who headed out to Howard Beach to find her got a door slammed in their faces. I can't imagine how she feels about me, after the ruse I pulled on her. Maybe, knowing how desperate my circumstances were, she understands.

With or without fame, life goes on, and Carl Dorfmeyer's death is still a big part of mine.

Elizabeth Hurley and I passed each other on the stairs of the courthouse the day I was released. Though by then she surely knew who I was, and that my only interest in her husband was in seeing him behind bars, she looked away as I approached. Embarrassment could account for that. Dazzled by my fleeting fame, the Codwallader sisters, avid readers of the *Record*, admitted to me that they told a "lovely lady"—Eunice's words—in a brown coat my name. Armed with that information, Elizabeth had only to dial information for my telephone number so she could make those hang-up calls. Silly of her, but I've often been pretty silly myself.

I heard through Tony that Detective Givens has met with Elizabeth several times. Over the years she put up with a lot from her husband. Apparently Elizabeth learned early on that lying, even about inconsequential things, was a way of life with Tom. He did it to manipulate, to seduce, to sway, to save his hide, or just for the pure hell of it.

Whatever happens with Tom, Elizabeth isn't going to stand by her man. When I saw her at the courthouse, where I expect she was headed for Tom's arraignment, the attorney Gladys Obus was at her side. Later that afternoon, prodded by lingering curiosity, I called Ms. Obus's office.

"I'm contemplating buying a condo," I said to the woman who answered the lawyer's line. "Does Ms. Obus handle real-estate matters?"

"No," the woman responded. "Ms. Obus specializes in divorce law. She might be able to refer . . ."

Another loose end tied up.

There are others, of course, but they involve far larger issues, and as we all know, the larger the issue, the more time it takes to get to the bottom of it.

One of those issues is the confession that I caught on tape. After Tom was arraigned, his lawyer, a button-down type who has made a reputation for himself by defending slithering worms, tried to claim that his client had been "entrapped." He wanted my tape barred from evidence. That didn't work, but from what I understand, he's sure to try more tricky moves.

And there's the issue of Louise's death, a major loose end. Tom has denied any involvement in it. "At no time after returning from lunch did my client see Ms. Gruber," the lawyer claims. I am not convinced, and have heard through the NYPD grapevine that Detective Givens isn't either. Apparently a bit of skin that was found under one of Louise's fingernails is being examined by the forensics people as we speak.

One way or another, whether it's for one murder or two, Tom "Terrific" Hurley is going to have to say good-bye to his ascent up the corporate ladder. Maybe Sing Sing can use a good human-resources person.

As for Givens the Exterminator . . .

I half expected an apology. My mistake. But next week "Reggie" and I are both expected at a Christmas party at the LaMarcas'. I have this wonderful fantasy. Reginald Givens and I just happen to run into each other in the kitchen when no one else is around. Maybe we're both waiting for the cappuccino machine to produce. Racked by guilt, Givens grovels and crawls, and being a humane type, I say, "Oh, don't give it another thought. It's over."

Ha!

But it will end for both of us, and that's nice to know. Givens will go on to other cases. As for me . . .

Mom and Dad have mounted the *Record's* front-page picture of me smiling in victory over the fake fireplace in their living room. My big happy smile says it all. Life is sweet. The thing is, though, I haven't quite decided what I'm going to do with the rest of mine.

There are any number of choices. Sam still thinks we can work things out, and he may be right. Mike, however, has tempted me by talking about a business deal in the Caribbean that could set both of us, and Moses, up in the land of palm trees for a long time. Knowing Mike, this business could be a little funny, but you never can tell.

What to do? In the end, I'll probably do the same thing that you would. For now, I'm going to slow down and take a deep breath, go out for a good meal, and finish with a big dessert.

CARROLL LACHNIT

MURDER IN BRIEF   0-425-14790-8/$4.99

For rich, good-looking Bradley Cogburn, law school seemed to be a lark. Everything came easy to him—including his sparkling academic record. Even an accusation of plagiarism didn't faze him: he was sure he could prove his innocence.

But for ex-cop Hannah Barlow, law school was her last chance. As Bradley's moot-court partner, she was tainted by the same accusation—and unlike him, she didn't have family money to fall back on.

Now Bradley Cogburn is dead, and Hannah has to act like a cop again. This time, it's her own life that's at stake...

A BLESSED DEATH   0-425-1534-7/$5.99

Lawyer Hannah Barlow's connection to the Church is strictly legal. But as she explores the strange disappearances—and confronts her own spiritual longings—she finds that crime, too, works in mysterious ways...

AKIN TO DEATH   0-425-16409-8/$5.99

Hannah Barlow's first case is to finalize an adoption. It's a no-brainer that is supposed to be a formality—until a man bursts into their office, claiming to be the baby's biological father. So Hannah delves into the mystery—and what she finds is an elaborate web of deceit...

Prices slightly higher in Canada